CONCRETE ANGELS

A C.T. FERGUSON CRIME NOVEL

THE C.T. FERGUSON MYSTERIES
BOOK 14

TOM FOWLER

WIDENINGGYREMEDIA

Library of Congress Control Number: 2023907796

Paperback ISBN: 978-1-953603-57-9

Editing by Chase Nottingham

Cover Design by 100Covers

Published by Widening Gyre Media

For Lisa and Isabel.

And to our favorite uncles—a Jack on each side of the family. We're lucky to have these men in our lives. Both—Fowler and Klein—have been awesome, accepting, and great examples of a fun uncle or "funcle." We love them both.

CHAPTER 1

"I'M JUST NERVOUS, YOU KNOW?"

My secretary T.J. could be described with many words. Nervous would rarely be among them. Still not twenty-one, she'd already turned around a rough life. Her current plans involved checking a significant box: getting her GED.

"You'll smash the test," I told her.

"I'm glad you're so confident. Wanna share a little?"

"If only it were so easy." She frowned. "Look . . . the exam is going to measure things you should've learned in high school, right?" Her head bobbed a little, though not enough to make her blonde ponytail move. "You've been doing all those and more since you started here. You write every day, and I almost never find something I'd want to correct."

T.J. grinned. "And I know you're pedantic."

"All part of my charm," I said. "There's another point in your favor. I wouldn't consider *pedantic* a super advanced word, but I'll bet a bunch of people taking the test don't know what it means. You even used it correctly." I raised my coffee mug to her. "I'm a pedant from way back."

"Thanks." She held up a large paperback. It was one of

those mass-produced test prep books I felt mostly served to part people from their money. "I really want to pass."

"It's not going to matter to me. You've done great work here already. A piece of paper isn't going to change anything."

"I know." T.J. put the book back in a side drawer of her desk. It landed with a thud. "I'm not doing it for you." She grinned again. "Not everything is about you, you know."

"My name's on the door," I said. "I beg to differ." The heavy metallic door in question, bearing writing which said *C.T. Ferguson, Private Investigator*, remained closed. We'd resolved a couple small cases recently but hadn't seen anything big this month. Thanks to a clever rate schedule T.J. devised, we remained in the black. It felt nice to have the windows open on a spring morning even if bangs and clangs from the body shop downstairs sounded louder. Still, I would've preferred hitting the mean streets of Baltimore with my sleuthing cap on.

"What about you?" T.J. asked. "You've rushed through two cups of coffee, and I think you were about ten percent crabbier than normal this morning."

"I'm not crabby."

"You always are when you come in before nine-fifteen."

"No one should be bright and chipper so early. Morning people are a plague on our country."

"I'm a morning person."

"Except you," I added.

T.J. leaned back and fixed me with an inscrutable look. "Something's going on. Trouble in paradise already?"

"No."

"Come on. You've been married almost six months now. I'm sure you and Gloria have argued about something."

"The number of bags she takes when we go anywhere," I said.

"You don't want to talk about it?" She shrugged. "All right." T.J. returned her attention to her monitor. We didn't have a lot of work to do—the light caseload and all—so I couldn't imagine what would occupy her time. She wasn't big on using social media other than for research—a rarity among people her age who typically broadcast every detail of their lives. I realized these thoughts made me sound much older than my thirty-two years.

"Fine," I said. "Gloria seems to want us to sell one of our houses."

T.J. chuckled. "Wow. That might be the biggest first-world problem I've ever heard."

"I know." I waved a hand. "It's kind of ridiculous when I say it out loud."

"No doubt." She affected a deeper voice in some absurd attempt to try and sound like me. "It's terrible. We might have to sell one of our million-dollar homes."

Mine would sell for less, while Gloria's would probably fetch a fair bit more. In the interests of not being branded as pedantic again, however, I didn't quibble with T.J.'s real estate valuations. "We both like our current places. It's not like we had a long engagement to figure these things out." At the conclusion of a harrowed case—one in which I felt Gloria's life could've been in danger—I suggested we do an impromptu courthouse wedding. She agreed. Our engagement would go down as among the briefest on record.

"The answer is obvious," T.J. said.

"Is it?"

"Sure. Get rid of yours."

"I like my place."

"You could fit it inside your wife's two or three times over."

"Probably three," I agreed. Gloria's much larger home in the posh Brooklandville neighborhood of Baltimore County could indeed swallow my Federal Hill rowhouse several times. Its proximity to I-83 South would also afford me a relatively easy commute into downtown. "I'm a city boy at heart. It's also hard to beat my location. I can't walk to the Abbey or the Cross Street Market from Gloria's."

"I'm sure you two will work it out," she said. "By which I mean your house will go on the market in a few days."

I had a snappy retort queued up and ready to go when the door swung open.

———

I rarely get visited by priests.

I prefer it this way, of course, and any men of the cloth I know probably feel the same. Our visitor wore the classic black shirt and pants with the white collar of a Catholic priest. I recognized him after a moment. "Father David." I stood and shook his hand. "If you came by to bless the place, we've been open for a while without anything too bad going down. I think I'll take my chances at this point."

Father David Abbott looked a few years older than me. He also stood a little shorter, though I had an advantage over most people at six-two. His hair was a lighter shade of brown, and the green of his eyes probably matched mine. He shook T.J.'s hand as well when she stood and greeted him with a smile. "I'm afraid I came by on something more serious today," he said. He dropped into a guest chair on the opposite side of my desk. T.J. sat and wheeled herself to us.

"What can we do for you?" I asked. "Everything good at the Esperanza Center?"

"Yes, fine." He paused. "Did you hear about the murder?"

"This is Baltimore, Father. You're going to need to be a lot more specific."

He showed a small smile. "You're right, of course. Very unfortunate. I'm referring to Sean Cooper. A priest murdered in the courtyard of his own church."

Normally, I would've made a crack about someone not being too worried about spending the afterlife in hell, but— my own beliefs on damnation aside—Father David was a nice guy who didn't need the barb. "How long ago?" I said.

"About a week and a half." The priest shook his head. "I know things don't always go as quickly as we want them to. The mills of God grind slowly, so I presume the same is true for the men and women trying to solve a homicide."

T.J. wheeled her chair back to her own desk and tapped on the keyboard. "Have the cops mentioned any leads?"

"Not to my knowledge," Father David said. "They don't necessarily need to talk to me, of course. I didn't work at his parish, and I'm certainly not the archbishop."

"How did you know Father Cooper?"

"We were seminarians together. For about a year, we overlapped at Saint Anthony's. He's . . . he was . . . a good priest and a good man. I'm well aware we don't always get both in the same person."

My secretary turned her screen around. "Found it." She wrinkled her nose. "Awfully gruesome, I have to say." A photo filled the monitor. T.J. provided an accurate description of the scene. A priest lay on the ground, arms out at his sides. Two concrete angels stood just past his head. Blood darkened the grass around the body, and even from a few feet away, I counted numerous stab wounds. "Someone clearly had it in for this guy."

"Yes." Father David sighed. "The medical examiner says the injuries alone probably wouldn't have been fatal. He . . . "

"Bled out," I said. The darkest splotches on the late priest's clothes corresponded with areas a sadist would target. They would cause pain and bleeding with eventually loss of consciousness. Death would only come after several agonizing minutes.

"Yes." He closed his eyes and took a deep breath. "Among the few facts I've managed to learn is someone posed him after his death." His brows knitted. "A final indignity, I imagine, to arrange him like our Savior on the cross."

The detail Father David shared meant the city's medical examiner finished a report. I could go online and look for it later . . . if I decided to take the case. "I need to ask something," I said, "and there's really no delicate way of doing it."

"No," Father David said, shaking his head. "I resent the sad implication there are so many in the priesthood, but Sean Cooper definitely wasn't a pedophile." His expression remained sour. "I understand you need to know. If he was, it probably means more people could've had it in for him."

"Exactly."

"He was a good guy. If every priest tried to be like Sean Cooper, we'd have a lot fewer problems." Father David lapsed into silence. T.J. shot me a meaningful look. I gave her a fractional shrug. She frowned.

"There's not much to go on here," I said. "Even if we round up to two weeks, it might seem like a long time, but a lot of homicides take a while for all the details to shake out."

"I'm tired of waiting, and so is the archdiocese. Because I know you, I volunteered to come down here and be the liaison. We want this solved, and we're willing to pay your rate to do it."

"I only accept actual money. Not blessings, communion wafers, or bad church wine."

Father David chuckled in spite of his visit's serious nature. "It's not exactly a great vintage, is it? Our budget's not unlimited, obviously, but we're hoping we can buy your time for a few days."

"I need to see what I'd be wandering into," I said. "While I'd like to think I work fast and solve cases the police can't, a few days isn't often enough time. If you were here for some faceless corporation, I'd be happy to take your money. You're not, so I want to be sure there's something to pursue before I say yes."

"Treading carefully with the church's money," the priest said. "Maybe I'll even see you at Mass one of these weekends."

"Let's not get crazy, Father," I said.

————

Father David left a few minutes later. T.J. wheeled her chair to my desk again. Friction from the carpet forced her to push off a second time to make it around to the business side. "I've never heard you tell someone you wanted to see what was out there first," she said. "Usually, you either dive in or tell them to pound sand."

I shrugged. "I like Father David. The Catholic Church as a global entity is huge, but one particular diocese really isn't. They're probably paying for this with money raised from the collections. If there's not much to go on, I don't want to deplete their coffers."

"I'm not sure you've ever been so positive toward the church, either." T.J. frowned. "You feeling all right, boss?"

"As well as ever."

"Okay," she said. "Where's our search begin?"

When T.J. first came to work for me through a program started by my friend Melinda, the idea was she would strictly be a secretary. I didn't think I was busy enough to need one, but I've always hated doing office administrivia, so I took her on. We were briefly acquainted on a prior case, and T.J. showed a willingness to do what needed to be done. She took quickly to everything I put before her, and her natural curiosity led to her wanting to know more about the things I did and how I accomplished them. I was happy to share knowledge with her. If she could knock out certain things in a pinch, my business benefited from it. "Normally, I would want to see the police report. Considering we got an update on it, however, I want to skip it for the ME's findings."

My secretary pursed her lips. "He mentioned knowing the body had been moved . . . or posed at least."

"Right. It's not a common position for someone to die in, but he obviously knows something. Not surprising the ME's office would share basic details with him. The archdiocese still has a lot of sway in the city." A few months ago, a ransomware attack knocked many city systems offline. The medical examiner came away largely unscathed. As such, I was able to access the report with no trouble. The folder held a PDF and a bunch of photos. I started with the images.

While the article T.J. found contained only one, the ME amassed a dozen and a half. They snapped shots of the body from every reasonable angle and probably a few unreasonable ones, too. Father Cooper lay with his arms out wide. The combination of grass and dark flagstones meant the blood didn't stand out as much as it would've if he got killed in winter. It made the scene appear a little tamer than it really was. A closer look at the body would show a bunch of tears in clothing and stab wounds underneath them.

"A very sharp and slender blade," T.J. said, pointing at the screen to show me where she read it. "Don't you have one like that?"

"I didn't kill the priest," I said.

"You might need an alibi." T.J. tried to give me a cop's practiced stare and came up comically short. "Where were you on the night he died?"

"Probably having sex with my wife."

Her face twisted like she'd been eating sour candy for hours. "Gross."

"I do have a blade like this because it's easy to conceal," I said. "Though the description would probably fit any good kitchen utility knife in the city. It doesn't exactly narrow the suspect pool."

"That part is for the police to puzzle out," T.J. said. "Or us."

I nodded as I scrolled through the pictures. "Lots of stab wounds."

"Someone hated this guy."

"It's why I needed to ask the pedo question. At least then, we have a convenient reason for someone to despise this man. But he was clean. This is a ton of venom against anyone but especially a priest."

"Does this mean we're taking the case?" T.J. asked with a grin.

"I know it sounds a little ghoulish, but I'm intrigued. Who stabs a priest a dozen times and leaves him to bleed out in a church courtyard?"

"We'll figure it out. We're on the case."

"We're on the case," I confirmed.

CHAPTER 2

ONCE WE FINISHED PERUSING the ME's findings, I went looking for the police report. The case had been active long enough for there to be copious notes. The BPD keeps their network locked down reasonably well. On my first case, my cousin Rich, then a uniformed sergeant, committed the grievous sin of leaving me alone at his computer for a few minutes. Armed with the information I obtained, I've been able to pass one of my virtual machines off as a BPD resource ever since.

Until today.

"They finally caught up to you," T.J. said with a snicker.

"I doubt it."

"You going to head down and talk to Rich?"

"Might as well. I'll bring you some lunch." I left the office, walked down the metal staircase, and climbed into my black Audi S4 sedan. It hailed from the prior generation, so while it lacked cutting-edge technology, it made up for it with the manual transmission the current version lacked. I headed to BPD headquarters where Rich now toiled away as a lieutenant in the homicide division. The elevator dumped me outside the bullpen.

A couple years ago, the whole area got updated and refreshed. Some overpaid consultant emphasized the concept of an open floor plan. Cubicle walls were a thing of the past. The advantage was I could see clear to the far end. Rich's door was open. I skirted the outside of the desks, exchanged pleasantries with a few cops I knew, and stood outside my cousin's door. He looked up and rolled his eyes. "What now?"

"The usual," I said, stepping inside. "Someone hired me to solve a case languishing here."

He snorted. "Which one?"

"The priest."

"Tough one," Rich said with a grimace. "Not an easy crime scene, either."

"I looked for the report online, but it wasn't there."

"Ransomware fallout. We're still getting everything back where it needs to be." The city got hit pretty hard a few months ago. Thanks to the help of yours truly, the attackers landed in jail just in time for Christmas. The police network went down more than once, and others across Baltimore suffered similar fates.

"I could help get things back online," I said. "Usurious consulting rates apply. Mockery included at no extra charge."

"I think we'll be all right," Rich said with a smirk. "So sorry to inconvenience you by making you drive down here, though."

"You could at least have some fresh coffee ready."

"Let's walk and get some." Rich stood. He was about two inches shorter than me and twenty or so pounds heavier. His time as a lieutenant added a little extra gray to his dark brown hair. Rich would turn thirty-nine soon, and then I'd get a year of cracks about him almost going over the hill. We'd been a distant sort of close over the years, but the relationship improved despite my frequent reminders of how Rich earned commendations on cases I helped him close. "We'll see if King is here," he added as he shrugged into his suit jacket.

Sergeant Paul King dropped into his desk chair as we approached. He took Rich's old position both in title and desk when my cousin got the well-deserved promotion. King was a good cop even though he looked more like a failed rock star than an investigator. He was tall and slender with a mop of dirty blond hair he could never seem to tame. "Rich is buying coffee," I said. My cousin frowned.

"I'm in." King got back to his feet. We left the building and walked to a Starbucks about a block away. Somewhere in the bullpen, a pot of old coffee sat turning into mud. None us were willing to risk a sip. The java shop wasn't crowded. Once we all had our drinks, I pushed the door open, and we headed back toward BPD headquarters.

"C.T. has graciously agreed to solve the priest case for us," Rich told King.

"Thank Christ," King said.

"I'd rather you thank me when I'm done," I said. "Not going well so far?"

King snorted. "We don't have shit. The ME told us it was a thin, sharp blade like this is some kind of revelation. Six hundred thousand people live in the city, and I'll bet two-thirds of them own a knife which might be the murder weapon."

"Maybe a chef killed him."

"I doubt it."

"People can get very angry over bad Yelp reviews," I said. They weren't buying my theory. This was fair—I didn't, either. "I know you don't have a lot, but I'd like to see the file anyway."

"I'll have to ask my lieutenant," King said.

"I hear he's kind of a prick."

King shrugged. "People tell me he's jealous of his cousin."

"Who could blame him?"

"You both can go to hell," Rich said, amusement playing on his thin lips. "King can print out the file for you. You want it? Scan it and email it back to me so I can get the damn thing online."

"Literally anyone in the building could do those steps," I pointed out.

Rich pushed the door open, and we walked into the lobby of police headquarters. "The only way I can overcome my jealousy is to give you busywork." I smiled as we passed the security area—which I cleared in record time thanks to walking in with two plainclothes cops.

"Fine," I said as we stepped into the elevator again. "I don't have a scanner since it's not two thousand ten, but I'll get it done."

"Good." Rich stepped off first once we arrived at the right floor. "King will get you the file." He walked back to his office. I headed to King's desk.

"Any piercing insights you want to share?" I asked as a nearby printer whirred to life.

King snorted. "I don't even have any dull ones. Wish I did. I ain't religious, but someone killing a priest like this is some bad shit. Who asked you to look into it?"

"Another man of the cloth. Someone I've known for a little while. I asked the obvious questions. There's no apparent reason someone should've hated the vic so much."

"Yet somebody clearly did." King collected the pages and handed them to me. "Guy seemed well-liked. Not a kid toucher or anything. No complaints from female parishioners, so he wasn't trying to mack on them. Who the hell stabs a priest a dozen times?"

"I guess I get to puzzle this out now."

"Yeah." King grinned. "Good luck."

I got the feeling I would need it.

———

I called T.J. when I left and told her to meet me at the church courtyard. The passage of time would not do wonders for the crime scene, but it always helped to get visuals. She wondered about her lunch, and I said I would pick up something en route. Thankfully, there was a fried chicken joint across the street from St. Ann's Catholic Church. I picked us each up a three-piece meal with a biscuit and ate mine in the parking lot. I needed to put a towel under the food as grease turned the paper bags translucent. The smell would linger in my car for a while, and I would enjoy it.

T.J.'s Mustang pulled beside my S4 a couple minutes later. She opened my passenger door, picked up the remaining paper bag, and plopped onto the seat. "Fried chicken?" she said as she peered inside.

"Embrace the grease," I said. "It's damn good."

She started with the biscuit, scarfed it down, and then moved on to the bird. "It's a good thing we're here," she said around a mouthful of drumstick. "I might be having a religious experience." We waited a few minutes. T.J. used every napkin in the bag—plus a couple more from the stash in my glove compartment—to wipe her hands and mouth. We got out of the car. St. Ann's sat at the corner of Route 45 and East 22nd Street. The exterior was brownish-gray stone. It was more long than tall, though a leap from the roof onto the concrete below would be ill-advised. I didn't keep a catalog of steeples in my head, but if I did, St. Ann's ranked in the middle of the pack at best. An attached rectory sat adjacent to the main structure, and the Mother Seton Academy—a middle school currently in session—stood on the opposite side of the courtyard we came to see. Scaffolding lined the exterior wall of the rectory.

We walked around the corner past the large red front doors and turned right onto a sidewalk running between the church and school. A black iron fence surrounded the courtyard. Despite its ominous look, the gate was open, so we headed in. T.J. snapped a few pictures with her phone while I pondered the wisdom of allowing unfettered access to an area which butted up against a building full of children. "You think we'll find anything?" she wanted to know.

"I doubt it," I admitted. "It's been long enough, and it's rained at least a couple times. Even if the cops missed something, it could have been washed away or picked up by some kid." I felt T.J. staring at me as I looked around. "You want to know why we're here in light of what I just told you."

"Duh."

"We may not find a clue to crack the case. Or much of anything, really. But you can't get the sense of a place from crime scene photos. They're clinical and designed to tell a story about how someone died." The courtyard was a mix of grass and brown gravel, the latter making a path from front to back and swelling into a hexagonal clearing around the center. There, one concrete angel kept watch over each of six directions. Despite being all the same size, none of them looked alike. Some were contemplative. Others held swords and looked ready to take flight and battle demons. "You have any of the ME's photos handy?"

"Sure," my secretary said. She joined me in the hexagon. "Huh. None of them are the same."

"Right," I said. "We can at least know which way he faced when he died . . . or when someone posed him."

"Does that tell us anything?"

"Today, right now? Probably not. Later when we have more info?" I shrugged. "You never know when a detail will matter."

"I guess." After T.J. and I determined where the priest lay after his death, we poked around the area. Nothing of interest remained from Father Cooper's murder. Time, the elements, and a bunch of other factors conspired against us. "Should we go inside? The guy who hired us didn't work here, right?"

"No," I said, "he's at the Esperanza Center. I'm sure the cops have already talked to the local guy, but it can't hurt." I'd only skimmed the police report since getting it, and if they talked to anyone else at St. Ann's, I didn't read those pages yet. The side door from the courtyard was locked, so we walked around to the front and entered via a large red door. I spotted a couple cameras mounted above the entryway. Black plastic domes housed them, so they stood out.

"You gonna catch on fire?" T.J. asked as we crossed the threshold.

"I hope not," I said. "I'll steer clear of the holy water just in case." Three rows of dark wooden pews ran from the altar to the rear of the church. A high ceiling yielded to pillars spaced out on each side. Most of the interior was cream colored. Stained glass windows and the stations of the cross lined the walls. The church was mostly empty with only a few older ladies sitting in a pew near the entrance. A priest stood near the front. We saw the man in profile as he lit a few small votive candles. He turned to face us, and I recognized him. "Oh, fuck." Alarmed looks I received from the women told me my *sotto voce* needed some work.

When I woke up this morning, I hadn't expected to go two-for-two on recognizing reverends associated with my case. "You know him?" T.J. whispered as one of the elderly ladies continued staring at me as if I'd kicked her cat.

"Unfortunately, yes," I said. The priest walked closer, and a grimace conveyed the fact he recognized me, too.

"Mister Ferguson," Father Lawrence Toohey said. "Why am I not surprised?"

CHAPTER 3

FATHER LAWRENCE TOOHEY hadn't changed much in the last four years. He'd remained slender, no easy feat for a man on the wrong side of fifty. More gray intruded on his black hair now, and less of it remained regardless of color. He kept his hands folded in front of him. It made him look priestly, and it was a good way to prevent himself from giving me the finger. "Father Larry," I said. "This is my assistant, T.J."

He showed a quick smile and inclined his head to T.J. At five-nine, she was almost as tall as he was. "An assistant? You've done well for yourself."

I spread my hands and looked around the interior. "So have you. Quite an upgrade over where you were four years ago."

"All is possible through faith in our Lord," he said.

"Of course," I agreed to be congenial. We were in a church, after all. I'd been raised Lutheran. I could go through the motions. Heck, I still remembered a few hymns, though no one needed to hear my singing voice. "I take it you can infer why we're here."

"Father Cooper. God rest his soul."

"Yes. Is there someplace else we might talk?"

"Sure. Follow me." Father Larry looked at the assembled women and gave them a friendly nod. "Ladies." They smiled, though the one who took the most offense at me still fixed me with a sour look as we moved away. He led us up the main aisle and then past the altar on the right. A heavy white wooden door led to a hallway which needed more lighting. The recessed ones overhead weren't getting it done, and the area was closed off to the outside. "Assistant, huh?" T.J. whispered as we walked. "Does this new title come with a raise?"

"Only if you're an executive assistant," I said. She elbowed me in the side. About a hundred feet later, Father Larry opened an identical door, and we stepped through. Based on the distance, I estimated we were now in the rectory. A central corridor ran for a while with doors on either side. We headed through the second on the right. I'd been in Father Larry's office at his old church. This one felt a little bigger, even if the setup was basically the same. The dark brown desk occupied the center of the room. Two tall matching bookcases stood behind it, each packed with tomes on religion and theology. Father Larry took his seat, and T.J. and I settled onto the cloth guest chairs.

"Your boss and I are acquainted," he said to T.J. before his eyes flicked to me "What was it . . . about four years ago?"

"More or less," I said. "It was one of my earlier cases. We're here today on the current one, however."

"Of course." Father Larry leaned back and blew out a deep breath. "Just terrible what happened. We only started services again this past Sunday."

"A worker here found the body on a Saturday morning, right?"

"Yes. Isidora. She's one of our cleaning staff." Father Larry grimaced and shook his head. "Poor woman. She really liked Father Cooper. Everyone did. I don't think she'd ever seen a dead body before. If there's a saving grace in all of this, I'd say the discovery on a Saturday is it. I can't imagine children at the school coming across it." He paused. "We kept the school open. Counselors were onsite. We didn't hold any Masses here the weekend it happened, obviously."

"How many other priests are here?" I asked.

"Right now, I'm it. Father Wallace is in chemo, and Father Belt is on a mission."

"Is he a spy?"

Father Larry rolled his eyes as T.J. fought a snicker. "I'd forgotten your wit. No. He's working with the underprivileged in Africa. The archdiocese sent us someone to help this weekend. I'm sure they will until we're properly staffed again."

"How are you handling all this?" T.J. wanted to know.

"I'm devastated," Father Larry said. He must have seen my skeptical expression. "I am. Sean was my friend."

"Where were you before? Saint Mark's?" His head bobbed. "This seems like quite an upgrade. Bigger building, better location . . . many more parishioners, I'm sure. Now, you're the man here."

"I'm not a killer, Mister Ferguson." A hard edge crept into Father Larry's tone. "I'll remind you how you thought I might have been four years ago. I wasn't. In fact, I helped you catch the man who was responsible despite my objection to your methods. Hopefully, they've improved."

"They have. For whatever it's worth, I wasn't accusing you. I have to ask certain questions in situations like this."

"I know." Father Larry composed himself with a long, slow breath. "The police basically did the same. I suppose it's the nature of the job even if it feels a little unseemly."

"Anything you can think of which didn't make it into the police report?"

"No. I told the detectives everything I knew and whatever I could reasonably speculate."

"Speculation interests me," I said. "Considering the brutality of the murder, I had to ask the obvious question."

"I understand," Father Larry said, "as much as I wish it weren't necessary. Father Cooper's file was blemish-free. He'd been here for years, and everyone loved him, including the teachers and students next door."

I considered asking Father Larry how involved he was with the school. Years before coming to Baltimore, he got accused of improper conduct with an altar boy. He already seemed salty to be dealing with me again, and I needed to keep him as a source of information, so I let it go. "Twelve stab wounds. I read the ME's report. None were fatal on their own. Someone wanted Father Cooper to suffer."

"I can't imagine who."

"You mentioned his involvement at the school," I said. "What else did he do?"

"The normal activities of a priest." Father Larry shrugged. "Masses, marriages, baptisms, funerals, counseling, sacraments for the sick. We don't turn people away if they need help."

"Did he help someone he shouldn't have?" T.J. said, posing the question I'd been about to ask.

"I don't think so," Father Larry said.

"All right." I took out a business card and placed it on the desk. Father Larry eyed it like I dropped a scorpion in front of him. "If you hear or think of anything, please let us know."

"I will."

"We'll see ourselves out." T.J. and I walked from the rectory. Despite the scaffolding outside, I didn't notice any signs of recent construction. It made me wonder how promptly the archdiocese paid its bills—and what this meant for my agency's bank account once our business concluded. We headed back through the church. The old ladies still sat near the door, and the woman who glared at me before did so again.

"You make friends everywhere we go," T.J. said as I held the front door open for her.

"At least she didn't ask me to pray the rosary," I said. "Who has the time?"

———

Later in the afternoon, I headed home. At this point, I figured we would take the case. T.J. and I already visited the scene of the crime, and I'd even gotten to spar a little with Father Larry. It reminded me of the earlier case when I'd first met him. I hoped not to involve him again, and he probably shared the sentiment. As my end rowhouse neared, I turned into the alley running behind the homes and swung onto the concrete parking pad.

Gloria's Mercedes AMG coupe sat to one side. In case the sleek shape and throaty sound of the car didn't give its rocketlike nature, the red color sealed the deal. I preferred my metallic black paint job. I'd added the parking pad after buying the house. It was one more touch I liked. The place ended up being perfect. The previous owner ran a psychology practice, so the main floor featured an addition to accommodate an office. I eventually separated home and business, but it was a great setup for a while.

As I walked in the back door, Gloria came into the kitchen. She pushed me against the door and kissed me aggressively. "Welcome home."

"Thanks. Maybe I can go back outside and we can do the whole thing again?"

She smiled. "How about dinner first?"

We'd ordered out a lot recently, so I rummaged through the fridge to see what I could cook. A package of ground beef, a box of pasta, a jar of sauce, and some spices later, I worked on spaghetti and meatballs. While two burners boiled and simmered, I heated the oven and sliced a relatively fresh baguette to make garlic bread. About ten minutes later, I assembled everything and set it on the kitchen table. The configuration of the first floor and its office meant kitchen space ended up a little pinched. My table seated two comfortably and four if I were desperate.

Gloria poured two glasses of iced tea and joined me. She cut her meatballs into tiny slivers. A couple years ago, she changed the way she ate to help her conditioning for tennis tournaments. It all worked, but a side effect was I sometimes lapped her during a meal. This would probably be another of those times. I cut my meatballs in half—the only acceptable way to slice them—and enjoyed dinner. By the time I'd eaten most of my food, Gloria hadn't even made it halfway. She'd probably have leftovers.

"I've been thinking more about our housing," she said as she worked on her last few bites. I remained quiet. It was common for married people to have a single house where they lived. If they owned an additional property, it was usually for something like vacations and set in a desirable location. She filled the gap my silence left in the conversation. "I love your place. It's full of character, and this neighborhood is hard to beat." Gloria smiled and squeezed my hand. "I really think we ought to sell it, however."

"Those are all reasons why I want to keep it."

"We don't need two houses. Especially with both of us working, expenses become important." After years of resisting the pull of a job, Gloria put her smarts and socialite contacts to good use by starting a fundraising company. She'd already hosted a few events which raised money for charities and got a lot of good press. We were both business owners whose jobs and revenues were unpredictable. What she said made sense.

I just didn't want to hear it.

"I get it," I said after a moment. "This place is great. I like your house, too, but for completely different reasons. I wouldn't want you to give it up. It fits you . . . just like mine fits me."

"I know." She nodded. "We both picked great places. I'm just trying to be practical. Your agency is doing well, but what if you get hurt? Or what if there's a recession, and people don't want to hold fundraisers? We got married all of a sudden." She grinned. "I'd always pictured a long engagement. A big wedding at a really nice venue. Now, I wouldn't trade what we did for anything. One of the side effects is not doing much in the way of consolidation in advance."

"Maybe I'll make a lot on my current case." I recapped the murder of the priest by hitting only the important points. "If I can work it for a while, maybe I can make the pope sell a painting to pay the bill." My wife chuckled. "I think we can afford both houses for now. As long as we can, I think we should keep them."

"Maybe we could," Gloria said. "I'm only trying to look at the big picture."

I understood even if I found the conversation unpleasant. Thankfully, she dropped the subject and took a few more mousy bites before packing the rest of her meal into a container. I hoped it wouldn't come up again.

———

After dinner, I texted T.J. about the case we'd yet to tell the client we accepted formally. I felt there was enough for us to investigate. While I'd never be confused for a religious person, I was raised Lutheran, and the idea of someone killing a priest still put me ill at ease.

I'm in on the Cooper case.

Cool. I thought we already were.

Haven't told Father David yet. I will.

As your executive assistant, I concur.

If we book enough hours to make the Vatican sell something to afford the bill, you can have any title you want.

And the raise that comes with it?

Sure.

What's up with you and Father Larry, btw? I know there's some history there because he mentioned an old case.

Yeah. One of my early ones. He had the kind of history you don't want a priest to carry. Someone got killed near his church. Turns out he was acquainted with the victim . . . and allegations were he knew him biblically years before. He turned out not to be the killer, but he was a good suspect no matter what he wants to say now.

Damn. I can see why he's a little leery around you. He def thought you were accusing him again earlier.

I know. It's why I tried to defuse it. I don't know if we'll need him for anything, but making an enemy could hurt our investigation.

Good call, boss. I'll talk to you tomorrow after I draft the proposal for my new title and raise.

I had to smile. While I'd met her before, T.J. represented a total unknown when I agreed to take a chance on her. She rarely came up short in skills, and she never lacked in personality. The only other person to inform about my official acceptance of the case was the man who came to see me in the first place. I called Father David. "You have yourself a detective," I told him.

"Excellent. Thank you, C.T. I know you don't want to hear it, but may God bless your efforts."

"I'll take all the help I can get, Father. We visited the crime scene earlier. By now, there was nothing left to see. We're basically starting from scratch with the exception of the police report and the ME's notes."

"I'll be sure the archdiocese gives you any help you need." He paused. "Did you speak with Father Larry?"

"Yes," I said. "We'd run into one another before. An old case." Father David didn't need to know all the details of my previous interactions with—and suspicions of—his colleague. I risked the sin of a little white lie. "I wasn't sure he'd remember me, but he did."

"Great. I don't know what he'll be able to tell you, but if you need anything from Saint Ann's, I'm sure he'll be happy to arrange it."

"All right. I need to be honest and not just because I'm talking to a priest. I don't know how long this is going to take.

You have a budget, I'm sure. How often do you want me to keep you in the loop?"

"Whenever you learn something significant, of course," Father David said. "Tomorrow's Wednesday. I think we can afford you for a few days. Check with me at the close of business on Thursday, and let's see where we stand."

The issue of payment rarely came up before when I worked for my parents' foundation. Since striking out fully on my own, I needed to be mindful of my rates and what clients could afford. "If you put in a good word with the Big Guy, maybe we can wrap this up quickly," I said. The priest told me he would, and we mutually ended the call.

I hoped Father David's blessings wouldn't matter, but like I told him, I would accept all the help I could get.

CHAPTER 4

T.J. TOSSED her car keys into the plain wooden bowl near her front door.

She liked coming home to this apartment. She'd even bought a few basic flower paintings and hung them on the otherwise bare walls. When Melinda initially got her off the street, T.J. shared a space with two other young women. She didn't care for the location. Too close to some of her old haunts. Once she landed a job and earned a raise, she moved to a much better building. Her place was a small one-bedroom model, but it was close to lots of markets and eateries.

A quick check of the fridge showed not very much to work with. The weather was still nice on a spring evening, so she got back in the elevator and headed out. Her building, the 501, stood on Franklin Street. From here, she enjoyed a pretty easy commute to work most mornings and access to many restaurants which stretched her budget if she visited them too often. T.J. walked a couple blocks to Eutaw Street and popped into Massey's Real Greek Food. Almost all the menu was Italian fare of some sort—pasta and pizza, plus other common items—but she came for the gyro. T.J. chatted with Ted the cashier for a moment, placed her order, and waited.

She looked out the squat front window onto Eutaw Street. Across the way, she thought she spotted a familiar face. Velvet. She hadn't seen the girl in at least a couple years. Back when they both spent way too much time on the streets doing things she wasn't proud of. As quickly as Velvet appeared, however, she was gone after a city bus rolled by. T.J. kept looking out the window and hoping her friend would reappear. She'd lost touch with most of the girls she used to work with. In many cases, this was a good thing, but Velvet had always been decent. If she were still in the life, she'd be a good candidate for Melinda and the Nightlight Foundation.

T.J. snickered at herself. It almost sounded like she worked as a recruiter for a cult. She jumped when Ted dropped a bag on the table. "Sorry . . . I guess I was spacing out a little." The plastic bag held a paper one. T.J. inhaled the aromas of lamb, onions, and fries. If she went easy, there would be enough left over for lunch or dinner tomorrow. Two meals for the price of one turned out to be good for the budget. As she pushed the door open and stepped onto the sidewalk, T.J. thought she saw Velvet again.

She dashed across the street, ignoring the long honk from a car she ran in front of. When she reached the opposite side, she didn't see anyone. T.J. poked her head in to a Chinese restaurant and looked behind the short row of buildings. Velvet was gone. Had she ever really been there? Maybe it was just someone who looked like her. She didn't exactly have a unique look. Lots of girls were short with dark wavy hair. T.J. made sure her bag of food survived the sprint across Eutaw Street intact and then headed back to her apartment.

Her unit's floor plan basically consisted of two areas. One

was the bedroom with an attached bathroom. The other might have been called "open concept" if it were a house. The modestly-furnished living room and kitchen blended together. Theoretically, there was space for a small dining room table, but T.J. didn't own one. She ate her meals on the couch. The brown fabric was thin and patchy in spots. Maybe if she kept angling for raises and bonuses, she could buy a new one.

Despite being hungry, T.J. picked at her meal. She took a couple small bites of the gyro and ate maybe a handful of fries. Seeing Velvet—or someone who could've been her stunt double—proved more unnerving than she thought. T.J. sighed, closed the container, and shoved it into the fridge.

————

T.J. looked at her phone. She thought about calling or texting C.T. When she first met him a couple years ago, two other prostitutes accompanied her: Velvet and Alex. She really hadn't kept up with either of them since getting out of the life and starting over. Clean breaks were best. Two therapists told her this repeatedly, and she agreed. Some of what they spouted was bullshit, but they got the big thing right. C.T. took a chance on her, never once tried to take advantage of her checkered past, and he'd acknowledged several times how well she did, including in the form of a $3000 Christmas bonus a few months ago.

He had his own issues now, however. Married. A wife who wanted to get rid of one of their houses. Sure, it was a major first-world problem, but when you liked a place, you didn't want to leave it. T.J. lived the inverse for years, and she knew it to be true from that side. She scrolled up past her boss' contact information and instead called Melinda. As usual, the woman picked up quickly. "Hi, T.J. Is everything all right?"

"Yeah." T.J. hesitated. "Well . . . not really."

"Something at your job?"

"No. I think I saw someone I used to work with."

Melinda fell silent for a few seconds. While her foundation helped a variety of women and families, she herself harbored a soft spot for hookers who wanted to go straight. Melinda herself did it—with some help from C.T.—over two years before. Since then, she'd tried to spare other girls many of the things she'd been forced to endure. "I'm sure it wasn't easy," Melinda eventually said.

"It was surprising at first," T.J. admitted. "I've tried to avoid the people and the areas I used to know as much as I can. There's still some leftover baggage there, I think." She sighed. "I was just getting dinner. Popped into a place I go to, and there she was."

"Who?"

"Velvet."

"I remember her."

"Did she ever come to see you?" T.J. asked.

"No. I don't think she was ready to move on like you were."

"Really? She seemed kind of burned out on the life toward the end before I got out."

"She may have been," Melinda said. "That doesn't make her ready to start over. You were, and I'm so proud of who you've become. Some people need more time."

"Maybe she'll be ready soon, then. I can try to find her again."

"Are you sure it was Velvet?"

"Pretty much," T.J. said, and she heard the uncertainty in her tone. "It was through a restaurant window and across the street. I guess it could've been someone else." She frowned. "I really wanted it to be Velvet. I want her to get the chance I did."

"I'm sure you do," Melinda said. "I think it would be great." She chuckled. "You know I want to try and save everybody."

"I do." T.J. smiled. It was a fool's errand, but Melinda's relentless positivity could overcome a great deal.

"If you think you can reach out to her safely, go ahead and do it. It's not worth putting yourself in danger. Don't do anything which might trigger you too much."

T.J. closed her eyes. She fondly recalled working with Velvet. Some of the circumstances turned out to be nice, and others were memories she would've preferred to avoid stirring up. "Life's pretty triggering," she said after a moment. "I think I have a handle on it."

"I'm sure you do," Melinda said softly. "You're strong."

"I'll let you know if I find Velvet again." T.J. wished Melinda a good night and ended the call. She turned the phone over in her hand. Fidgeting wasn't like her. Seeing someone from the old life rattled her more than she cared to admit . . . even to Melinda. She set her mobile on the drab coffee table. A knock at the door made her jump. Who the hell would be coming to see her?

Whoever it was knocked again. "Yeah, yeah," T.J. said as she moved across the room to the door. She stood to the side and looked through the small peephole.

Velvet stood on the welcome mat.

———

Velvet smiled as T.J. opened the door. "Hey," she said. "Thought it was you in the restaurant."

"I looked for you." T.J. crossed her arms. "I went across the street and checked around. Where were you?"

Velvet didn't answer the question. "I saw you walk up Eutaw and then into this building." She nodded appreciably. "Not bad, Tami Jean."

"Don't call me that," T.J. snapped.

"All right, all right." Velvet put up her hands. "Sorry. Can I come in?" She looked much the same as she did when T.J. saw her last. She wasn't very tall—five-four at most—but her pretty face, dark eyes, and terrific body always made her popular among the johns. Whatever she did for work now, it allowed her to buy fashionable jeans, a Polo V-neck T-shirt which showed more than enough cleavage to catch the eye, and a North Face jacket.

"How'd you know which apartment was mine?"

"The guy at the front desk told me." Velvet smirked. "How many times did we bat our eyelashes at a guy and get him to do something?"

T.J. smiled at a few memories and inclined her head toward Velvet's chest. "I'm sure the clothes helped, too." She moved to the side and swept her arm toward the interior.

Velvet walked in and looked around. "Not bad." She headed through the kitchen. T.J. couldn't help but notice the way her friend's butt moved and her hips sashayed. Velvet looked like she'd been poured into her form-fitting jeans. She always wore booty shorts, tiny skirts, or something skintight. T.J. hated how quickly she remembered feeling like she needed to compete on the corners against someone with a better body. She pushed the old memories down as Velvet plopped onto the couch. "I guess you got a job now?"

"Yeah." T.J. locked the door and joined her friend. For as much as she wanted to see Velvet earlier, having the woman in her apartment felt weird. "Remember the detective who was looking for Libby a couple years ago?"

"Sort of."

"I'm his assistant."

"Wow." Velvet grinned like a woman who knew exactly what she wanted. "I remember him looking pretty fine. Alex was into him. You fuck him yet?"

"No!" T.J. wrinkled her nose. "I'm out of the life. Out all the way."

Velvet patted the cushion beside her. T.J. had dropped onto the opposite end of the couch. "You look like you're about to crawl into the sofa. What the hell is going on?"

"I'm all right." T.J. scooted down. "Just surprised to see you is all. What are you doing now?"

"This and that," Velvet said. "I've upgraded. Can't say I've left the life yet, but I got one foot out the door. I put a bunch of content on OnlyFans now. When I need to, I take some escort work. Nothing like what we used to do. These are guys who can *pay*."

"If you want to make a clean break, I can help you."

"Trying to save my soul, Tam . . . T.J.?"

"I landed in a good situation," T.J. said. "Got clean. Had some people help me sort my shit out and get my life together."

"You don't miss it?" Velvet leaned in a little closer and dropped her voice to a husky whisper. "Not even a little?"

"No."

"I still feel the pull." She took a pack of long cigarettes from her purse. "Mind if I smoke?"

This was a new habit. When T.J. last saw Velvet, the girl hated smoking and even carried mouthwash in case she picked up a tobacco-loving john. "Outside, sure" T.J. said. "I can't have it in here. It's in my lease."

Velvet rolled her eyes. "Fine. Whatever. Who helped you make your break?"

"It's a place called the Nightlight Foundation. The lady who runs it used to do what we did, so she gets it."

"And now it's her mission to save wayward girls?"

"She's doing good work." T.J. frowned. "I have an apartment and a job. Soon, I'll get my GED. It all seemed so far away a couple years ago."

"I got goals, too, you know," Velvet said.

"Good. What are they?"

"For now, I'm trying to drive my online content. Selling special sets and packages kinda feels like suckering a john back in the day, but they pay time and time again." She paused for a light chuckle. "I guess men never change. Anyway, I'd like to get out, and I'm working on it. Trying to find people to look up to. Right now, I've got my eye on a local businesswoman. I think she's going to be a real mover and shaker . . . especially if she can ditch her husband."

"That's great," T.J. said with a smile. "It's always nice to aspire to something. If you want me to refer you to the foundation at some point, let me know."

"I'll think about it," Velvet said, but her knitted brows and pursed lips suggested she'd already formed an opinion. "Not sure I'm into all that soul saving."

"It's not like that."

Velvet stood. "I gotta go. It was nice to see you again. Don't be a stranger."

"You, too." T.J. got to her feet, and the two shared a long embrace. Velvet left, and T.J. locked up behind her. She crossed the apartment and looked out the back window as Velvet walked away. T.J. hoped she would be all right. Not everyone landed on their feet.

CHAPTER 5

I AWOKE before Gloria the next morning. This was typical. Despite the changes she made to her eating and other routines for tennis, she remained someone who enjoyed her sleep. I did, too, but since turning thirty, I struggled to remain in bed past nine. Considering the shade my secretary threw at me every time I came into the office after nine-thirty, I was usually up by eight.

It was a nice spring morning to go for a run on the mean streets of Federal Hill. Another point in favor of my house: the access and scenery for constitutionals. Gloria's winding road connected to others, and the whole neighborhood was surrounded by trees. Anything interesting was on Falls Road —reachable but several blocks away. Federal Hill featured classic rowhouses, a bunch of pubs, restaurants, and shops, and the eponymous park overlooking the Baltimore Harbor.

Not even a contest.

I spent a couple minutes warming up at a brisk walk, then hit my stride and did some laps around the park. Even though the pavilions at Harborplace were in receivership, the view across the water remained terrific, and the sun glinting off it spread light onto the carousel and Maryland Science

Center. After about thirty minutes, I headed back up River-side Avenue with my hands on my hips. Ever since getting shot and losing a lung lobe afterward, my fitness never quite returned to its former levels. Still, ninety-something percent from a strong baseline remained good.

After a shower, I put on jeans and a button-down shirt. Gloria was in the kitchen filling a travel mug with coffee. "Gotta get an early start," she said. After a glance at her watch, her cheeks colored a little. "Well, early-ish at least. I'll get breakfast on the way."

"All right. I might, too."

"Let's do my house tonight, all right?" She kissed me before I could answer. A sound tactic. With enough kisses and follow-on activity, I would probably agree to a great many things.

"Sounds good," I said. Gloria left, and her Mercedes rumbled to life a moment later. I swigged some coffee, poured more into a tall travel mug, and walked out the door a few minutes later. It was close to nine. I stopped at a nearby Royal Farms store and grabbed a breakfast sandwich each for me and T.J. When I pulled into the lot, her yellow Mustang was conspicuous by its absence. A bunch of vehicles waited for Manny and his crew to work on, and metallic thunks as I walked closer told me they were well underway.

At the top of the steps, I unlocked the door and walked into a dark office. No T.J. This was odd. She never took time off and always got to the office before me. Even on days I tried to be early, she'd be sitting at her desk by the time I arrived. She didn't mention anything yesterday about being late or not coming in. I put the food down and checked our shared Google calendar on my phone. Also nothing. I called her, and it went to voicemail. Now, I was concerned. I dashed off a text. *Hey, wondering what's going on. You're always here before me. Hope you're OK.*

As I sat and unwrapped my sausage, egg, and cheese sandwich, T.J. called. "I'm coming in a couple hours late," she said.

"No problem. Everything good with you?"

"Rough night. See you soon." She ended the call. My level of concern didn't diminish. At least I knew she was all right. I left the other breakfast sandwich on her desk and got to work. Father David told me his murdered colleague had been an excellent priest and—most importantly in today's climate—never faced any accusations over his behavior. I couldn't simply take his word for it, however, so I started digging. Thinking it might take a while, I brewed a half-pot of coffee before settling in to work.

One of the reasons the Catholic Church was able to hide a lot of facts from the public was because they kept so many documents internal. They only saw the light of day under subpoena. Even after the fallout from the scandals and cover-ups, the church still kept things close to the vest. Thankfully, the Archdiocese of Baltimore didn't practice great security. During a routine probe of their network, I found a server running the very old and insecure Telnet protocol. I connected, poked around, and found a document containing administrative credentials.

Sometimes, it really is so easy.

Sean Cooper had indeed studied at the seminary with Father David. He'd served at a number of stops since his ordination. None of the files I found for him indicated he'd ever been involved or even suspected of anything inappropriate or untoward. From the central office, I could even check records for all the churches where he'd been stationed. Nothing contradicted the assessment indicating Sean

Cooper had been a model priest and a credit to the profession.

Someone wanted to kill him badly enough to draw out the process and make him suffer. The answer to why wouldn't be found in his personnel file, however.

———

A few minutes later, footsteps clanged up the metal stairs. The door opened, and T.J. walked in. She flashed a quick smile and sat at her desk. "Morning, boss."

"Everything good?" I asked.

"Yeah." She unlocked her laptop and stared at the screen. I waited for her to elaborate, tell me off for prying, or anything else, but she remained silent.

"You sure?"

"I'm fine."

"You haven't even looked at the breakfast sandwich I left on your desk."

Her eyes flicked to it for a second. "Thanks. I'll heat it up later." She turned to look at me. "How are things this morning?"

"A little slow," I said. "I had to make my own coffee. It set me back a few minutes."

"I'm not sure how you've survived." I expected the barb. Hell, I set T.J. up to deliver it—not usually a requirement considering how freely she hurled them. Her delivery lacked some of its usual zing and humor.

"All right, what's really going on? You seem a little off this morning."

"I'm fine," she said again.

"The hell you are."

T.J. closed her eyes and sighed. "You'll think it's silly."

"Try me."

It took her a few seconds, but she said, "Fine. Remember Velvet?"

I shrugged. "It was a phase when I was eighteen. The blazer looked good on me, though."

A small grin accompanied the eye roll I expected—and deserved. "She was one of the girls you met with me in the coffee shop. You were looking into Libby's disappearance."

I thought about the case. It ended tragically like a lot of them do. Libby wound up dead, but at least I caught the men responsible with an eleventh-hour assist from T.J. "She was the brunette, right?"

T.J. nodded. "We were pretty tight. As much as you could be when you're basically competing for thirsty men's cash, at least." She snickered. "Not that it was much of a competition. Velvet was always the favorite. I'm tall. I wouldn't want it any other way, but average or short guys don't want to be with a woman who can look down on them. In the right heels, I'm as tall as you." She was right. The five-inch gap between our flat-footed heights could be overcome by the right pair of stilettos or platform boots. "Velvet is shorter. Great tits. Perfect ass. She was always the big earner."

"You're not still competing with her, you know."

"I know. I discovered I fell back into those old thought processes very quickly."

"Where did you see her?" I asked.

"I picked up some food last night. Thought I saw her across the street, but when I got there, she was gone. A little while later, she knocks on my apartment door."

"Is she the first person you've run into from . . . before?"

"Yeah," T.J. said. "I try to keep myself away from people and places that would remind me too much of the old life.

We had a nice chat, at least. She's moved to OnlyFans and what sounds like higher-end escorting. I mentioned Nightlight and Melinda, but I don't think Velvet is ready yet."

"People move at their own speed especially when it comes to major changes."

"I know." She paused and smiled. "Thanks for listening. I guess it was weighing on me a little this morning."

"It's all good."

"Where are we on the priest?"

"I independently confirmed he wasn't a kid toucher," I said.

"You didn't believe your friend?"

"I did, but the whole mess was a scandal in part because of the cover-up. Father David doesn't have any special title or rank. He could have been kept in the dark. Turns out he wasn't."

"Not about this one at least," T.J. pointed out.

"True. I looked through the police report and didn't see any mention of security footage."

"Usually means there wasn't any."

"Right. Maybe there isn't of the courtyard, but I saw a couple cameras above the church's front doors. They could have others. We may not get to see Father Sean knifed on film, but it doesn't mean we can't learn something."

"Worth a try. You going to break in?"

"I'm going to try doing it the right way first," I said.

"Working with all these priests is rubbing off on you," T.J. said.

"Go to hell," I said.

———

Unfortunately, doing this part right meant calling Father Larry. As the lone priest available at St. Ann's, he was the only person I could contact about it. I didn't expect him to know much about the setup, but I held out hope he could direct me to someone who at least knew how to turn a computer on.

Paul's Epistle to the Romans told us to rejoice in hope. If only I could.

"I don't know anything about it," Father Larry said.

"No offense, but I didn't expect you to. Is there someone else there who might've configured the system? Your sacristan?"

"Timothy?" The priest snorted. "He's a good kid, but it would be pretty far outside his wheelhouse."

"All right," I said, "let's start with a little information. Are there any other cameras at the church?"

"There's another one at the side door."

"The one which opens to the courtyard?"

"Yes."

I hadn't noticed it on our visit, but we'd focused more on the crime scene. Still, spotting details was something an investigator should do well. "No others?"

"I don't think so, no," he said.

"What about at the school?" If it also had one across from the church's courtyard cam, we might be able to get a decent video or pull some good stills.

"Only two, I think. One at the front door and one at the back where the recess yard is."

I bit down a blasphemy and thought about how Father Larry might be helpful. The archdiocese probably installed and maintained the security system. While they wanted the murder solved, they were also an institution. They'd value things like proper procedure. Police could ask for footage with a warrant. A private investigator would be unlikely to receive a warm response. I thought about checking with Father David but decided to play the hand I'd been dealt. "You're at your desk, right?"

"Yes, why?"

"Your computer runs Windows?"

"Yes. What's this all about, Mister Ferguson? I don't want to get wrapped up in one of your schemes again."

"The last one you helped me with worked pretty well," I said. "Besides, I simply want some information from you."

"What are you going to do with it?"

"Request the footage." Which I would—in a manner of speaking.

Father Larry harrumphed but eventually said, "Okay, what do you need?"

I talked him through the process of launching a command prompt, typing something specific, and reading me the results, which I entered into a text file on my computer. "I think I have everything," I told him when we'd finished. "Thanks for your help."

"I hope it bears some fruit," he said and ended the call.

"He was actually able to help you?" T.J. wanted to know.

"In a roundabout way." I jerked my head to the side. "Roll yourself over here. You can watch me access their cameras."

"Cool." T.J. wheeled her chair to me.

"As I figured, he didn't know anything about the security system. Instead, I got him to read off some information from his PC." I pointed at the text file on my screen. "What does it tell you?"

"Looks like his hostname, IP address, MAC address, and DNS servers."

"You're right. Look at the numbers, though." She did and shrugged a couple seconds later. "They're public."

"Ohhhh," T.J. said. "So you can try and find the cameras this way."

"Yes." One of the limitations inherent in IP addressing is the number of supported hosts. A workaround is to use a private scheme. Certain blocks and ranges are reserved for this, and most home networks use one. Businesses adopted the tactic more and more over the years, as well. From a risk management perspective, most machines didn't need a public-facing address. The Archdiocese of Baltimore, on the other hand, took an old-school approach. I didn't yet know if it extended to devices like cameras, but we would soon find out.

"What's this?" T.J. asked as I brought up Shodan.

"Think of it as a search engine which can point you to just about any Internet-connected device."

"You can control them from here?"

"No," I said. "It will tell me more about them, though. IP address. Make and model. We can use those to look for things like vulnerabilities and default credentials."

T.J. rubbed her hands together. It was good to see her come out of her mini-funk. It didn't take long to find what we needed. Filtering results by IP range showed us some devices, and picking the cameras out proved easy from there. They came from a popular manufacturer. At least the archdiocese didn't skimp on the equipment. It remained to be seen if they skimped on the setup and management.

With the make and model in hand, we searched for open vulnerabilities. The most recent was a year old. Still, odds were good of finding unpatched cameras in the wild. Enterprises paid attention when it came to updating their computers. Other devices . . . not so much. Another major problem was default credentials. They're necessary to enable initial setup out of the box. Competent organizations change them. "Let's find out what kind of a return on their IT investment the archdiocese is getting," I said as I keyed in the built-in username and password.

The answer: pretty poor.

No one bothered changing the initial credentials, so I gained access to the camera. The first thing I cared about was storage. If it offloaded and deleted data, we would need to track down the video files elsewhere. Thankfully, the policy proved favorable: files got backed up to the cloud overnight, but they also remained local for thirty days. T.J. rattled off the day Father Cooper was murdered.

"Friday night into Saturday," I said. "No services except for later in the afternoon."

"So if anyone comes to see him, it's probably not good."

We soon learned someone would actually need to visit to get caught by the cameras. The front pair could only see to the bottom of the stairs. Anyone who hurried past the front of St. Ann's via the sidewalk would be invisible. The side unit similarly lacked range. Unless someone killed the priest a few feet in front of the door, we'd never get a look at it.

T.J. and I watched the playback at a high rate of speed starting in the morning. People filed into the church leading up to a service at nine AM Friday morning. About forty-five minutes later, they left. An occasional person came and went throughout the rest of the day. Each time, I paused the video during the best glimpse of them we could get and took a screenshot. T.J. also snapped a photo of each with her phone.

Nothing much happened until the evening. At about six-thirty, two guys neared St. Ann's. I slowed the playback speed to real time. As one pulled a front door open, the other was courteous enough to look at the camera. I screencapped the event, and T.J. also took a photo of it. She tapped away on her phone as I sped the video up. We saw the same two men leave about twenty minutes later. They didn't look bloody or hurried.

"I don't know who they are yet," my secretary said, "but the guy who looked up has a large neck tattoo. It's for a Mexican gang."

"This case just got a lot worse," I said.

CHAPTER 6

AFTER CONFIRMING Father David was in, T.J. drove us to the Esperanza Center. It stood on Broadway just north of Eastern Avenue. While most of Fells Point earned a reputation for pubs, eateries, and shops, the Esperanza Center provided important services for recent immigrants to the United States. This made it a bit out of place in the neighborhood. When I first returned from Hong Kong over four years ago, I volunteered for a couple weeks before beginning my PI career and sporadically in the years since.

"How's your Spanish?" T.J. asked as we approached. Rather than the brick facade featured on many other buildings in the area, the Esperanza Center's three-story front was made of tan stone. The only visible name was in the form of a blue awning with small white letters over the main entrance. A smaller placard identified the service provider as Catholic Charities of Maryland.

"Probably a little rusty but good enough," I said, "though I doubt we'll get a lot of use out of it today." We moved through the lobby and past a room full of children playing with each other while their parents talked nearby. Father David's office door was open, so I knocked on it. He waved us in with a smile. T.J. and I took seats on the cloth task chairs in front of his desk. The small office remained spartan. Other than the desk and a crucifix on the wall, its major feature was a bookcase packed with tomes on immigration, social work, and spirituality.

"How can I help you today?" Father David asked, folding his hands in front of him on the desktop.

"We watched some security footage from St. Ann's," I said.

"The archdiocese released it to you?"

"In a manner of speaking, yes." I put up my hand to head off Father David's forthcoming objection. "You came to me. My methods aren't always by the book, but I'll get you results. It's probably better for all of us if you don't focus too much on how I do things."

Father David frowned but bobbed his head. "All right. What did you see?"

T.J. took an Android tablet from her purse and pulled up a couple still images from the video feed. "These two men were the only visitors anywhere near the time your friend was killed. We don't know if they came to see him or not, but I can tell you the tattoos we can see indicate these guys are in a Mexican gang."

"Not uncommon, I'm afraid. We don't discriminate based on circumstance. Father Sean was adamant about it. 'We need to meet people where they are,' he would say." He smiled. "I know he didn't come up with the quote, but he certainly used it enough. He was big on understanding people's circumstances as a part of helping them. Sometimes, this meant acknowledging someone was in a gang. You can still try to make their situation better, but it's all in the approach."

"Do you know who these two guys are?" I said.

Father David shrugged. "By sight, no, but I'm sure we can figure it out. I doubt they would've had anything to do with Father Cooper's murder, however."

"Because gang members are renowned for their dedication to nonviolence?"

"Because he was helping them. You may be cynical, Mister Ferguson. Maybe I am a little, too, sometimes. God knows this job isn't always easy. But Father Cooper never let it get to him. He wanted to help the people who came to him. Immigrants. Refugees. Some of them were in gangs when they immigrated. Others found them here. He didn't care. He even let people do work at the church. There have been a bunch of issues and delays with the construction, so he would give jobs to people who needed the work and the money."

"Maybe those two saw something," T.J. said. "Or someone. It would still be good to talk to them."

"If they visited Father Cooper, they probably signed the guestbook."

"I guess we're making another stop at Saint Ann's," I said. "Father Larry will be thrilled."

"Do the two of you not get along?" Father David asked.

I shrugged. "We're acquainted from a case a few years ago. Let's just say there's a little personality conflict at play."

"He's committed to finding the killers, too. We all want to see them pay for what they did."

"I guess we're off to the church, then." T.J. and I stood. "Thanks. We'll stop by again if we need anything else."

"Thank you, Mister Ferguson," Father David said. "God be with you both." T.J. and I left his office and exited the Esperanza Center. As far as I could tell, we were alone.

———

The sacristan at St. Ann's didn't want to let us look around.

"It's all very irregular," Timothy said. Despite looking like a scruffy college freshman, he sounded like a prim and proper butler weary after forty years on the job. Showing him my ID did little to change his mind or demeanor.

"Murder is an irregular business," I said. Timothy's expression remained neutral.

"The police were already here. They went over everything."

"Apparently not because the archdiocese hired me to move the investigation along."

"I just don't think—"

"Look, Timothy," I broke in. "You can either stand in my way or stand aside. Regardless, we're going to check out Father Cooper's room and office. I'm sure Father Larry can tell you we're official if you have questions." I shouldered past him, and T.J. followed me.

"He's just doing his job," she whispered as we walked along. "How many times have you told me not to put someone through to you?"

"He doesn't get to keep us from doing what we came here to do," I said. "Besides, your voice is more pleasant on the phone than mine."

"No, it's not."

"Sure it is." We took the stairs to the second floor. I wanted to see the bedroom first. It wasn't generally accessible to the public, so it made a better place for anything Father Cooper might have wanted to hide. "People probably think you're better-looking than me, too, even though I might push back a little there."

T.J. punched me in the shoulder, and I grinned. She rolled her eyes. We stood outside Father Cooper's bedroom on the second floor. Other than the restroom, all four of the doors here looked the same. Drab brown broke up the same-ness of the off-white walls. A small sign to the right of the entryway identified the room as belonging to Rev. Sean Cooper. It was unlocked. "Good thing," T.J. said as I swung the door in. "I don't think Timothy would've unlocked it for you."

"Who needs him?" The quarters were larger than I expected. I figured priests would have dinky accommodations akin to the fourth bedroom in a townhouse—maybe ten feet square with a modest closet and builder-grade window. This was at least fifty percent bigger. A queen bed stood at the far corner. Two dressers lined the walls, and an exercise bike and mat consumed a bunch of the remaining floor space. Some of the drawers remained slightly ajar . . . probably a result of the cops rifling through them.

"I'll take this one," I told T.J. The dresser in front of me was squat and long. The one she would search through was tall and narrow. A few framed pictures clustered near the center. I imagined they were arranged differently and put back indiscriminately by the BPD. All showed Father Cooper with people he bore some resemblance to. I guessed his parents and a sister who looked to be around his age. It made me recall my own sister Samantha who died when I was sixteen. I checked each frame but found nothing other than the photos inside.

T.J. and I got down to business with our searches. I'd never considered what kinds of other clothes priests might own. In the case of Sean Cooper, his extracurricular wardrobe consisted of several pairs of identical jeans, an impressive array of T-shirts, and enough underwear to outfit a football team. The officers who searched through here before me didn't take much care in putting things back. If anything had been here, they would've found it. I even pulled the drawers out, looked behind them, and checked for false bottoms.

"Nothing of interest here," T.J. said a moment later. "Just a bunch of socks, workout clothes, and hoodies." We checked the closet next. It wasn't very big. Probably why Father Cooper rocked the double dresser setup. Most of the clothes hanging up were the standard black shirt and pants worn by priests all across the country. Also on hangers were a few other colors of slacks as well as some sweaters. I checked the walls of the modest space for any hidden items or secret doors but came up empty.

We left the bedroom and returned to the first floor. Timothy kept an eye on things as we walked into Father Cooper's office, but he didn't try to stop us. If the cops searched this room, they took a lot more care in keeping it neat. "I'll take the desk," T.J. said, and she cut me off to get there. This left me with the overcrowded bookcase.

"I guess I'll work here," I said. She stuck her tongue out at me and opened a drawer. I'd never seen so many books on religion, theology, and the like, and I went to private schools my whole life. Despite holding approximately nine tons of old tomes, the bookcase remained in good shape. I checked the back and sides for hiding places and whiffed on all. Would Father Cooper hide something in the books?

I took a step back and appraised the situation. If he did, any of the titles would make a good hiding spot. Odds were slim of anyone getting here to begin with, and even if they did, most people wouldn't pick up thick religious books out of genuine interest. Anyone conducting a proper search would start with the top left. If I were going to conceal something, I would make sure to do it farther down and hope whoever rifled through my stuff got bored and gave up.

I began my search on the second shelf from the bottom.

"There are some letters in here," T.J. said. "Some in English, some in Spanish. A few pictures, too." She flipped through them. "Everyone looks happy." Her eyes scanned a few papers. "These are all thanking Father Cooper for things he did."

"If he got a different kind of correspondence, I hope he kept it over here."

"You just want to be the one to find it."

"Fair," I admitted. "I'd also hate to think I crouched at a shelf of dusty old theology books for nothing." I started with the first volume on the shelf and worked my way down. Toward the far end, I picked up a book with the thrilling title *Explaining Theology While Living It.* Even looking at the cover made me want to yawn. I held the tome spine up and shook it. A folded paper fell out. "Hello." I picked it up and unfolded it.

> *Father Cooper,*
> *You need to stop. You're endangering people . . . most of all yourself. This is your only warning.*

"Wow," T.J. said. She walked over to check out the note. It was handwritten in very neat cursive on a plain sheet of white paper.

"I'm not sure I've ever seen a death threat with perfect penmanship before," I said.

"Maybe a woman wrote it."

"Men can have nice handwriting, too."

"Yours is kind of a mess."

"I didn't pay much attention in cursive class," I said.

"I think we need to pay attention to this," T.J. said.

"Definitely. It's our only lead so far." I checked for the presence of Timothy. He wasn't anywhere nearby. "Let's grab it and go." T.J. slipped the paper into her purse. On the way out, we ran into Timothy again. He inserted himself between us and the door. "Is there another exit?"

"Sir?"

"From the rectory," I said. "Is there another way in or out?"

"There's a back door, yes."

"Where does it lead?"

He shrugged. "There's a small grotto there, and then it winds around to the courtyard. Why?"

"Just trying to get the lay of the land. Thanks." He moved aside, and T.J. and I left.

"Are you thinking what I'm thinking?" she asked.

"Does it involve calculating how many times Timothy got stuffed into a locker?"

She grinned. "No. If there's a back door, Father Cooper could've walked outside without anyone else knowing about it."

"Yeah," I said. "It wouldn't even get caught on camera."

CHAPTER 7

WE MADE another stop while we were out.

I did some research on my phone once we left St. Ann's. The archdiocese originally signed a large contract to renovate the exterior and interior of both the church and sacristy. The first company they hired folded before work began, so another company picked it up under the same terms. Thanks to some staffing issues on the contractor's end and funding challenges from the Church—both reported in the *Baltimore Sun*—the project saw more delays and problems than progress. A recent report said everything would be up for another round of bids soon.

We would get the runaround from the archdiocese. They'd barely commented in the articles I found. "Father Cooper apparently let some of the people he helped do work around the church," I said as I dug for some more information. "Not just sweeping and straightening, either. He'd give them money from collections for performing real labor."

"You think the construction company wanted him dead?" T.J. asked.

"Maybe, but the contract had been a debacle pretty much from the start. They brought their own share of problems to it. No, I think we should look at the union. If a priest was giving meaningful jobs to other people, they're the ones who stand to lose."

"Where are we headed?"

I didn't know much about trade unions, so I became fluent as T.J. drove. The people who did the work behind the walls—plumbers and electricians, mostly—had their own separate representation. The folks who hung the drywall and screwed the floorboards into place belonged to Local 79, the Baltimore-area chapter of the International Building Workers Union. "They're actually not far from our office," I said. "Looks like they're in Greektown. About two miles farther along Eastern Avenue near Hopkins Bayview."

T.J. said she knew the area, and we headed there. Despite only being twenty, she was a good driver. The Mustang helped. T.J. didn't like lingering behind slow drivers, and the turbocharged engine provided plenty of passing power. I would have preferred the V8 and a few more creature comforts—not to mention the manual transmission—but the car suited T.J. It was no frills. Dependable. What you saw was what you got. She replaced an old and battered Civic with this faster model a few months ago and seemed happy for the change.

The headquarters of Local 79 must have served as a pub in a previous life. It featured a wide front and was deeper than the rowhouses near it. A parking lot packed with a couple cars and a bunch of pickup trucks lay out back. T.J. left the Mustang in one of two remaining spots. We walked around to the front entrance. Floors were polished dark hardwood. Impractical for a trade union office but ideal for a bar. The walls needed to be repainted. Spots where posters or paintings hung previously were obvious thanks to the slight color difference.

They'd done a good job converting the place to an open floor plan, at least. A bunch of men milled around desks in the back. A lone woman sat at a large desk near the entry. She had a round face and wore her dark hair up in a bun. After scrutinizing T.J. and me, she didn't offer a smile. "What can I do for you?"

"We'd like to speak to Mister Teller," I said, referring to the union boss.

"Do you have an appointment?"

"No."

"Mister Teller doesn't see anyone without an appointment."

"Let's not pretend he's a head of state . . . " I glanced at her desk for a name. ". . . Rebecca." I showed her my ID. "It's about a murder investigation. If you'd rather the police come here, I'm happy to tell them how uncooperative everyone in your office is."

"We're busy."

"Right. You have two guys back there playing paper football on a desk. Two others are making coffee. It's always struck me as a one-person job, but I've never been a part of a union. The rest don't look like they're doing anything except converting oxygen into carbon dioxide. Can we dispense with the bullshit?"

She turned around, shouted, "Hey!" into the rear of the office, and all the men did their best to look busy. One even picked up a clipboard. "I'll call." She stared at me the whole time she lifted the phone and keyed in a three-digit extension —201. "You got a private detective here to see you." She paused. I couldn't hear the other end of the conversation. "He says it's about a murder investigation . . . all right." She replaced the handset. "You can head up the stairs. He's on the right."

"Thanks," T.J. said. Probably a professional courtesy. Rebecca didn't really earn our gratitude. We climbed the stairs. They led to a hallway running to the rear wall. Besides the restroom, there was one door on each side. The boss was supposed to be on the right. We knocked. "Come in," he called, and I opened the door. The union's website said Brent Teller had been in charge for five years, recently winning another four-year term. He was a tall and broad man who looked like he could still carry a pile of two-by-fours and frame a house. His hair remained brown, but his goatee was mostly gray. He shook my hand and made sure to apply a strong grip.

"You told Rebecca this was about a murder?" he said.

"Yes," I said as T.J. and I sat in front of his desk, and I showed Teller my credentials. There was a lot of unused space in the office. The desk sat around the center. There was a bookcase on both walls around it. In the far corner, a smaller desk held a few rolled-up blueprints. The rest was all paneling, carpet, and air. Maybe Teller liked having a large floor plan to help him feel important.

"We haven't lost any members recently."

"Not one of yours. Sean Cooper, a priest at St. Ann's Church."

Teller folded his hands in his lap. "I'm afraid I don't see the connection."

"Bad contract," I said. "The first company couldn't live up to it. There's scaffolding there, so I presume work was at least set to begin at some point. Once the project ran into some problems, the priest gave jobs to refugees in the parish." I spread my hands. "Turns out you don't need four hundred square feet to delegate tasks."

"What are you getting at, Mister . . . Ferguson, was it?"

"Yes. He wasn't just letting people sweep the floor in the

mornings. This was real work. The kind which might normally go to your union."

"And you think I murdered a priest because he handed out jobs following a bad contract?"

"It's a theory," I said.

"Have you said it out loud?" he asked. "It sounded a little ridiculous to me a few seconds ago."

Before I could answer, the door opened, and a beautiful woman walked in. If she'd been sitting at the desk downstairs, the line of men interested in toiling for the union would've wrapped around the building. She looked to be about five-six but taller in the four-inch stilettos she wore. Her skirt stopped a couple inches above the knees, showcasing legs which suggested she wore heels often. Dark hair spilled over her shoulders, and the button-down shirt was probably a size too big to ensure it properly closed over her breasts. "Oh. Sorry, hon. I didn't know you were busy." I couldn't place her accent, but she didn't sound like a local even though she used the popular 'hon.'

"It's fine," Teller said. "These investigators are here about the priest who was murdered a while ago." He smiled and extended a hand toward the recent arrival, revealing a Rolex around his wrist. "This is my wife, Mary."

She showed an automatic smile. "Nice to meet you both."

"Oh, I remembered. Kyle told me he needs a new polo before his appearance tonight. Can you make sure one's waiting for him?"

"Sure. What size does he use?"

"Just a large." She nodded and left the room. "She helps me out a few days a week. This is a much busier job than I first thought it would be, but it's also very rewarding." I didn't say anything. Teller was no doubt used to pontificating and overstating how much he loved what he did. "You offered a theory a couple minutes ago. Do you think I'm a murderer?"

"It doesn't have to be you," I said, "but your workers stand to lose the most."

"The people who work for me aren't killers."

"I've found the question of who's a killer or not often comes down to motivation."

"I guess you'll need to find a different motive, then," Teller said. "Look, no one was happy to lose work. We've seen some . . . flakiness with the archdiocese before. The money doesn't always come when it needs to. The problem is they're not completely in control of the purse. I hope the contract situation at Saint Ann's gets resolved so my guys can go there again. If it doesn't, there's plenty of other jobs to go around." He glanced at his fancy watch again. "Now, if you'll excuse me, I do need to get back to work of my own."

"Thanks for your time," T.J. said. We walked down the stairs and outside the building. I saw a couple Greek restaurants across the street, and I knew Ikaros was a couple blocks up. "Good area to grab lunch," she suggested.

"It is," I said. "All this talk of construction makes me think of another place, though. Let's head back. I'll bring you something."

"You don't want me to come with you?"

I shook my head. "Not this time."

———

After returning to the office, I enjoyed the nice spring day and hoofed it to Little Italy. It was a little over a mile to the front door of Rizzo's. I'd known the owners my whole life. Tony Rizzo ran the place under its original name of *Il Buon Cibo*. His daughter Gabriella took over about a year ago, modernized the menu and décor, and simplified the name. Like many restaurants, Rizzo's occupied what was originally a brick rowhouse.

The first floor looked more like a Brooklyn pizza bistro than ever. A few diners ate at tables. I was late enough to avoid the lunch rush. Tony kept a table near the fireplace on the lower level. His daughter preferred the second floor, so I climbed the stairs and found her at her usual spot. Two large men with no necks shared the table with her. In addition to inheriting the *ristorante* from her late father, Gabriella also took over organized crime in the city.

We were close in age and grew up as friends. She'd always been beautiful, but we remained only friends because I didn't want her father to have me drawn and quartered after the inevitable breakup. Gabriella had a darker, classic Italian complexion, but otherwise looked a lot like Mary Teller. They even dressed in similar button-downs, and my old friend's needed to size up to do the same restraint job. The pair of enforcers knew me enough to remain seated as I walked to her table. "Can I join you?" I asked.

Gabriella shrugged. "It's a free country." She glanced at the muscle twins. "Take a walk, guys." They got up and left without complaint. Once they were out of earshot, she said, "You know, when we devised our truce, I didn't expect to see you very often." Her dark eyes flicked to the ring finger on my left hand for an instant. "Congratulations, by the way."

"Thanks," I said. "I would've invited you, but it all came together quickly. I also didn't want anyone to poison the wine."

"Oh, please." Gabriella grinned. "I could come up with something far more creative." Our truce became necessary when Gabriella grew obsessed with her father's death. Two of her men abducted me and questioned me about it in a decidedly unfriendly fashion. Eventually, I told Gabriella in person what I knew about her dad and his attempt to take me out in his final weeks on earth. We'd been in a kind of frosty *détente*—or *rilassamento* in her Italian roots—ever since. "I'm happy for you, really."

"It's permissible to send a gift up to a year later, you know."

"I still have a few months, then, don't I?"

"I guess you do," I said.

"What brings you in today, C.T.?"

"Your dad used to have his hand in construction. I'm wondering if your modernization efforts have kept it in play."

She crossed her arms and leaned back as much as the chair would allow. The interior refresh hadn't quite made it to the second level yet. The dark wood and exposed beams presented a stylistic contrast with the ground floor. Paintings of Italian vistas on the wall were effective in setting the mood, at least. "He started scaling back on that a while ago," she said. "I've followed his example. One of the things he told me is construction got more popular with people laundering money. It brought more scrutiny than before." She paused. "Why do you ask?"

"A priest hired me to look into the murder of one his compatriots."

"Saint Ann's?" I nodded. "Wow. The Church hired you. I'm a little surprised you'd take the case."

"I may not be Catholic like you," I said, "but the murder of a priest still sits wrong with me."

"You're Lutheran." Gabriella flashed a warm smile. "As you might say, that's within the error bars of being Catholic."

"I do admire someone who could look at a major institution and write a list of ninety-five things wrong with it. I can't get past thirty with the current mayor."

She chuckled. "Still. You're adjacent to Catholic. And you're right . . . it doesn't sit well with me, either. I've never been to Saint Ann's, but I don't want to see a priest killed unless he was a major pedo."

"He wasn't."

"If you want to know if I've heard anything about it, I haven't," Gabriella said. "What's the construction tie-in?"

"Saint Ann's was supposed to be undergoing renovations. There were contract issues, and the priest who got killed handed some serious work to refugees at the church."

Gabriella spread her hands. "People have been murdered in this city for less. I'll keep an ear out. If I hear anything, I'll let you know."

"Thanks."

"You're still not getting a free meal." The corner of my longtime friend's mouth turned up slightly, betraying her stern tone. Maybe a layer of ice defrosted.

"It's expensive with me getting carry-out for two now."

"It's nice of you to get lunch for your secretary."

"Yeah," I said. "If only I could keep her out of my leftovers."

CHAPTER 8

T.J. STAYED in to make dinner this time. A quick stop at the grocery store on the way home boosted her supplies. No one ever taught her much about cooking, so she tended to stay with simple fare. Sometimes, C.T. would tell her about things he made for dinner, and they'd talk a little about the recipe— if he actually had one—and techniques. For the most part, however, she stuck to easy dishes. The property management company probably didn't want a new tenant tripping the fire alarm.

Tonight, she boiled water for rice and heated a frozen Chinese entree in another pan. While those moved along, she diced a tomato and sliced part of a cucumber, adding both to a bowl of lettuce. For a few years, she didn't eat very well. Sometimes not very often. A salad might not be the classic pairing with sesame chicken, but it represented a much better class of food than she'd gotten used to in her teens.

When everything was ready, T.J. carried her dinner to the living room and ate in front of the TV. She flipped on the local news. Despite the generally depressing nature of coverage—it seemed the anchors spent half the runtime talking about murders and other violent acts—she liked knowing what happened in Baltimore. Even when it was depressing. Besides, some people who made the news for unfortunate reasons today could turn out to be clients in a week or two.

She was almost finished with her meal when someone knocked on the door. T.J. checked her phone. She didn't miss any calls or texts. Whoever it was rapped again. She got up, moved to the entryway, and looked through the peephole. Velvet again. "Shit," T.J. muttered under her breath before unlocking and opening the door. Tonight, Velvet opted for a short skirt and a white button-down shirt worn low enough to show the top half of her breasts to the world. A purse which was barely bigger than a clutch lay around her shoulder on a thin strap.

"Can I come in?" Velvet asked. T.J. stood aside and swept her arm into the apartment. "This place is close to the college. Lot of students live here?"

T.J. shrugged. "I guess."

"Plenty of potential boyfriends to test out."

"I haven't tried yet."

"You should." Velvet moved into the living room and sat on the opposite end of the couch from the last bites of T.J.'s dinner.

T.J. picked up her plate. "What do you want, Velvet?" She realized she'd never known the girl's real name. Some in their former profession offered them up after a while if they built some trust with co-workers. Velvet never did. The other girls all knew T.J.'s initials even if they never learned the actual names behind them. Her pimp's enforcer settled on the incorrect Tami Jean which was why she still hated it.

"I got curious about that foundation you mentioned."

"Nightlight?" Velvet nodded. T.J. set her plate down, the last few bites still uneaten. "It was great for me. Best thing

I've ever done in my life. I'll tell you anything you want to know."

"How long did it take?"

"For what?"

"To get . . . " Velvet gestured absently around the room. ". . . the life out of your head."

"There's no brainwashing," T.J. said. "They can't *Eternal Sunshine* anything away." She shrugged again. "It's more about building a present where you can live with your past."

"Sounds like something on a brochure," Velvet said.

"It's not, but maybe it could be."

"And you can live with yours?"

"Even when people I haven't seen in a couple years randomly turn up at my door." T.J. smiled. "Yeah. I know who I was. More importantly, I know who I am now."

"You've been at it for a while from what I see."

"It's a process," T.J. said. "It's not just getting you off the streets and out of the life. It's about helping you build skills to do something else."

"I might be ready sometime soon," Velvet said. "I told you I've been . . . cutting back. There's something I'm working on now. It's a little different. Once I'm done, I may want to meet your friend."

T.J. never considered Melinda a friend before. Inspiration. Mentor. She thought friend fit really well, too. "When you think the time is right, come talk to me."

"Hey, you wanna take a walk with me?" When T.J. glanced at her watch, Velvet added, "Don't be an old lady. It's barely dusk."

"Where are you headed?"

"I want to find someone. We can talk more on the way." She stood, and T.J. copied the movement without thinking. Following the popular Velvet again. She chided herself for it. "Let's go." T.J. hesitated a moment but joined her friend.

———

They headed south from T.J.'s apartment and picked up Saratoga Street going east. Massey's was on the left. Did Velvet know the area well? It would've helped her disappear when T.J. saw her last night. Within a couple blocks, they also passed a nail salon, and St. Alphonsus Catholic Church. It looked nothing like St. Ann's, but T.J. still thought about the current case. The headquarters of the archdiocese wasn't far from where they stood, either.

Velvet kept walking. After being quiet for a while, she finally spoke up. "I have an ulterior motive here." T.J.'s stomach clenched. "Well, two, really. How much do you like your new life?"

"I love it," T.J. said. Velvet snorted. "I do. I make honest money for honest work. My boss trusts me. I've been able to get a decent apartment and a car."

"Great." While they waited for a light, Velvet took a pack of long, thin cigarettes from her purse and lit one. "Want a smoke?"

"No."

"Suit yourself," Velvet said. "You're a worker bee now, T.J. If you're happy, great, but—"

"I am."

"I have an offer for you."

"Not interested," T.J. said.

"Hear me out." T.J. stopped and crossed her arms. It took a couple seconds, but Velvet paused and doubled back a few steps. "I told you I was working on getting out, and I am. This is a good gig. You work a high-end party."

"Work how?"

"You know how."

"No way," T.J. said. "Never again. Hard pass."

"You sure? Pay's great."

"I'm sure." She shook her head. "I can't believe you'd ask me something like that after what we've talked about last night and tonight. What the hell?"

"Fine, fine." Velvet put up her hands. The right one still held her mostly untouched cigarette. "You're right. I shouldn't have mentioned it. At least walk a little farther with me."

"Where are we going?"

"There's a friend I want to see."

"I'm not sure I'm in the mood to meet any of your friends tonight," T.J. said.

"Here he comes." Two men approached from farther along Saratoga. "Hey, babe." As they got closer and stood under a street light, T.J. got a good look at the newcomers. Both were white, tall, and slender. One sported a full head of shaggy blond hair, and the other went bald. The bald one grabbed Velvet and kissed her. She led the group into a nearby alley behind an apartment building where Chrome Dome pushed her against the wall to make out some more.

A moment later after being groped a few times, Velvet said to T.J., "You want anything?"

"Yeah. To go home."

"No. I mean weed."

"I got stronger stuff, too," the clean-shaven one said.

"I'm out. Don't come by again until you're ready for what we talked about earlier, Velvet. I don't need this kind of shit."

"What the hell?" the blond one said. He moved in front of T.J. "Where you think you're going?"

"Home." T.J. heard her pulse in her ears. "Get out of my way."

"Maybe it ain't time for you to leave yet." Blondie took a step forward. Even during her days working the streets, T.J. and the other girls who hustled for Weasel Boy—his name got a little more ridiculous every time she thought about it— learned basic self-defense. She'd resumed occasional studies since working for C.T. This would be the first field test, however. When the guy menacing her reached out, T.J. raised her leg and slammed her heel down on the top of his foot. He howled and started to hop.

He didn't get to do it for long. While the guy cursed at her, T.J. drove her knee into his groin. While he was doubled over, she shoved him, and his face bounced off the wall of the apartment building. "What the hell?" his friend said.

"T.J., what are you doing?" Velvet asked.

"Screw this," T.J. said. She backed away, keeping an eye on everyone else. "You want to talk about the foundation, fine. Anything else, stay away." Before the other guy could give chase, T.J. sprinted back toward her apartment.

————

After locking her door, T.J. slammed her keys into the bowl in the entryway.

"Dammit, Velvet," she growled to the empty apartment. Was the whole evening some kind of setup? When she first arrived, Velvet seemed interested in getting out of the life for good. Then, she talked about a party she was working. "Did she really think I would say yes?" Maybe the weed was a ploy to make an affirmative answer easier. T.J. remembered Melinda talking about how seeing people from the old life might feel good at first, but it often doesn't go well.

"No one's ready until they're ready," Melinda said several times. It always sounded self-evident to T.J., but now she understood. Velvet could talk about reducing her exposure, changing the way she worked, and a desire to springboard into a clean break. None of it meant she was really prepared. She called Melinda. It rang a few times but went to voicemail. T.J. thought about calling C.T. but decided against it. He had his own issues to handle, and she didn't want to appear weak to her boss.

T.J. opened her closet and hefted the heavy bag out. She didn't want to keep it on display in case the building manager ever saw it and objected. With the help of a stepstool, she hung it over a beam in her bedroom. T.J. changed into a T-shirt and shorts, slipped on a pair of MMA gloves, and got to work.

She opened as she always did—by picturing Weasel Boy's face and punching it repeatedly. The guy who first taught her some self-defense accused her of punching like a girl. Over the last few years, T.J. practiced hard to lengthen and strengthen her strikes. She didn't have a formal trainer anymore, and so she'd come to rely on YouTube for instruction. With a raise or bonus at work, T.J. could take proper classes.

Once her hands stung, T.J. moved on to elbow attacks. C.T. told her the value of them—not breaking your fingers or the small bones in your hands chief among them—and she'd worked them into her routine. T.J. thought about Velvet again. Despite being in the same stable, they competed for work. The exceptions were a few johns who paid handsomely for both of them at the same time. *Never again*, T.J. thought as she planted her left foot, rotated her hips, and put a hard elbow into the bag.

T.J. took a deep breath and backed off a step. A perk of

being tall was having long legs. Most girls needed to get closer to an opponent to kick them. T.J. could stay farther away. She raised her fists and started with basic snap kicks. Why was Velvet around all of a sudden? T.J. lived in this apartment for a couple months and had never seen her before last night. She wasn't working the streets anymore. While she might have been extra friendly with the guy selling weed, drugs were available all over the city.

It didn't make sense. The girl could do OnlyFans work from anywhere. She'd just need a phone and an Internet connection. High-end escorting was the only possibility. T.J. liked her apartment, but there were many nicer buildings in other parts of Baltimore. They'd be full of rich men who would pay through the nose for a night with a girl like Velvet. It made T.J. wonder again why Velvet was around here.

She didn't know if she'd ever get an answer. Velvet was reckless tonight. In addition to trying to pitch a job she should have known T.J. would never accept, she led them to a dangerous situation. The pot dealer would be handsy until Velvet didn't want to buy from him anymore. Or until her new friend kicked his buddy in the balls. Then, he might escalate his demands. T.J. sighed and launched a few more kicks. Velvet was a grown woman. She was probably about the same age as T.J., but the street added years. Velvet could take care of herself.

If she wanted to have a serious conversation about Nightlight and getting out of the life for good, T.J. would be ready to help her. Otherwise, she wouldn't open the door for her former companion on the concrete again.

CHAPTER 9

IN THE MORNING, I changed into my Under Armour gear and went for a run. It was a few degrees warmer today, so I saw another couple people in my travels. A slender blonde woman and a beefy black man did laps around Federal Hill Park, as well. We were on my home turf because Gloria wanted a shorter drive after a long day at her job. I was happy to oblige. A few people walking their dogs came and went with one small yapper growling and snapping at everyone who jogged by—me included. After about thirty minutes of exercise, I finished my final lap at a walk and headed back up Riverside Avenue.

It was when I spotted the two large guys standing on the sidewalk.

They did a decent enough job of not looking like goons. As much as two tall, broad-shouldered guys with empty stares and no necks could appear non-threatening, at least. One leaned against a small car he could only enter or exit at great pain, and the other stood against a house. I slowed my pace a little to get some more breath back. The pair watched me the whole way. They barely seemed interested in anyone else, though both turned to eye the blonde jogger as she went by up the opposite side.

"You guys need directions to the gym?" I said as I drew closer. Neither responded. "If you tell me you don't take mirror selfies, I'm not going to believe you."

"Believe this," the brown-haired one said as he pushed his large frame off the tiny car. "You're asking too many questions."

I started counting on my fingers. "So far, I've only come up with one. You're setting a really difficult bar."

"Not today," the shaved-headed one said, his voice full of annoyance. I fought to hide my smirk. "In general. You need to drop what you're working on."

"If I say I will, do you guys just leave?" They looked at each other. The bald one scowled. My needling was paying off. "What if I'm a liar? How do you verify I've stopped?"

"You know what?" Mister Clean said. "Screw you. How about I just beat your ass for being an annoying son of a bitch?"

I raised my fists and smiled. "You're welcome to try."

As I figured, Chrome Dome came at me first. His T-shirt showed muscles large enough to end most fights with a single blow. The problem with one-punch guys is they fall into the habit of ending encounters quickly. When they run into someone who doesn't fit the pattern, they get out of their depth quickly. A few max-effort whiffs later, my clean-shaven foe was already breathing hard. The second moved closer. I didn't want to deal with both of them at the same time.

I backed off a couple steps, and Baldy followed me. I caught the extended fist he threw, turned my hips, and flipped him onto his back. His left elbow cracked against the concrete steps of a rowhouse, and he howled in pain. Only for a second, however, as I kicked him in the face. His head bounced off the sidewalk, and he went quiet.

By now, the brown-haired one was almost on top of me. I pivoted back around and turned a couple punches aside. He launched a side kick. I blocked it, and he followed up with a right jab before I thought he could. I turned my body enough to turn it into a glancing blow off the ribs. He put more power into the follow-up, but he was a little off-balance. I dodged the punch and shoved him aside. The guy stumbled forward. I kicked him in the back of the knee, and his leg went out from under him.

He managed to avoid capsizing completely, but he had no defense for a sharp elbow to the face. My opponent was splayed out on the sidewalk a few feet from his friend, who breathed but otherwise lay still. We hadn't attracted much attention yet. A couple cars went by. Someone hustled up the opposite sidewalk. I didn't see anyone on a phone. No sirens approached. The brown-haired enforcer rubbed his face, so I kicked him in the gut. He sputtered and cursed. "Who sent you after me?" When he didn't answer, I tried the tactic again.

"Piss off," he grunted.

Neither man carried a weapon. In fact, their jeans hugged their legs. No wallets or keys, either. If this guy didn't want to talk, I wasn't getting anything out of them. "Last chance," I said. "By now, someone's called the cops. If you'd rather talk to them, you're an idiot."

"Piss off," he said again.

I shrugged. "Have it your way." I gave him another elbow in the face, and he joined his goonish friend in dreamland. As I walked back up the street toward my house, I dialed 9-1-1 and reported two injured men lying on the sidewalk. When the dispatcher asked what happened to them, I played dumb.

It took considerable effort.

———

I returned home to find Gloria already in the kitchen. Usually, the smells of coffee and whatever I'm cooking on the stove woke her. She still wore her pajamas and yawned before kissing me. "Have a nice run?" she asked as the brew machine did its glorious work.

"Yeah." I flipped open my refillable water bottle and took a long pull. "Even got a little constitutional after." She arched a delicate eyebrow. "Two guys tried to talk me out of continuing my current case."

"What happened?"

"Well, I'm here and about to have coffee and breakfast with you." I glanced at my smartwatch, which displayed the stats for my recent run around the park. "By now, they're probably getting checked out by the paramedics." I got two coffee mugs down from the cabinet. "I was nice enough to call nine-one-one after I left them lying on the sidewalk."

Gloria grinned. "Very thoughtful of you."

"I'll beat your ass, but at least I'm courteous enough to call the paramedics afterward. What do you think of it as a jingle . . . maybe with a little piano in the background?"

"Needs a lot of work," my wife said.

"I've never been much of a songwriter," I admitted. The coffee maker beeped its completion, and I filled both mugs. The matter of breakfast remained. I took a carton of eggs and a package of bacon from the fridge. Once a pan finished heating, I put the bacon in first.

"You have any idea who would've sent two guys after you?" Gloria said.

I shrugged. "Presuming it's related to what we're currently working on, there are a few possibilities."

"The priest's murder?" I nodded as I flipped pork strips. "Doing it was bad enough. Now, it seems whoever did doesn't want to stop there."

"Some killings are random," I said. "With over three hundred homicides a year, you're going to have a bunch fall into the category. It also means many more were deliberate. No one's going to send two goons to keep tabs on a random or accidental murder, but stabbing anyone—priest or not—a dozen times is a very deliberate act."

Gloria sipped her coffee and sat at the round kitchen table. "Have you talked to anyone who might want to keep it quiet?"

"Hard to say. We may not have identified the guilty party yet, so I don't want to assume someone we've talked to sent those two idiots after me. Word could have reached whoever did it."

"So you're no closer to a logical answer?" Gloria wanted to know.

"Unfortunately, no." I took the bacon from the pan, set it on a plate, and cracked the eggs. Frying them in the pork grease made them taste even better. It was science. "Neither guy had a wallet or anything on him. Not even car keys. I couldn't run an ID or license plate." I added a little salt and pepper to the eggs and inhaled the aroma. While they sizzled, I dropped a couple slices of sourdough bread into the toaster. A few minutes later, I carried two plates of bacon, eggs, and toast to the table.

Gloria smiled as she looked at her breakfast. "Thanks. Nice and hearty."

"You might need it to survive another day in the cutthroat world of fundraising."

"All my fistfights are metaphorical," she said.

We ate in silence for a couple minutes. Gloria cut her fried eggs into small pieces like she did with everything. From my table, we enjoyed a nice view of the parking pad outside the back door and the alley running past the rear of the house. "You can't get these views in Brooklandville," I pointed out.

Gloria looked out the window and grinned. "This is true."

"All the concrete and brick you could want."

"And to think I've been enjoying trees and nature all this time."

While the conversation remained pleasant, I knew this was a sticking point. I didn't want to belabor the matter, so I didn't say anything else.

———

When I got to the office, T.J.'s Mustang occupied its usual spot. Manny didn't reserve any for us, but his crew used certain parts of the lot for cars they worked on, and customers tended to cluster near the entrance. My secretary and I parked more on the side. I opened the door and inhaled the aroma of fresh coffee. I would have some when I finished my travel mug. Part of any successful morning routine is making a seamless transition from home java to work java. "You seem happier this morning," I said as I sat in my chair.

T.J. smiled, and she had a nice one when it looked sincere. She was pretty but not so much potential clients would walk in to stare at her. "I am."

I expected some elaboration after our much longer chat yesterday, but I didn't push it. "A couple of guys tried to discourage me from working on the case after my run this morning."

Her eyes widened. "You all right?"

"Sure." I'd probably have a bruise from where the one guy hit me but nothing else. "They got the worse end of it."

"You know who they were?"

"No," I said. "No wallets, IDs, or car keys."

"Hmm." T.J. frowned. "I'll bet the union boss sent them."

"Teller?" She bobbed her head. "Why?"

"The morning after we talk to him about the dead priest, two guys are leaning on you to drop it? The timing is too coincidental."

"Which is why we can't presume it's him."

"I thought you didn't believe in coincidences," T.J. said.

"It depends on context. We're all only here through the unlikely occurrence of our parents meeting, liking each other enough to have sex, and giving birth to a child."

"Can you take it easy on the philosophy, boss?" T.J. raised her mug. "I don't like to dive in before I've had my second cup."

I smiled. "Sure. What I mean is we've talked to several people so far. The priest has been dead a couple weeks. News of our investigation is going to make the rounds in certain circles. Yes, it's possible Teller sent those two. They certainly looked like they could have carried a lot of drywall. He doesn't strike me as dumb or careless, however, and he'd need to be some of both to do it the morning after we came to see him."

"Or desperate," my secretary said.

"Maybe."

"Didn't you also visit your friend the mob lady?"

"I'm not sure we're so tight anymore, but yes."

"You think she could've done it?"

"No," I said.

T.J. furrowed her brows. "It's not like I'm spitballing here. There's precedent for her doing shit like this."

"I know." The confrontation several months ago in Gabriella's father's house—now hers—played in my mind. Our truce seemed intact. "I think she and I have moved past the sending goons stage of . . . wherever we are."

"Describe the two enforcers." I did. "You get a picture of either?"

"No." I chided myself. Should've thought of it even in the moment. "I didn't want to attract a bunch of attention. I was nice enough to call nine-one-one for them, though."

"Any serious injuries we could check hospitals for?" T.J.'s fingers hovered over the keyboard. She soaked up knowledge quickly and was always eager to use what she'd learned. If I wanted to call her my assistant, she'd certainly earned the title.

"Doubt it. Maybe a concussion."

"You're not giving me a lot to work with here."

"Welcome to the world of investigations," I said. "Now, let's see if we can come up with some more legit angles to pursue."

CHAPTER 10

WHO WAS SEAN COOPER?

T.J. and I spent a lot of time trying to figure out his last days and final hours. Who came to see him? Why did he go into the courtyard? Who would want to stab a priest a dozen times? "I think we need to start sooner," I said. "Maybe whoever killed him is someone he came across recently. It's also possible it was someone he'd known for quite a while. I think we need to know as much as we can about who he was. The whole story. Let's do a lot of digging."

We both got to work. T.J. looked into his professional life, and I would take the personal side. "Pretty boring," she said after a minute. "He worked a few jobs in college . . . the bookstore and stuff like that. Then, he went into the seminary. He's been a priest ever since. Never did anything else."

"I'm sure he didn't find it boring," I said. "If anything, he probably considered the priesthood his calling."

"Your Christian roots are showing," T.J. said with a grin.

I shrugged. "It's not really a profession you stumble into or wind up at. We can quibble about the purity and worthiness of some of the men who've put on the vestments, but the vast majority of them got into it because they believed in it."

"You going to church after this?"

"No," I said. "I've lived dangerously enough for one day."

T.J. chuckled and got back to work. "We've already looked into his time in the priesthood. No allegations of anything improper. He did a lot of work with immigrants for the archdiocese, too, not just during his time at Saint Ann's. Seems like it's something of a passion project for him." She tapped the keys. "I don't see a good reason in his work history. I guess it's something you'll have to uncover."

"Might as well get started, then." T.J. wheeled her chair over as I dug into the personal history of the late Father Sean Cooper. He came into the world thirty-seven years ago. "Wow. Way too young to die."

"Yeah," T.J. agreed.

His father Glen was mostly Irish, and his mother Sylvie was French. Glen met her during a trip to Europe, and he stayed there for a year before they returned to the States as husband and wife. "His mother might be the genesis of his working with immigrants," I said.

"Pretty different coming from France versus south of the border here."

"In some ways. She was probably better off than a lot of our Hispanic immigrants, sure. But they'd both face language barriers and challenges adapting to a different country and culture."

"She was a western European woman. She looks white." T.J. pointed at Sylvie's picture on the screen. From what I'd seen of Sean Cooper, he inherited his mother's eyes and nose but his father's sharp jawline. "That alone would mean she'd face less discrimination."

"Probably," I admitted. "Some Latinos look Caucasian, too, you know . . . but I get your point. Still, I think this is a good impetus for him wanting to work with immigrants. His mother was a pretty European lady, but it doesn't mean she had an easy time of things."

"What about the dad?" T.J. asked.

"American citizen. Stayed overseas for a while after meeting Sylvie, but he didn't travel much otherwise. Worked in a few different industries but settled in finance. No criminal record. Died three years ago . . . only a couple months after his wife."

"Any other family?"

A couple more clicks gave me the answer. "A brother. Older by eight years." I searched for Glen Cooper Junior and got a few results. Not all of them were positive. "Seems he's had a few run-ins with the law over the years. Started with solicitation when he was twenty."

"Going into the priesthood looks pretty stable by comparison," T.J. said.

"Yeah. Eight years is a pretty big gap when you're growing up." Rich was my cousin and the closest thing I'd have to a brother, and he was almost seven years my senior. It seemed like a massive difference when he was already involved with a bunch of things I wanted to do. As adults whose professions often overlapped, the gap didn't seem bad at all. "The brother probably served as a role model of what not to do."

"He local?"

"Southern Maryland."

"Road trip?"

"Let's go," I said.

———

We hit the highway ahead of traffic, but it caught up to us en route. Each of the three major arteries we drove—I-95 South, the Baltimore-Washington Parkway, and the Capital Beltway —was more congested than the last. I figured we'd be going in the wrong direction for a slowdown on the Capital Beltway, but never underestimate the volume of cars on I-495 during daylight hours. What should have been a two-hour drive took twenty minutes more.

Steven Cooper lived on Pensive Street in Leonardtown in the shadow of a large community center. For a rural area, it looked much more suburban than exurban. Single-family homes stood on streets running in a neat grid with an occasional cul-de-sac. Parklands broke up the monotony of the sprawl. People played pickleball on a converted tennis court. It almost made me want to get a Starbucks coffee and a Hydro Flask.

Almost.

I curbed the S4 in front of Steven Cooper's house. His was a touch smaller than the ones around it, but they'd all clearly come from the same set of cookie cutters. A double-wide driveway ran up to a single-car garage on the right side of the house. A couple trees which needed a few decades to reach maturity sprang from the manicured front lawn. I wondered how often the homeowners association sent people around with rulers to measure the grass. Anyone over a half-inch would get a fine in the mail.

In some ways, it reminded me of Brooklandville. Gloria's area was tonier and posher with a lot more space between houses, but the overall vibe struck me as similar. A bunch of people with nothing better to do forced their ideas of neighborhood bliss on everyone else. Once we got out of the car, T.J. must have seen my expression, because she walked close and said, "You all right?"

"Yeah. Let's pay this guy a visit."

We headed up the asphalt walkway. It yielded to three

steps and a small stone porch with two packages waiting to be taken inside. I knocked on the door and waited. No answer. I waited some more. Still nothing. I rang the bell and heard a loud *ding-dong* even with everything closed. After another minute passed, T.J. said, "Maybe he's not home."

I shrugged. "No newspapers on the porch or yard, so maybe he's not a subscriber."

"He's not eighty."

"Fair point. Two boxes here." I looked at my watch. "He could still be at work."

"I ain't seen him for a few days," a man said. T.J. and I turned toward the newcomer. He was about sixty and reed thin, dressed in a T-shirt and sweats which hung loose on his frame. A small dog yapped at the end of a leash.

"You live nearby?" I asked.

"Yeah. Next door."

"Does Mister Cooper go away a lot?"

"Hardly ever. He works early, so he's normally home around three." It was after four now. "I usually see him come and go, but nothing for a few days now. It's kinda weird. If he was gonna go somewhere, I think he woulda told me."

"You friends?" T.J. said.

"As much as two people living next door to each other for a few years can be," the man said. "We play pickleball sometimes." He frowned and scrutinized us. "Who are you two?"

"Private investigator," I said. "Mister Cooper's brother died a couple weeks ago, and I wanted to ask him a few questions."

"Jesus. He never said anything."

"Some people grieve privately."

"Yeah." The dog pulled at its leash. "Tell him I said I'm sorry for his loss."

"We will," T.J. said. The man and his pet moved along—

slowly because the dog wanted to sniff every blade of grass along the way.

Once he was well out of earshot, I said, "Can you get the snap gun from the car?"

"We're going in?"

"I think we need to based on what the neighbor told us."

"All right." She opened the passenger's side rear door and fetched the tool. While she did, I slipped on a pair of thin black gloves. I performed a nosy neighbor check, didn't see anyone paying attention to us, and popped the front lock in a couple seconds.

As soon as I pushed the door open a couple inches, I knew something was wrong.

CHAPTER 11

"IS that smell what I think it is?" T.J. asked as she covered her nose and mouth with her elbow.

"I'm afraid so." I pulled the collar of my T-shirt up. It didn't do a lot. The stench of death was strong. "You want to wait outside?" She shook her head and moved into the foyer. I kicked the door shut.

T.J. put her arm down and copied my move of covering her nose and mouth with her T-shirt. "What the hell does it mean that the brother's dead, too?"

"Maybe nothing," I said. "He could have had a heart attack for all we know. Let's look around."

"Shouldn't we call the police?"

"What are they going to do besides take evidence we might be able to use? If the smell is this bad, our guy has been dead for a while. If someone killed him, they haven't set up camp in his house. Let's look around. Based on what we find, we can decide to call the cops or not."

"All right." T.J. remained in place, so I led the way into the home. The entryway spilled into the living room, with smooth tile giving way to plush carpet. A sectional sofa and coffee table took up a great deal of the floor space. A new and large TV I would've loved to take with me hung on the wall. Near the window, a recliner sat facing the TV at an angle.

"It's a lot for one person," I said. "There's seating here for at least six."

"Maybe he has friends over to watch sports," T.J. offered.

I shrugged. "Maybe." Steven Cooper kept the place neat. The only things sitting out on any surfaces were the TV remote and two coasters. We walked into the similarly pristine dining room next. A table with seating for six was the main feature. A buffet and wine rack stood against the side walls. As with the living room, nothing looked out of place. We moved in to the kitchen. It boasted of counter space in abundance, including a freestanding island. Two plain chairs sat around a small wooden table.

For once, something looked out of place.

A plastic bowl held three cigarette butts and some ash. T.J. noticed it, too, and she peered at the contents. "I didn't peg him for a smoker."

"He's probably not," I said. "House doesn't smell like it . . . though it may be hard to tell right now. No little burns in the furniture." I pointed at the arrangement. "Also, this is a plain bowl. Probably for whisking an egg or two. It's definitely not an ashtray." On closer inspection, faded purple lipstick rimmed the cigarette butts. Another factor which pointed to someone else being the smoker. I read the small print on a label near the filter. "Virginia Slims 120 GM."

"Gold menthol," T.J. said.

"You used to partake?"

"God, no. Hated the things. I stayed as clean as I could. I knew a bunch of girls who smoked. Virginia Slims is mainly a woman's brand." She glanced down at the bowl. "What are we doing with this?"

"I want to take at least one."

"You have a DNA lab somewhere?"

I chuckled. "There are times I wish I did. Even then, getting an untainted sample from a cigarette butt is pretty hard as far as I understand it. Probably beyond what the county can do. My guess is they'll send whatever they find to the state or maybe even the FBI."

"So we won't get results quickly." T.J. crossed her arms. Her white shirt slipped from her lower face, so she pulled it back up. "You still want to grab one?"

"Can't hurt." I patted my pockets. "I don't have any bags or anything."

"Me, either."

Since I was the one wearing gloves, I opened a couple drawers until I found plastic bags of varying sizes. I plucked a sandwich baggie from a box, gently picked up the butt, and dropped it inside. Once I made sure yellow and blue made green on the zipper, I placed it in my pocket. "The bowl is cold, so whoever came here and smoked did it a while ago."

"Probably his last visitor," T.J. said.

"Doesn't mean whoever came here is the killer," I pointed out. "Leaving this behind is pretty careless. Still, I think we need to work from the assumption a woman visited Steven Cooper and murdered him."

"Let's at least look at the body."

We found it upstairs. The stench was much more potent on the second floor. T.J. and I both covered our noses and mouths with our elbows. It did some good but not enough. The bloated and discolored corpse of Steven Cooper lay on the carpeted floor beside his bed. Flies buzzed around the area. Dried blood caked his neck below a single stab wound to the jugular. "Looks like a slender blade," I said. T.J. leaned closer and examined it. "Same weapon?"

"No way to know until a report comes back, but I'd say it's likely."

"Now, we can presume a woman killed the priest, too." Her brows knitted. "With him being a good reverend, it kind of takes a love triangle off the table."

"I tend to agree. Let's get the authorities out here."

"We sticking around?" T.J. asked as we headed back down to the lower level.

"We found the body," I said. "It's only right. Besides, it might create some goodwill when I ask for things like a police or coroner's report."

T.J. sighed. "Fine."

I called 9-1-1.

———

While we waited for the county cops, I stashed the stolen cigarette butt in the car. They could probably twist the law into pretzels and search T.J. or me because we were in the house alone. Extending probable cause to my car would be a different challenge. A few minutes later, two marked Ford Explorers rolled up. A white van plain except for the CORONER label on the side followed a moment behind.

Four uniformed deputies entered the house. They were all men ranging from an inch or two shorter than T.J. up to a couple inches taller than me. The lone black guy on the team was the shortest, but his compact build and loose movements suggested he could take his three friends in a fight. A man in a white Tyvek suit walked in behind them. One pair climbed the stairs with the coroner's man while the other duo strongly suggested T.J. and I join them in the living room. They left the front and rear doors open, and the breeze blew away the worst of the remaining smell.

Deputies Finch and Walker remained standing while my secretary and I sat on the sectional. Making a clean break with his namesake bird, Finch was the taller and heavier of the two. Walker wore his hair short and his mustache full. Both were gray. Once we established who everyone was—both men scrutinized my PI license—we got down to business. "Why did you enter the house?" Finch said.

"No answer at the door," I said. "We ran in to the neighbor who told us he hadn't seen Mister Cooper in days. Add to this the murder of Mister Cooper's brother in Baltimore about two weeks ago, and we were concerned."

"You didn't think to call us?"

"I did."

"Once you ransacked the place," Walker said.

"You and I must define the term very differently," I said. "We didn't touch anything."

"The smell didn't tip you off?"

"It did. We wanted to know what we were walking into before calling. My assistant and I are also looking into the brother's murder. He was a priest."

"Pedo?" asked Finch.

"No."

"You sure?"

"As sure as I can be," I said. "Besides, it was a small percentage. Odds are extremely strong any individual reverend did nothing wrong."

Finch shrugged. I didn't relish being in the position of defending the Catholic Church, but he didn't belabor the point. "How long have you been on the case in Baltimore?"

"Only a couple days," T.J. said.

Walker snorted. "Took you two days to figure out he had a brother?"

"We got here before you, didn't we?" She smiled sweetly

as both men's expressions shifted to ones suggesting they'd been sucking lemons all afternoon. I don't ever recall feeling more proud of her.

"Why do I think you're holding out on us?" Finch said, crossing his arms.

I tried to keep the peace. As much as I enjoyed T.J.'s barb, we didn't need these two complicating matters. "What do you want to know, Deputy?"

"You have any suspects in the priest's murder?"

"Not yet, no."

The coroner's man came down the steps and joined us. "Single stab wound," he said in a curt tone. "Right into the jugular. He would've bled out quick."

"Professional job?" Walker asked.

"Doubt it. Most people know it's a vulnerability. Nothing suggests any sophistication." Before Walker could get another word in, the technician continued. "Been dead two days and change. Maybe three. I'll know more after an autopsy." He moved to another first-floor room.

"This fit in with what you know?" Walker said.

"The first vic was stabbed a dozen times," I said.

"Someone must've hated him," Finch said. "Probably a pedo." Walker left the room to follow the crime scene guy.

"I told you he wasn't."

"Maybe he was just good at hiding it."

"Even if he was, why would someone drive two hours and murder his brother some eleven or twelve days later?"

"I don't know." Finch shrugged. "Sounds like it's your problem to . . . uh, privately investigate."

"Couple cigarette butts in the kitchen," Walker said as he re-entered the room. "Virginia Slims. My ex-wife smoked those. Seems our vic had a visitor."

"Don't mean she killed him," Finch pointed out.

"Sounds like you now have a problem to investigate," I said. Both deputies frowned. "Can we go?"

"Leave a card." I took one from my wallet and handed it to Finch. "We might need to ask you more questions later."

"I'm sure you will." T.J. and I left before the two caught on to the insult.

CHAPTER 12

AFTER WORK, T.J. looked through her closet for a nice dress.

She didn't own many—fancy or otherwise—so the search wrapped up quickly. The winner was a long strapless royal blue number. Whoever owned it originally probably shelled out a lot of cash. T.J. picked it up for ten dollars at a thrift store. She got a speedy shower and put extra conditioner in her hair.

During her working girl days, T.J. often had to be ready for the next john quickly. She didn't like rushing through her routine now. Being able to take the time to make herself look nice was yet another perk of her improved circumstances. T.J. slipped on a strapless bra. She'd never been a fan of them but needed one with the dress. While she wouldn't threaten to bust out of it like Mary Teller or Velvet, she also didn't need a wardrobe malfunction tonight.

Velvet. T.J. thought about her friend for the first time since running away from whatever the hell the woman involved herself in. Once T.J. put the dress on and verified its fit in several key areas, she looked at her phone. All quiet. She remembered Melinda's advice about no one being ready until they're ready. It was certainly true of Velvet. Maybe she just needed a little push. T.J. tapped out a message.

Hey. There's a fundraiser for Nightlight in about 90 minutes. It's at the Hilton downtown. No pressure, but I think you should come. You can meet Melinda and see what kind of work we do. It was the royal "we," but T.J. knew Melinda wouldn't mind. Besides, she wanted to be more involved in helping girls new to the fold if her job allowed the time. Her cell vibrated with an incoming text from Velvet.

> Not sure. What's the dress code?

It's a fundraiser. I'm sure people will come in gowns, but I'm wearing a dress.

> Not sure how many dresses or gowns I have. My closet is still pretty limited.

Girl, I know you have options. Pick something nice.

> In other words don't look like a hooker?

Probably best if you don't, yeah. :)

> Alright. I'll try and make it. And sorry about those guys. I didn't expect them to be so forward.

Just be careful.

> I always am, T. xx

Hopefully, Velvet would show up. It would be good for her to see how things worked and how the foundation could help her turn her life around. She'd probably dismiss some of what she heard as the sort of platitudes one would expect to be said at a fundraiser. In her more cynical days, T.J. might have thought the same thing. The life turned hopeful young girls into bitter women, and the sooner Velvet could get out of it, the better.

As T.J. worked on her long blonde hair, she decided she would stop trying to recruit Velvet if she didn't pop in tonight. She would come aboard on her own schedule or not. Gentle pushes didn't always work. People were only ready when they were ready, after all.

———

She'd gotten dressed and styled her hair quickly, so T.J. was among the first to arrive. Melinda, of course, already patrolled the ballroom. Did she ever sleep? Melinda gave directions to a few hotel workers as they finalized the smaller details. The venue looked great. White cloths with gold trim covered the round tables. Eight dark wooden chairs sat around each with a black napkin and cutlery at each spot.

Melinda turned around and smiled at T.J. Her mentor looked great, too. Her red hair hung long and straight except for being curled at the ends—similar to how T.J. styled hers before she arrived. The hostess wore a cream-colored gown and a necklace with a prominent ruby—her name when she worked the streets—just below her throat. While the gown wasn't lascivious or revealing, it did little to disguise Melinda's terrific figure. T.J. tugged the top hemline of her dress a little higher. "Don't hide 'em if you got 'em," Melinda said with a grin.

"I don't *got 'em* quite like you."

"You're doing all right."

T.J. grinned, too. "I'm trying to look professional tonight."

"You're a beautiful young woman, T.J. Don't hide it because you think you need to uphold a certain standard." Melinda held her hands out and raised her eyebrows. T.J.

nodded, and Melinda gently tugged the top of the younger woman's dress back down to where it was before and even a touch below. A little cleavage now showed over the blue cotton. "There. I understand you don't want to appear like you used to. I don't, either . . . but there's nothing wrong with looking good. There's power in knowing your own appeal."

"I'll keep it in mind," T.J. said. She fought the urge to adjust her clothes again.

People filed in, and the noise level in the ballroom increased. Still too young to order a real drink, T.J. burned through a couple of diet sodas as she sat at the featured table. Melinda was going to tout her as the foundation's initial success story tonight. The first girl rescued from the streets, trained, and placed in a productive job. It all sounded great except for the fact she was expected to get up and say a few words. Maybe Melinda would cover the bulk of the talking.

A few minutes before the scheduled start time, several police officers walked into the room. The mayor followed them. Vincent Davenport was Melinda's father. They hadn't always enjoyed the best relationship, but things seemed to be looking up since she started the foundation and he went to City Hall. The elder Davenport was about sixty. His hair remained mostly black, and his glasses made him look somewhat professorial.

It also lent an air of sternness. On some level, Davenport reminded T.J. of some of the men who came to see her in her old job. Too old for the coeds and too boring for the wife. She'd heard the sob stories before. T.J. shook her head. This was the mayor, not some random john. He came decked out in an expensive tuxedo. Before becoming mayor, Davenport ran one of the largest businesses in the state. He could certainly afford nice threads. Vincent Davenport and one of his retinue joined Melinda, T.J., and a few board members from Nightlight at the main table.

A couple minutes past the designated hour, the mayor stood and walked to the podium. He tapped the mike once to make sure it worked. "Good evening." Well-concealed speakers helped his voice fill the room. "Thank you all for coming tonight. I never ran for mayor for any of the benefits, but I must admit one of the perks is being able to come here in my official capacity and introduce my daughter. Many of you know her already, I'm sure. She's done a lot of great work these last few years, and I'm proud of the turnout her foundation is getting tonight." A round of applause went up. "None of you came to see me, so let me introduce my daughter and the president of the Nightlight Foundation . . . Melinda Davenport!"

Loud applause rose as Melinda followed her father to the podium. They did the European air-kissing thing, and the mayor took his seat again. Melinda smiled as the ovation continued. Once it ebbed, she finally started to speak. "Thank you. It means a great deal. Thank you all for coming tonight. This is a huge event for the foundation. I'd like to thank our fundraiser Gloria Reading Ferguson."

T.J.'s eyes widened. She didn't know Gloria was involved in this. More applause circulated, and Gloria stood. Like Melinda, she opted for a gown, though hers was powder blue. She looked stunning. Her chestnut hair hung straight past her shoulders. C.T. smiled and clapped—as did his parents and another similarly-aged and well-dressed couple T.J. presumed were Gloria's folks—as his wife waved to the gathering for a moment before sitting back down.

"By now, many of you know my story. Maybe you all do. The girls we rescue mean so much to me because I used to be one of them. When I started this foundation, people told me I was crazy. No one cares about prostitutes. You can't redeem people who chose that path." A smattering of boos came from the back of the room. "The girls are junkies, so send them to rehab and hope for the best." She paused to shake her head. "I didn't listen to any of that because I know better."

A fresh round of loud clapping made Melinda pause again. "When my father decided to run for mayor, I was worried. Not for him per se, but for how people might try to use what happened to me to attack him. It happened here and there. A few people tried. I think they learned pretty quickly it wasn't going to stick. I wasn't going to run and hide. My father wasn't going to lie about what happened or try to paper over it. Honesty still matters.

"Now . . . I don't want to make this about me. It's about the foundation and the ladies we've been able to help so far. Our first success story is here with us tonight." T.J. felt heat come into her cheeks as fresh applause filled the room. "T.J., please stand up." She did. It felt awkward to have a couple hundred people looking at her, but she tried her best to smile through it and offer a polite wave. "She's been employed with one of our donors for almost a year now. Terrific. We also have two young women who should have good jobs soon. Katy and Chrissy, please stand up." Both did. T.J. met them once or twice at the foundation. They were both a year or two younger than she was, and their time off the streets brightened their complexions and returned their smiles.

Melinda talked for a few more minutes and explained what the money raised tonight would do. She wanted the means to rescue more troubled girls. T.J. tried to enjoy the meal as the venue staff brought food out to everyone. Thankfully, she didn't get put on display again.

———

Once the event wound down, T.J. spotted Velvet. She wore a black dress with a neckline low enough to make T.J. feel a little self-conscious. A red sash was tied around her waist, and red stitching ran up each side of the dress. Melinda's recent advice played in her head, and she smiled at her friend. "Glad you could make it."

"Thanks," said Velvet. "Looks like a pretty swanky affair."

"When you're trying to raise money, swank is the kind of thing you need."

"I guess. You got a little moment in the spotlight."

"Ugh." T.J. frowned. "I thought it might happen. At least I didn't have to make a speech."

"So if I do this," Velvet said, "is your friend going to point at me one day?"

"We can hope so." Melinda broke away from a well-wisher about twenty feet away. "Let's go say hi." She grabbed Velvet's hand before the other woman could protest and dragged her the short distance to where Melinda stood. "This is Velvet. I mentioned her a couple days ago."

"Oh, great to see you," Melinda said as the two women shook hands. "I'm glad you could come and see a little bit about how the foundation operates. Most of what we do isn't this glamorous, of course, but it pays the bills."

"Seems like you do good work." Velvet's voice dropped. "I think I'm going to be ready to make a break soon. I want to get out."

"How long have you been in?"

"Hell." Velvet snorted. "Officially? I guess close to six years. Unofficially another year or so. I was way underage when I started."

"Too many girls are." The three women moved to an unoccupied table while the last guests filed out. A few workers milled around the room. "If you don't mind me asking, how old are you now?"

"Twenty. I'll be twenty-one in a couple months."

"Honestly, you're a little older than most of the girls we see."

"Sad," Velvet said.

"It is," Melinda concurred. "We get some way under eighteen. Most of them are strung out or on their way."

"How do you decide who you'll work with?"

T.J. wondered, too. In the foundation's early days, there were only a few. Over the last year or more, word of their work spread, Melinda needed to onboard qualified new staff, and the client base increased accordingly. "I'd like to help everyone," Melinda said. "The reality, of course, is we can't. It's not even a resource problem. Some girls say they want help, and they never come back. It's hard to make a change when you feel entrenched in something . . . even if it's something terrible."

Velvet nodded. "All right. Give me a couple weeks, and I think I'll be coming your way."

"We'd love to see you whenever."

"Wanna head outside with me?" Velvet asked T.J.

"Sure," T.J. said. She hugged Melinda before walking through the lobby and out the front door with Velvet. "Why not get away now?"

"I'm in the middle of something." Velvet took a case from her purse. She grabbed a long, thin cigarette and lit it. "It's going well. I don't want to walk away right now."

T.J. bobbed her head as she recalled the kitchen table at Steven Cooper's house. "Hey, can I have one of those?"

"Really? I thought you didn't smoke."

"I don't." T.J. tried to inject a little humor into her

chuckle. "I also don't normally get called to stand up in front of two hundred strangers."

"All right." Velvet opened the case again. T.J. plucked out a cigarette, and Velvet lit it for her. T.J. inhaled and the taste of menthol filled her mouth. She pulled it from between her lips and looked at the filter. Small writing stood out above it.

Virginia Slims 120 GM.

CHAPTER 13

I WOKE up in Gloria's king-sized bed. My alarm was set to go off a few minutes before hers. Thanks to a nice meal at the gala last night, I felt I needed a morning constitutional. Brooklandville was a far cry from the mean streets of Federal Hill. If the roads here could be categorized as merely a trifle unpleasant, the homeowners association would stamp out the root cause and pass a new bylaw. Still, the scenery was nice. Trees stretched their branches of new leaves toward the morning sun.

When I walked back into Gloria's house, she was awake and in the kitchen. She handed me a mug of fresh coffee and planted a minty kiss on me. "Thanks," I said as I took the cup.

Her nose wrinkled. "You need a shower."

"I probably do. Want to join me?"

"The coffee's nice and hot."

"So are you." She blushed. "And you have a very fancy microwave perfect for reheating."

"I do, don't I?" Gloria grinned, grabbed my hand, and led me upstairs at a run. The shower took longer than it ordinarily would have, but neither of us minded. We returned downstairs dressed for the day. I wore jeans and a sweater. Gloria looked stunning in a white shirt and blue skirt. She heated up our coffees while I made us a quick breakfast of scrambled eggs, toast, and turkey sausage—the latter cooking quickly in the microwave. I couldn't recall the last time I'd seen Gloria's fridge so well stocked, and the cynic in me wondered if it was part of some larger point about moving to her house.

She didn't raise the issue over breakfast, however. We both needed to be out the door soon, so we ate more than we talked. Gloria actually cut her sausage into bites she wouldn't need an electron microscope to find. We each took a to-go mug of coffee and headed out the door. "Tell T.J. she was great last night," Gloria said before giving me a lingering kiss goodbye.

"I will." Her one-car garage meant the Mercedes rocket got to park indoors. I walked through and climbed into the S4. Gloria's coupe reversed past my car, and we both left Brooklandville for Baltimore. My commute was pretty easy, and T.J.'s Mustang sat in its usual spot. I finished off my Yeti of coffee and got out of the car.

"Morning," she said as I entered the office.

"I feel like I should ask for your autograph," I said.

"Twenty bucks. Thirty if you want a picture, too."

"Wow." I sat at my desk. "Inflation hits us lowly fans." T.J. smiled but didn't say anything else. "Gloria said you were great last night."

"Thanks."

Again, nothing else. T.J. never struck me as being comfortable in the spotlight, so I didn't press the issue. It was a shame—she made a great example of exactly what the Nightlight Foundation can do. Especially when paired with a supportive and handsome employer. "You all right?"

"Yeah," she said. "Just a little tired after being put on display, I guess."

"Melinda needs to show her foundation is a success," I pointed out. "I see you as a great employee, but to her, you're an example of the good she can do."

"With the right sponsors and more money."

"Those are part of running a foundation."

"I know." She sighed. "I know. I guess it was a bit of a late night."

"Did I spy Velvet making an appearance?"

"Yeah. I introduced her to Melinda." This was something T.J. wanted to do. I figured she'd be happy about it, but she might as well have been reading the stock report for all her enthusiasm. "I think it went well," she added. "Velvet's not quite ready yet, but she knows where to go when she is."

"Good," I said, not even convincing myself. I was about to ask T.J. what was really going on when footsteps came up the stairs, and the door opened.

———

A mousy man with a bald spot and John Lennon glasses walked in. He was about T.J.'s height and slender enough to make people think he was unwell. His suit looked at least a size too big on him. "Good morning," he said without making it sound like the first part of the day would be in any way pleasant.

"Can we help you?" T.J. asked as she stood. In medium heels, she was a couple inches taller than our visitor. He didn't appear happy about having to look up at her, but he struck me as a man who rarely wore a pleasant expression.

"Yes. I'm Gregory Mason. I work for the archdiocese."

"What can we do for you, Mister Mason?" I asked.

T.J. made two cups of coffee. Our guest told her he took his black. She carried both to my desk where Gregory Mason sat in the guest chair. "I understand you're investigating the death of Father Sean Cooper."

"We are, yes." T.J. grinned at my inclusive pronoun usage.

"I'm hoping I can help a bit."

"Trying to keep the bill down?"

"No." He fidgeted in the chair which was too wide for his frame. "Well, I don't want to see the archdiocese spend a lot of money if I can avoid it."

"Sure," I said. "Tell me the budget. I'm curious to know how much you value a priest's life these days."

He took a sip of his coffee and tried a smile. I didn't reciprocate. "We want to see justice done, of course. I'd like to tell you more about Sean Cooper if I may."

I spread my hands. "Please. Not only will we know the official worth the Archdiocese of Baltimore places on the life of a reverend, but we'll also learn how incompetent you think the investigators are."

Mason fell silent for a few seconds. "I just want to help. I'm not trying to place a price tag on anything."

"All right." T.J. wheeled her chair next to mine. "What do we need to know?"

"I'm sure you've done some looking around already," he said. "Oh, please make sure you're accounting for your time with Father David. Anyway . . . I think you should know Sean Cooper was deeply committed to bettering the lives of immigrants and refugees."

"We know," I said. "Like you mentioned, we've already started looking around."

"Right. Yes, of course." Mason cleared his throat. "He'd been at Saint Ann's for a while. The archdiocese is sympathetic to the cause of immigrants, of course, but we can only do so much. Father Cooper pushed those limits. Even when we tried talking to him and reminding him to work through official channels, he still did what he felt he was called to do."

I shrugged. "Sounds like a good priest, then."

"Are you Catholic, Mister Ferguson?"

"Does it matter?"

"I guess not." He smoothed his pants. "You're right. Sean Cooper was a model priest. He even made sure to work with gang members. The police don't want to do anything but arrest them, of course, and other priests are a little . . . reluctant to get involved."

"We know," I said. "A couple gang members came to see him shortly before he died."

"You don't suspect them, do you? As far as I know, he was able to get through to them."

"We're not ruling anyone out at this point," T.J. said, sounding like an old hand at PI work. "It's still early in the investigation."

"You want to know who I think you should look into?" He angled his body toward us, and his lean face looked sinister. "Father Cooper gave a bunch of jobs to immigrants when the construction contract dried up. I don't know all the details surrounding what happened there, but I know the union boss was unhappy about it. Teller's his name. At the risk of sounding very uncharitable, I think he's something of a smarmy prick."

"His job makes him something of a politician," I said. "Being a smarmy prick sort of comes with the territory."

"Did you know he paid a couple visits to Father Cooper?"

"No."

"We don't know what happened or what was said, of

course. I doubt the exchanges were pleasant. Men like Teller don't like seeing jobs taken away."

"If he gave immigrants and refugees all this work," I said, "where did the money come from?"

"Second collections," Mason said. "Most churches do them, and they're usually for special causes in the parish."

"Were the members of Saint Ann's supportive?"

Mason shrugged. "As much as we could reasonably expect, I suppose. They raised enough money to get some jobs done. I'm sure it made Teller very unhappy."

"Maybe we'll have to pay Mister Teller a visit," I said.

After Mason left, T.J. said, "You mean another visit?"

"Sure. It didn't hurt to let him think he told us something we didn't already know."

"I don't think Teller's going to be happy to see us."

"Probably not," I said as I grabbed my coat.

"Let's at least make sure he's there." T.J. looked up the union's office number and called. A minute later, she hung up and said, "He won't be there until later in the afternoon."

"We'll see him then."

———

A few hours later, I drove us to the office of Local 79. Rebecca the receptionist looked as unfriendly as before. She wore her hair in the exact same bun. As with our prior visit, men appeared to look busy in the back part of the first floor. "Twice without an appointment," she said, trying to sound like a disapproving teacher—and succeeding. "Mister Teller is very busy, you know."

I jerked my chin toward the clown crew at the back. "Someone needs to be." She rolled her eyes but refrained from yelling at them this time. "Can you tell him we're coming up?" Rebecca grunted and picked up her handset as T.J. and I ascended the stairs. In his office, Teller was dressed more like a foreman than the head of the union. He wore a Local 79 polo shirt with a nice pair of jeans and a well-used set of tan work boots. I wondered if dressing like one of the guys made them see their boss differently.

"You're here again," Teller said with a sigh as T.J. and I walked into his office.

"We have a few more questions," my secretary said.

Teller leaned back in his leather executive chair. At least he possessed good taste in one area. "Fine. If you're still looking into the priest from Saint Ann's, though, I don't know what else I can tell you."

"A man from the archdiocese came to see us," I said. "He mentioned the scope of the work Father Cooper gave to immigrants and refugees at the church. Even paid them out of a special second collection."

"How he accounted for the money isn't really my concern," Teller said. "I told you last time . . . contracts go sideways sometimes. We have a lot of good Catholic members who love their churches, but the archdiocese isn't always the most reliable client. We've had much better luck with private companies and even the city. It comes down to better control of the purse."

"Had to be a nice chunk of change. Old building . . . two if you count the rectory. A few stories tall. I'm sure it needed a lot of work. Seeing people who weren't in your union get those jobs must have been irritating."

"We weren't doing any work during those periods. Contract irregularities. I would've hoped anything on the list would have remained there, but at the end of the day, I can't control what a priest does. He's the one who needs to live and work there everyday. Sure, I can't say I'm thrilled about what he did, but no one in the union would kill the man over it."

"How many workers do you have?" I asked.

"A lot," Teller said. "I'd need to look up the exact number."

"We can wait."

Teller frowned. "It's thousands. I doubt the exact count is important."

"Probably not. My point is you can't tell me all your members are in lockstep with what you say. What if the guy who was supposed to be the foreman on the church job got really pissed?"

"He would've been assigned to a different job," Teller said. "Keep in mind they might be members of the union, but these men and women work for a variety of companies. How many jobs a certain firm has in the hopper isn't something I can control. I think I've been more than patient with you twice now. If you'll excuse me, I have a major quarterly event to finish planning."

Like in our first meeting, Teller's wife entered the office and commanded all eyes and attention. Today, she wore a form-hugging black dress. The neckline was low enough to ensure people looked at her breasts. A red sash hung around her waist, and as she moved, I noticed stitching in the identical shade of crimson running up the side. It was a great garment and seemed extremely out of place in the main office of Local 79. "Oh. The detectives are here again." She walked to the desk, picked up a slim letter opener, and used it on a plain white envelope.

"I think they were just leaving," Teller said.

T.J. stared at Mary Teller. When I spoke, she finally turned away. "I guess we don't have any other questions for now."

"I'd like to think you won't again."

I wondered which companies held the specific contracts on various aspects of St. Ann's. Teller probably wouldn't tell us, but it would be easy enough to research. "We know where you are in case we do." I tried to keep my eyes on Mary Teller's face as I stood and moved toward the door. It wasn't easy. "Have a nice day."

She flashed a quick and automatic smile. "You, too."

We walked downstairs and out of the building. "Okay, this is weird," T.J. said.

"You ogling his wife was weird," I said. "I'm supposed to be the one who stares at the beautiful women."

"I've seen that dress before. Velvet wore it to the gala last night."

"Really?"

"Yeah." We climbed into the car. "What do you think it means?"

"I have no idea," I said. "Maybe they shop in the same place." T.J. shrugged. "Maybe they're the same person."

She chuckled. "They're not."

"Have you ever seen them together?"

"No."

"There you go."

"It's just odd is all." I supposed it was, but like a few things with this case, I didn't know if it meant anything.

CHAPTER 14

WE STOPPED for a late lunch or early dinner on the way back. It was about three. Definitely a meal classification dead zone. When I first got my S4, I resisted eating anything in it. It was only a few years old at the time, and the interior remained pristine. Over time, the demands of certain cases have forced me to relax this rule. It's hard to keep your car immaculate when you might need to bring burgers to a long stakeout. If I could stomach the thought of being seen regularly in a non-luxury brand, I might have gotten something different.

T.J.'s car always contained a food bag of some sort, so she chowed down right away the second we left the drive-through. Early afternoon traffic gave us enough time to eat our sandwiches and fries. As an experienced three-pedal driver, I managed to feed my face, steer, and change gears without a problem. We arrived at the office to find Manny's shop closed early for the day. I gathered up our trash and carried the paper bag out of the car as we crossed the lot toward the front door.

I only saw the shooter in my peripheral vision.

"Get down!" I shouted and pushed T.J. forward. Three

bullets whizzed past us as we kept low and ran back toward the cars. I raised my head enough to look through the window of one. A man stood on a roof across the street holding a rifle of indeterminate make and model. He wore a gray hoodie, jeans, and a black baseball cap. His gun must have been a semiautomatic to put down the opening volley so quickly. As I pondered this, three more split the air above us.

I took my phone out and tried handing it to T.J. She stared at me with wide eyes. "Focus," I said. "We can get out of this, but we need to stay in the here and now." I sympathized with her shock. My own rapid heartbeat thudded in my ears. After taking a couple bullets last year, I didn't care to repeat the experience any time soon. "Take my phone." She did. "Remember the new security system I helped Manny install a few months ago?" Her head bobbed a little. "Get into it and try to get some photos of this asshole."

She was incredulous. "What about calling the cops?"

"There are a bunch of people across the street," I told her. "Someone else will."

"What are you going to do?"

Another few rounds slammed into the old junker SUV we squatted behind. I wondered if it would continue to provide adequate cover. So long as we stayed behind the engine, we should remain all right. The shooter moving to change his angle would represent a challenge. I drew the 9MM I carried on my hip. "Give this asshole something to think about." After another three-round burst, I stood and squeezed off four shots. All slammed into the brick at the top of the building where the gunman stood, the bullet strikes making him scamper back. At about two hundred feet, I didn't expect to hit him without a lot of time to sight and squeeze each shot. Making him dodge was enough. He'd be running out of time soon. Someone must have called the police by now.

When the shooter edged back toward his previous position, I opened fire again. He dashed away. Sirens sounded faint somewhere in the distance. A moment later, a man in a gray hoodie, jeans, and a black hat appeared on the sidewalk. He hopped into a car I didn't get much of a look at and sped away. I didn't risk shooting at him with pedestrians, cars, and other drivers in the area. People already ran from the scene. I put my gun away and crouched beside T.J. Her hands shook as she tried to use my phone.

"We're all right," I said, putting a hand on her shoulder. "Deep breaths. He's gone now."

"Thank goodness." T.J. inhaled and exhaled loudly a few times. "I think I managed to get the camera to face him and get a few stills."

The sirens grew louder. "Good job." Her trembles had decreased. "You okay?"

"I guess." She tried flashing a game smile. "I think this is the part of the job I might never get used to."

"The day I do is the day I give it up," I said.

"Who do you think was shooting at us?"

"I didn't get much of a look at him. With the hat and the distance, I could barely see any of his face."

"I think Teller sent him," T.J. said.

"Maybe. Like he told us, though, the specific companies the archdiocese hired for certain jobs would stand to be angrier than the union."

"I guess. Look at the timing. We leave his office a couple days ago, and two guys try to beat you up the next morning. We leave today, and there's a guy shooting at us when we get back." Police cars drove onto the lot. Red and blue flashing lights surrounded us.

"You make a compelling argument," I said and wondered what the hell we would tell the police.

A bunch of cops scurried around the parking lot.

Several more were positioned across the street. Some talked to witnesses—a couple of whom pointed in my direction—and others stood on the roof where the shooter opened fire on us. While a pair of female patrol cops talked to T.J., two officers who'd questioned me many times over the years stood before me now. Jennings was smaller than his partner Brennan, who looked a little older and like a recent immigrant from Ireland. "Tell us what happened," Jennings said.

"We pulled in to the lot." I pointed toward my car even though they probably recognized it. "On our way to the building, someone took a few shots at us. We ducked and hid behind the old SUV."

"Good call," Brennan said. "Big engine. Tall tires. You get much of a look at the shooter?"

"Not really. He was across the street on the roof where your friends are now. Gray hoodie, black hat, and jeans. A white guy from what I could see of his face. Past those basics, I don't know. We were focused more on trying not to get hit."

"And you returned fire," Jennings said as he jotted a few notes. It wasn't a question.

"Yes. Mostly to keep the shooter busy. At this distance without a lot of time to aim, I didn't think I could take him out. I more or less wanted to hit the brick at his feet and keep him from firing at us."

"Did you?"

"Every time," I said.

"Risky to shoot back," Brennan added. "Cars on the street. People in the area . . . including in the building."

"I understand, but I didn't hit any of them. All my bullets struck brick. I got the shooter to backpedal and eventually come down."

"Did you see what kind of car he got into?"

"Not very well," I admitted. "It was gray. Definitely a car and not an SUV. If I had to guess, I would say a sedan over a coupe, but it's speculating. Whatever he climbed into, he took off and was gone well before you got here."

"When did he shimmy down?" Jennings wanted to know.

"Around the same time I first heard the sirens." Neither man said anything. I shrugged. "Someone was bound to call. I'm sure he knew he wouldn't get more than a few chances."

"You're probably right," Brennan said. He handed me a card.

"You know I could wallpaper my office with all the cards you two have handed me over the years, right?"

"Might be a nice decorative touch," Jennings said as he closed his notebook. "Owner here?"

"No, he closed up the shop early today."

"He do it often?"

"I don't know," I said. "If you're asking because you think he might have been involved or known something in advance, don't bother. He wasn't, and he didn't. If anything, I think he'll be salty about what happened. This is a car repair shop not a shooting gallery."

"Well, I'm sure he has insurance," Brennan said. "The truck looks old, at least. Might be a junker he's scavenging for parts."

"You want to hand me a useful business card? How about someone who sells bulletproof fences?"

Both cops snickered. "Shit, you might've just given me an

idea for what to do when I retire," Jennings said. They walked away. T.J. wrapped up her interrogation a couple minutes later. I didn't try to chat with her while cops and technicians remained at the scene. I did call Manny to tell him what happened but left a voicemail. I liked our office, and while he'd shown a willingness to put up with some of the more interesting aspects of renting to a PI, another shooting in his parking lot might be too much. I couldn't blame him if he kicked me to the curb.

Once the BPD folks left, T.J. and I went inside. She walked directly to her chair and plopped down. I made a half pot of coffee. While it brewed, I asked her, "You all right?"

"I will be," she said after a deep breath. "Not every day I get shot at walking to work."

"I know. Obviously, we've pissed the wrong person off."

"Yeah. Brent Teller."

"We'll keep looking into him." I inhaled the aroma of fresh java. "I don't want to rule anyone out just because of the timing of when things happened." When the coffee machine's completion chime rang, I prepared two mugs and carried both to T.J.'s desk. "Since I'm doing your job, maybe you can do mine. Let's see what you got from the security system."

She grinned. "You presume I sent those images to myself."

"I do."

"I did." She logged in to her laptop and brought up her email as I sat on the corner of her desk. The most recent message carried three attachments. T.J. opened the first. We saw the shooter on the roof across the street, but the raised rifle blocked most of his face.

"Nothing much there. Next one?"

She opened the second. His head was turned a little, but

we got a decent enough shot of him. "Recognize him?" T.J. asked.

"He looks familiar, but I don't know from where."

"He's a pretty generic white guy. Lot of them around."

"Makes me happy to be exceptional."

She made a show of clearing her throat as the third image loaded. It offered a good view of his face. I leaned closer and scrutinized it. The gunman still looked familiar. It nagged at me, but I couldn't place where I'd seen him. "Can you rotate the image? Like have him facing more to the side?"

"Give me a minute." T.J. saved the picture from her email and opened it in a photo editing app. She pivoted the figure so we saw him mostly from the side.

"I've seen him before." I closed my eyes. "From this angle or pretty close to it." A picture formed in my head. He stood against a funeral home wall dressed in a cheap suit which made his profession obvious to everyone in attendance. I'd spotted him right away. I opened my eyes. "I heard his name once. Can't pull it, but I know where I've seen him."

"Where?" T.J. said.

"Originally at a funeral home. Since then, I've noticed him in passing a few other times." Before my secretary could repeat her question, I said, "In precincts."

Her brows knitted. "Oh, no."

"Yeah. He's a cop."

CHAPTER 15

WE CONDUCTED the next part of our research at my desk.

The BPD's network, even though it had recovered from the recent ransomware attack in some ways, still recognized my laptop. While I couldn't access police case files, I could reach their HR department. "I don't see a way to match his photo," T.J. said.

"Me, either," I said after another minute of hunting around. "No worries. We'll borrow the state's facial recognition system." I'd used it several times, and all my previous attempts came in the interests of finding a criminal. Police officers would also be registered, however, so the picture should lead to a result. I grabbed the image from TJ's computer, uploaded it to the system, and waited.

A result came back almost right away.

Patrick Kelly O'Hearn was a uniformed BPD police officer. He made sergeant two years ago and got busted back down after fifteen months due to a couple of excessive force complaints. "Sounds like a real charmer," T.J. said.

"I've never really dealt with him. He was extra security at a funeral home while I worked a gang case three years ago. Since then, I've seen him around here and there."

"Why's he taking shots at you, then?"

"He was shooting at you, too. Maybe he's one of those guys who's really insecure about tall women." I pointed at the screen. "He's listed at five-eleven."

My secretary grinned. "I doubt it. Someone doesn't want us nosing around, and they happened to have this cop on speed dial. The question is who?"

"Let's look into our friend here." A couple searches gave us a lot of intel on O'Hearn. He was thirty-eight even though he looked five years older, the eldest of three children, and carried nearly thirty grand in credit card debt. "There's motive. Pay off a card or two. Hell, maybe all of them. I'd like to think we're worth way over thirty thousand."

"He's clearly being low-balled."

Not much else stood out about O'Hearn. He'd never been married. His student loans were clear. He rented an apartment and owned an SUV. Other than his profession and debt structure, he was pretty typical. "I'm sure he won't go back to his apartment now." I remembered him climbing into a car to make his getaway. "Either he borrowed someone's ride or stole it."

"Do we go to Rich with this?" T.J. asked.

"At some point, yes," I said. "I'm not sure we're there yet." I moved the mouse to the section of the report which mentioned his family. "We can still learn more about this prick."

O'Hearn's brother Joseph—younger by three years—worked for a local construction company named The Johnson Corporation. "I'll bet they get some interesting crank calls," I said.

T.J. snickered. "Not every company should be named after the founder."

More important than the company which signed his

paychecks, Joseph O'Hearn was also a dues-paying member of Local 79. T.J. thrust her finger toward the screen several times. "See? I told you Teller's behind this."

"I get what you're saying," I told her. "The union has thousands of members. My guess is there's a connection because off-duty cops tend to do paid security work for private companies. There's an easy referral pipeline in this case."

"Did their company do any work at Saint Ann's?"

I brought up their website. It looked very basic and needed a redesign by someone competent. "It's not listed in their portfolio of work. In a good Catholic city like Baltimore, you'd want to trumpet every church you worked on." A job rebuilding the steeple at St. Isaac Jogues in Baltimore County appeared near the bottom of the list accompanied by a few pictures. "We'd need to do more research to know if they'd even gotten in on the contracts at Saint Ann's. It may not matter. Joseph could have mentioned his brother to Teller years ago for some security gig."

"It's certainly possible," T.J. said. "Do we go to Rich with this now?"

I shook my head. "I want to wait. Let's see if we can establish the real connection between them first. You should get home after the day you've had."

"So should you."

"You first. I'll follow you and make sure no one takes any more shots at us."

T.J. nodded. "Yeah. Probably a good idea. We've scared him off for today."

"'We' is doing an awful lot of work there."

She grinned. "Fine. You scared him off with your shooting and general machismo."

"Better."

"Can we get going now?"

"Yes," I said. "I'm ready for today to be over."

———

I followed T.J. back to her apartment building. It marked the first time I'd seen it. I knew where she lived because her address got processed by the small company I hired to manage payroll. The place suited her. It wasn't too plain or too fancy. Its proximity to the University of Baltimore meant a number of her fellow residents would be age peers. She waved from her Mustang as she turned into the lot, and I stayed straight. I completed a circuit of the surrounding streets but didn't see anyone or anything out of place.

Gloria had texted while I drove. She wanted us to stay at her house again tonight. I sighed and wondered if this would become the norm. Since we basically shacked up a couple years ago, we spent all but a night or two a week at my house. Gloria went home from time to time, but she'd already taken over some of my dresser, closet, and bathroom space. Remarkably, she dominated the same areas in her own house. I wondered how many clothes and beauty items she owned. All the grains of sand on Ocean City's beaches might not equal the number.

I jotted off a quick affirmative reply and headed out of the city toward Brooklandville. Despite a little traffic on the Jones Falls Expressway, I made good time. I pulled into her driveway and left the S4 to the right of the garage door. Inside, Gloria had a laptop on the couch. She stood and kissed me before getting right back to work. "Got a donor on the hook?" I asked.

"No." She grinned. "Just trying to finalize a couple scheduling things. Melinda's event was great. We've gotten a bunch of interest from new clients even though it's only been a couple days."

"I knew you'd be a success."

"How was your day?"

"Before we got shot at? Pretty good." Concern knitted Gloria's eyebrows. "Afterwards, it kind of sucked."

She set her computer aside and leaned forward. "Are you both all right?"

"We're fine. T.J. was a little shaken up."

"Weren't you?"

"I guess," I said. "Drawing fire isn't something I enjoy."

"Is this still the murdered priest case?" I nodded as I set my backpack down. "You must be on the right trail."

"Probably. It's getting more twisty and turny. T.J. is sure the construction union boss is behind it."

"You're not?" she wanted to know.

I shrugged. "It's possible. Convenient . . . but possible." I sat beside her on the couch. "There are moving parts in play. I'm still not sure how everything fits together yet. Might need to do some research this evening."

"I was going to try and knock out a little work, too. Should we order in?"

"Absolutely," I said.

"Pizza all right?"

"If I ever turn it down, you should immediately presume I've been replaced by a pod person."

"I don't think aliens will abduct you anytime soon."

"It doesn't need to be little green men. The government could swap me out for an android duplicate."

Gloria chuckled. "Why would they do that?"

"You know they'd want to replace the best-looking people first."

"I would've already been scooped up, then," she said with a grin.

In the absence of a drink to raise, I pointed at my wife and dropped thumb to forefinger. "*Touché*."

While Gloria ordered pizza, I unpacked my laptop. Mine was a black model with a green backlit keyboard and looked like it belonged in the office of a professional gamer. Hers was rose gold—a fancy term for pink which probably only served to increase retail prices—and looked like it belonged in a flower shop. I opened a secure tunnel to my desktop which sat at the office. Workers from across the city and surrounding counties belonged to Local 79. They probably drew checks from dozens if not over a hundred companies ranging from three-man operations to multimillion-dollar entities.

As any large organization, the Archdiocese of Baltimore tried to keep a lot of information private, but they made most of their contracts public. "In the interest of transparency," their web portal proclaimed, marking what might have been the first time the Catholic church used the phrase without irony. Saint Ann's needed quite a bit of renovations both to its main building and the rectory. The attached school was omitted.

I scrolled through a bunch of boring contracts and probably had a dozen or more PDFs open at once. If I'd found everything, it meant six companies shared pieces of the work. Those pieces ranged from pretty small to extensive. The largest deal covered four million dollars. If someone backed out of it, I'm sure I'd be salty. "It still doesn't make sense," I muttered under my breath.

"What doesn't?" Gloria asked.

I didn't think she'd be able to hear me. Gloria proved to be an effective sounding board several times before. "One company had a pretty big contract at the church. Four million. It's on hold as far as I can tell, and the priest handed off a bunch of jobs to immigrants." Unless Saint Ann's enjoyed the richest and most generous parishioners in the city, any figure close to or over a million was well out of scope for second collections.

"You've worked cases where people got killed for less."

"I know. I understand some people might be mad at Father Cooper, but the archdiocese is the one causing the problems in the first place. They're not exactly reliable when it comes to getting projects going on time." I checked on the company involved. They claimed over a hundred million in projects last year. "Sizable firm. The money isn't a huge percentage of their revenue."

"Someone could've lost out on a bonus," Gloria suggested.

"True." While it remained likely an individual company would harbor more enmity over a failed or delayed contract than the union, I couldn't identify a good suspect yet.

"Pizza will be here soon. You look tired. Why don't you save your work for later?"

I rubbed my eyes and closed the laptop lid. "Probably a good call."

———

After putting away three large slices of pizza and a salad, I wasn't in any mood to get back to work.

Neither was Gloria. She browsed Netflix for a moment and found a popular show she'd been meaning to watch. My excitement level didn't match hers, but I went along with it. A few minutes after the opening credits, my phone vibrated in my pocket. Father David's name appeared on the screen.

"This can't be good," I said as I got up and ducked out of the living room. "Hello?"

"Mister Ferguson. I'm glad I was able to reach you so late."

"I'd have to be at least twice my age to think it's late at the moment."

"Can you come to the Esperanza Center?"

My watch showed it was nearly eight-thirty. The Center would have closed for the day around five. In my brief time volunteering there, however, I knew it sometimes maintained unscheduled hours to help community members in need. "Why? What's going on?"

"There's been an unfortunate development in the case," the priest said. "I think the police are making a mistake."

"Wouldn't be the first time."

"Not really comforting."

"I'm sure," I said. "Did the cops arrest someone?"

"Yes, and I'm sure they have it wrong. I'm not alone in this, either. It's why I'd like you to come down here."

I got the impression Father David didn't want to go into more details over the phone. "All right," I said. "I'll head your way."

"Thank you, Mister Ferguson." I ended the call before he could pass on any blessings. I would likely need all the help I could get, but I preferred to confine the nebulous goodwill of deities to working hours.

"I have to run out," I told Gloria as I put my holster and jacket back on.

She frowned. "At this hour, it can't be good."

"Certainly fits with the rest of today, then." I kissed her goodbye and headed for the door.

CHAPTER 16

I KNOCKED at the entrance to Esperanza Center and heard bolts turning back. Father David opened up. After poking his head out to check both directions, he ushered me in and reengaged a couple locks. "I wasn't followed," I told him.

"Making sure."

"This feels a bit like a spy movie now."

He grinned in spite of the situation. "I'll let you pick your code name once this is all wrapped up. Come on." I followed him to his office where two Latino men waited in the guest chairs. Both looked short and compact, and I saw several tattoos peeking out from their collars and sleeves. "This is Juanito." The spiky-haired fellow nodded. "And Josue." The latter narrowed his eyes. It didn't make for a very pleasant greeting.

"We doing this in English or Spanish?" I asked.

"Better in Español," Juanito said.

"All right. Let's hope I'm not too rusty."

Father David continued in his guests' native tongue. "*Estos dos estan en una pandilla*" I translated into, "These two are in a gang." They both frowned and eyed me suspiciously. The priest did his best to placate them. "He's not going to turn you in."

"What happened to bring me down here at night?" I asked in my best Spanish.

"The police arrested one of their friends."

I leaned against the wall and rubbed the bridge of my nose. "He didn't do it," Josue said. "Carlos is innocent."

"Run through it with me," I said. "Talk a little slower for my *gringo* ears."

"He went to see the priest," Juanito said. "Father Sean."

"I know a couple of your friends were on camera."

"Carlos made another visit a couple days before. He didn't have an alibi for the night of the murder."

"Unfortunately," Father David added, "this was enough for the cops. They dragged Carlos off despite him telling them he didn't do it."

"I'm not trying to defend them, but they hear people say those words a lot."

"He didn't do it." Juanito shook his head hard enough to unmoor it from his neck. "No way. Josue must have thought remaining silent and staring would convince me. It did not.

"Can I talk to Father David alone?" I said. The two young men muttered among themselves but eventually got up and left the office to the priest and me. I closed the door.

"You're wondering if Carlos really did it," Father David said.

"Of course I am."

He shook his head. "I guess it's been a while since you volunteered here. You're judging them before knowing all the facts."

"Gangs haven't exactly earned the benefit of the doubt, Father."

"You have much experience with them?"

"Some. Mostly the West Baltimore kind."

"Mostly Black?" he asked. I nodded. "Some similarities, sure, but I think you'll find Latino gangs differ in a couple ways. We're talking about immigrants in most cases. No real sense of family. It's what they're really looking for. Once they find it . . . and once they meet someone who shows them compassion again and again . . . these men are not going to squander it."

"So it's tea and biscuits with a nice priest but knives for everyone else?"

"You're oversimplifying the situation."

"Then, I need you to complicate it for me." He pulled a face. "I want to believe you. Even if I do, the police aren't going to take you at your word." I jerked my thumb toward the door. "They certainly won't believe those two."

"They have to be able to make a case," Father David said.

"Really, all it takes is one assistant state's attorney who thinks it's an easy win," I said. "Someone who sees a gang member, knows judges and juries won't like him, and figures it's a nice victory to have in the file when promotion time comes around."

"Awfully cynical outlook."

"You've worked here for a while. It's shown you the good in a lot of people. Let's just say my job shows me some other sides."

The reverend put his head in his hands and sighed. It came out between his fingers like a hiss. "What do we do, then? I can't ask you to work double time."

"I'll keep my investigation going. If a better suspect turns up, the cops will cut Carlos free. They might also find an ASA who wants them to show some actual proof and not just a few bits of circumstantial evidence."

"Let's hope," he said. "How's it coming along?"

"Not too well." I debated telling him about T.J. and I ducking gunfire in the parking lot. In the end, he probably wanted to hear it. So long as he didn't launch into some long blessing, we'd be good. "We seem to be on the right track, at least. Two men tried to discourage me by force yesterday, and someone took a few shots at my secretary and me earlier today."

"Oh, dear." He crossed himself and folded his hands. "I pray for your safety as this continues."

"I'll talk to the police," I said. "My cousin is a lieutenant in Homicide. No guarantees, though. He might want to see a better suspect before cutting a decent one free."

"I appreciate whatever you can do."

I left his office. Juanito and Josue waited outside. "*Vaya con Dios*," Juanito said as I headed for the door.

"It would be a nice change," I said.

———

Despite it not being on the way home, I stopped by police headquarters. When I texted, Rich said he was still there. I decided to be courteous and showed up with a pair of fresh coffees. Anything would be better than the swill which always seemed to sit in the bottom of pots in the Homicide bullpen. I carried both to my cousin's office where he sat behind his desk. Sergeant Paul King occupied one of the guest chairs.

I handed a cup to Rich, and King snatched the other before I could protest and took a long drink. "Thanks."

"It wasn't for you, actually."

"Oh." He drank some more. "Want it back?"

"It's all yours now."

"Cool," King said. He moved toward the door. "I'll leave you two to have your latest tiff."

"It's like he knows us," I said. Despite the late hour, I really wanted the coffee King absconded with.

"What's going on?" Rich asked. "It's not like you to make a social call so late."

"You're the one staring down middle age in a few years, dear cousin. Let's not compare our bedtimes."

Rich snorted. "Christ, I wish I got a chance to go to sleep at the same time each night." He paused and sipped the java. "You gonna tell me why you're here?"

"The gang member you arrested for the priest's murder."

"What about him?"

"He didn't do it."

"Oh." Rich set his coffee down. "Let me alert the media and arrange for his immediate release."

"Could you?" I dropped onto one of the guest chairs. "I'm sure your PR people are used to working odd hours. Killers don't take many nights off in this city."

"Why do you think he's innocent?"

"The priest who hired me for this case works at the Esperanza Center," I said. "He's convinced the man in Central Booking is innocent."

Rich spread his hands. "I have good evidence against him. He's on camera going to Saint Ann's twice. He was seen arguing with the deceased on one of those trips. We've been to the church. There are plenty of ways to get into the courtyard without being seen by their system."

"So your theory is he argued with Father Cooper, snuck back to the church later one night, made it to the courtyard unseen, arranged for the priest to join him there, and killed him?"

A small frown pulled Rich's brows down. "Yes."

"Did it sound ridiculous when I said it out loud?"

"No," my cousin said.

"I think you're making a lot of logical leaps based on circumstantial evidence."

"You have a better suspect?"

"Working on it."

"Let me know when you do."

"You really think an ASA is going to take this one all the way?" I said. "You don't have very much besides a bunch of circumstantial evidence."

"What do you know about evidence?"

"Whatever I learned watching *CSI* and *Law and Order* reruns. If you can't dazzle a jury with fancy tech, you're not going to win."

"Winning an eventual case is above my pay grade," Rich said.

"Let me help you, then. You need a better suspect because the one you have didn't do it."

"Find me a better one, then." Rich sipped some more coffee. "Why are you so convinced he didn't do it, anyway? It's not like you to be so swayed after one conversation with the clergy."

Did the police know about the construction contract and the dead priest's tendency to pay immigrants for their work? If he didn't, part of me wanted to let him find out on his own. The other part didn't want to see an innocent man sit behind bars longer than necessary. I'd been in a cell at Central Booking. Zero out of ten. "Father Cooper gave people a bunch of jobs at the church," I said after a moment of deliberation. "He used a second collection to pay for it."

Rich shrugged. "So?"

"So the archdiocese had a contract to cover the work. There were some funding issues or whatever, and rather than waiting for it all to get sorted out, the priest paid immigrants in the community instead. I imagine we have some construction workers who are pretty pissed."

"Pissed enough to commit murder?"

"Seems more likely than someone killing a man who worked to make a bunch of people's lives better. How many murderers bite the hand feeding them?"

"You might be surprised," Rich said.

"After four-plus years of doing this . . . probably not."

"Let's not get into a comparison there. You say he's innocent. I say I can hold him for forty-eight hours. Maybe he didn't kill the priest, but he didn't exactly live a life of virtue. The ASA might find other things to charge him with."

I stood. "I guess I'd better get back to work, then." I left Rich's office. King sat at his desk not far from the door.

"Thanks for the coffee," he said, raising the cup and showing a shit-eating grin.

"I spat in it," I said.

As I walked toward the elevator, he called, "No, you didn't."

———

As I drove back to Brooklandville, I dialed T.J. "You never call this late," she said, unease tinging her voice. "What's going on?"

"A few things, and none of them are good." I ran down the list for her, focusing on my trip to the Esperanza Center, the gang member's arrest, Father David's insistence of innocence, and the police not really giving a shit without having a better suspect to fall back on.

"Maybe they shouldn't have arrested him for no good reason," T.J. said.

"You're probably right. I stopped by headquarters and talked to Rich. He's not exactly sympathetic to our position."

"Sounds like you've had a busy evening."

"I'm starting to wish I hadn't answered my phone. Gloria's Netflix show would've been preferable."

"What's our next step?"

"The goal remains the same . . . we need to figure out who really killed Sean Cooper. The cops can hold a suspect for forty-eight hours, and he is involved in a gang, so they might find something else to charge him with even if we pin the stabbing on someone else. Ultimately, we're trying to solve a murder. If we can get an innocent man out of the slammer at the same time, so much the better." I paused for a breath. "I did a little digging into the specific contracts a couple hours ago. Basically, six companies had pieces of the Saint Ann's pie ranging from tiny to pretty big. Four million was the largest amount I found."

"I'd probably knife someone for four million dollars," T.J. said.

"Remind me to get an anti stab vest if we ever investigate a billionaire."

She chuckled. "You know what I mean. It's a lot of money."

"It is, but the company pulled in twenty-five times as much last year. They may not want to lose the revenue, but it won't break them. I'm wondering if someone lost out on a bonus or something because the jobs never got off the ground."

"It's possible. Not a bad motive."

"No, it's not," I said. "Let's start running it down tomorrow."

"Anything else we can do tonight?"

"Probably not much. I'll hit the ground running in the morning. I'm tired."

"At your advanced age," T.J. said, "I'm not surprised."

"You're fired," I said and ended the call. She sounded a little weary, too. Among getting shot at, the gala the prior night, and the re-emergence of Velvet, T.J. had a lot on her plate besides whatever we did at the office. I wondered if she would still nose around tonight. Odds were good she would.

CHAPTER 17

T.J. STILL WANTED to focus on the union leader.

Drilling down to the individual companies which earned the contracts made sense. They'd potentially have reasons for killing a priest who was giving their work away—up to four million reasons in the case of one firm. Even a foreman who stood to make a ten-thousand-dollar bonus would have ample motivation to take out a knife.

On some level, most of these guys paid dues to Brent Teller and Local 79. He talked a good game, but he sounded like a politician while doing it. T.J. didn't trust most people who ran for office. She'd met a few in her earlier life, and they were all self-interested and slimy. Brent Teller was cut from the same cloth. Despite his protestations of innocence, she figured he was involved somehow, even if he didn't actually do the stabbing himself.

Despite giving C.T. grief for working late and being over thirty, T.J. felt tired at the ripe old age of twenty. She'd been through a few eventful days. There was more work to be done, however. She put water on for hot tea and opened her laptop. Teller made himself easy enough to find. Local papers and magazines wrote him up from time to time, and he was all over LinkedIn and more traditional social media sites.

Teller was an educated man, earning his bachelor's from Penn State and an MBA from the University of Maryland. He made sure to let everyone know he used to be a regular construction worker before deciding to get involved in the union. "For the betterment of my fellow workers," as his biographical page—probably self-written—proclaimed. Teller posted many pictures over the years. The most recent sets featured him playing golf, shaking hands with the mayor and governor, and shirtless on the beach.

At least he kept himself in shape. His wife probably demanded it. T.J. remembered C.T.'s eyes nearly bulging out of his head when Mary Teller walked in during their first visit. She was certainly beautiful, and as much as she didn't like them, T.J. had to admit they made an attractive couple. And an interesting one. Teller wasn't a bad-looking guy, but he married well above his station. Mary also looked quite a bit younger.

A little more research revealed she was—twelve years, in fact. A recent "30 Under 30" feature in *Baltimore Magazine* profiled Mary Teller. She was twenty-nine, and her husband had recently turned forty-one. The article was a total puff piece and didn't get into much detail about Mary Teller's life. It mentioned her role in the union's operations, her charitable endeavors, and her frequent appearances at Baltimore's swankiest parties and gatherings.

"Great," T.J. muttered. "A socialite."

The kettle whistling snapped T.J. out of her work. She prepared a mug of Lady Grey tea with a splash of milk and carried it back to the couch. Was Mary Teller's socialite status something they could use? She moved in a lot of exclusive circles. It would probably be easy to find someone who would stab a priest to death for the right price.

The more T.J. looked at photos of Mary Teller—and there were many—the more she thought of Velvet. The two women were built similarly and looked a little alike. Mary was older and a little taller, but a resemblance was there. Including in their clothes. T.J. remembered seeing them in similar dresses as well as a nearly identical shirt and skirt combo. Did it mean anything? Did Velvet run into Mary while working as a high-end escort?

T.J.'s phone vibrated. She checked the notification. A text from Velvet. "Speak of the devil," she said to her empty apartment. Velvet wondered if she wanted to meet for a drink. Just the two of them. Being a year underage wouldn't matter especially to someone with connections. T.J. replied and told her friend she'd love to.

———

T.J. walked a few blocks to a bar called The Golden Row. It looked retro and not in a good way. Dark wooden floors, paneling on the walls, and overhead lighting that came straight from a pool hall contributed to the outdated vibe. Of course, Velvet was a prostitute scoring drinks despite being under twenty-one, and this was exactly the kind of place to make such an arrangement. T.J.'s friend sat at the far end of the long bar. The crowd was sparse.

Velvet offered a small smile. "Thanks for coming."

"Sure." T.J. sidled onto a bar stool. Other than picking up carryout, she hadn't been in a place like this for a couple years. A pair of men played billiards on a table in the corner. The cue ball banging into others made more noise than anything else. T.J. remembered Velvet's cigarettes. "What's going on?"

"I just felt like I needed a drink. Thought you might, too."

The bartender came down to their end. He was tall and wiry, with sleeves of tattoos down both arms and spiky black hair with blue highlights. Velvet smiled when he approached. "I'll have another," she said. "One for my friend, too."

"I'm all right," T.J. said, shaking her head. "Just club soda with lime."

"Seriously?"

"I don't drink."

"Don't tell me it's because you're too young." Velvet snorted. "I remember a few times you put away a good bit."

"Yeah. It's why I don't anymore." The bartender dropped off another martini for Velvet and T.J.'s sparkling water.

"Jerry takes care of me." Velvet winked. "And I take care of him." It explained the arrangement. Velvet might have carried a fake ID, anyway, but T.J. wasn't surprised she'd sleep with the bartender in exchange for not getting carded. "You have a very judgy face sometimes."

"Sorry," T.J. said. She plucked the lime wedge out of her club soda and squeezed it. After stirring it with the straw, she took a drink. "What do you want to talk about?"

"I told your friend Melinda I might be ready in a couple weeks. You know . . . to make a clean break." Velvet paused and stared into her glass. "I think I'll be ready sooner."

"Is something bad happening?" T.J. lowered her voice and leaned closer. "Are you in trouble? We can help you if you are."

"No. I'm all right. I . . . got a job coming up. It's sooner than expected, and it's going to pay really well. Once it's done, I think I will be, too."

"What's the job?"

"This guy likes to throw big parties for his workers every quarter. Fancy hotel and all." T.J. remained silent while Velvet took occasional sips of her martini. "They have the ballroom, a DJ, open bar. It's really great." Her voice grew quieter. "They also rent out a block of rooms. Some other girls and I are there for . . . entertainment. The pay is awesome."

"Is this what you invited me to work a few days ago?" T.J. wanted to know.

"Yeah." Velvet grinned. "You'd be popular. Lots of big and tall guys." She chuckled. "The guy who puts these on . . . I'm not sure what exactly he does. If I had to guess, I'd say politics, but I don't ask. A bunch of people work for him. His wife comes, too. I don't think she knows about the rooms and all. She's beautiful. Brunette." Velvet touched her own hair. "Classy. Younger than her man for sure. I'd say she's in her twenties and he's forty or more. She could make a million dollars or more doing what I do. Instead, she wears killer dresses and supports her husband. It's something to aspire to."

"It's nice to have goals. I wasn't sure what I wanted when I left. I just knew I had to get off the streets. Melinda told me I'd make a great secretary or assistant." T.J. shrugged. "I went along with it. Even if I didn't like it right away, it was a ton better than where I'd come from."

"Do you like it?"

"I love it," T.J. said. "My boss is great. I told you we met him when he was looking into Libby's murder, right?" Velvet nodded. "Right now, we're investigating the murder of a priest. It's a pretty grisly job sometimes, but I enjoy the hell out of it. I think C.T. was a little skeptical of hiring me at first, but I know he values what I do now."

"I don't want to be someone's secretary," Velvet said.

"There are other things you could do." T.J. patted Velvet's hand, and her friend smiled. "Melinda is good at figuring out where you'd fit in best. Then, it's a matter of making sure you have the skills you need. I took a bunch of training classes to learn all about working in an office. Some of them seemed like bullshit, but I use the stuff I learned every day. You'll find something, too."

"Thanks." Velvet downed the rest of her martini and put a twenty on the bar. "I think I want to go. I'm glad we could talk again."

"Me, too." T.J. took another drink of her club soda and left the rest. She followed Velvet outside.

"See you later." Velvet opened her arms, and the two hugged. She took a long cigarette out of her case. "Want another?"

T.J. put up a hand. "Not this time." Velvet walked away, and her heels clattered on the concrete sidewalk. The long cigarettes. T.J. never found the right moment to ask about them. Even if she had, she doubted a straight answer would have been forthcoming. She thought back to what Velvet said about the parties. A guy who put them on once a quarter. His beautiful and younger brunette wife. It all added up to something suspicious. T.J. waited for Velvet to get about a hundred yards away before following her. Her tennis shoes didn't clatter.

———

T.J. had to stop when Velvet did.

The other woman got a phone call and paused to answer it. She was a fair distance ahead, but if she turned around, T.J. would be exposed. This was one time when it was a disadvantage to being tall and blonde. She moved into the doorway of a rowhouse law office while Velvet talked. She was too far away to hear anything, but the conversation didn't seem animated. Velvet put her phone away, lit another cigarette, and kept walking.

T.J. followed again. Could Velvet really be a killer? T.J. didn't think so. They'd worked together for a couple years and become the closest thing to friends two girls in a bad situation could be. Velvet had seen a lot of violence in her life and overcome many challenges. The fact she'd made even a partial break from who she used to be deserved praise. It was hard to think of her as a murderer. If the cigarette had been a Marlboro, T.J. wouldn't harbor any doubts. How many women smoked that particular variety of Virginia Slims, however?

The party angle was another thing to add to the investigation. Velvet played coy about who hired her, and it could have been a number of people, but the description fit the Tellers pretty well. Brent certainly seemed slimy enough to throw swanky parties and encourage his workers to sleep with escorts. His wife couldn't have signed off on the sleazier aspects. Still, she was a socialite. She'd be in her element at fancy soirees even if she didn't know what went on a floor or two above. T.J. shook her head to clear her racing thoughts. One day and investigative avenue at a time. Right now, she was following Velvet.

They'd walked about a half-mile from the bar. Ahead, the divided Franklin Street crossed St. Paul and Preston Gardens Park before combining and continuing as Orleans Street. If T.J. knew her Baltimore neighborhoods, this was Mount Vernon. Velvet crossed the park at St. Paul Place and headed into a white building called The Courtland. T.J. found a bench near a tree and sat where she could keep the place in sight. A quick search on her phone told her it was a luxury apartment building offering the best of Mount Vernon's entertainment and amenities.

A light came on at the corner of the first floor a minute after Velvet went inside. T.J. kept waiting even as a cool breeze forced her to zip her coat up to the neck. The front of the building didn't make it look like an apartment. T.J.'s first guess would have been boutique hotel. It was the right size and in a good area. Velvet must have been doing pretty well for herself if she was living here. T.J. chafed at her rent in The 501 some months, and it was maybe half what a place like the Courtland would charge.

The lone light remained on. Curtains covered the interior, however, and T.J.couldn't see anyone moving around. A few minutes later, the apartment went dark. T.J. remained on the bench a little while longer, but no one else came or went. She didn't want to walk back to her apartment now that it felt cold, so she summoned an Uber. Tomorrow would be an interesting day at the office.

CHAPTER 18

RUNNING in Brooklandville could never be the same as doing it in Baltimore.

Still, miles were miles, and I had to admit I could get used to the scenic backdrop. I missed Federal Hill Park and the view across the Harbor, but this would be a close second. The lack of goons waiting for me as I walked back up Riverside Avenue was another perk. After doing about a three-mile loop on the streets near Gloria's house, I walked back.

Seeing her already in the kitchen was a surprise. "You stink," she said, holding her nose theatrically as she kissed me.

"Want to help me get clean in the shower?"

"Mmm. Not this time. I need to get out of here early." Percolating coffee filled the kitchen with its wonderful aroma. "I'll probably get breakfast on the way."

"Another day in the cutthroat world of fundraising," I said. "Pretty soon, you're going to have goonettes waiting for you."

She smiled. "Let's hope not."

I trotted upstairs and showered. Over time, I'd carved out a space in Gloria's walk-in closet. It was the size of my second bedroom. I kept clothes hanging on one bar and a few shirts on small shelves. She'd also given me half a drawer in one of her two dressers. If we really were going to combine to one house, there would need to be a serious rearrangement of the clothing spaces. I had enough to fill Gloria's closet. The problem, of course, was she did, too. And then some.

Freshly clad in clean jeans and a sweater, I headed downstairs. Gloria had already left. I guzzled a mug of coffee, packed my bag, and left. En route to the office, I picked up fresh java and a couple breakfast sandwiches from a place near Gloria's. They cost triple what I would pay at Royal Farms, and I doubted they were three times as good. Such would be life if I moved to Brooklandville.

At the office, a construction van occupied the spot I would normally park in. I grabbed the next one. T.J. was already at her desk. I dropped one of the sandwiches in front of her. "Thanks," she said.

"I got it at some shop in Brooklandville," I said. "I hope you can taste the price premium."

"Is the bagel organic?"

"I think a law requires it. Punishable by submerging the merchant in common tap water."

T.J. snickered. "I'm sure it'll be great." She unwrapped the paper—which I presumed was recycled in the most upscale facility available—and inhaled the aroma before taking a big bite. A moment later, she added, "While you were being old and turning in early, I had a pretty interesting night. Might have even learned a thing or two about our case."

I sipped more of the Brooklandville shop's coffee. It was good. Probably on par with Royal Farms who brewed a pretty mean cup. Considering it cost almost double, I'd hoped for better. "Do tell."

"I met up with Velvet again."

I frowned. "You're certainly seeing a lot of her."

T.J. put up a hand. "Don't worry about me. I'm fine. She's not going to suck me back into the old life. The fact she's still sort of in it is actually helping us." Rather than elaborate, T.J. chomped more of her sandwich. While I wanted her to continue, I summoned the willpower to remain silent and not take the bait. After another bite, she did. "She talked about working some swanky parties."

"Well, she claims to be a high-end escort," I said. "Makes sense."

"She didn't name any names," T.J. went on. "I'm not sure if it was out of discretion or just not knowing. Anyway, she talked about a guy who likes to put on parties for his workers every quarter. He rents the ballroom in a nice hotel . . . plus a block of rooms so his guys can take advantage of the entertainment."

I recalled our second visit to the union boss. "Teller said he had some quarterly thing to finish planning." My secretary smiled and nodded. "Could be a coincidence."

"Velvet also mentioned the man's beautiful and younger wife is in attendance."

"The coincidence is deepening."

"Let me add a little more to it," T.J. said. "You know I've been on Teller from the beginning. He's not a bad-looking guy, but he's a six, and his wife is a nine."

"Probably a nine-point-five," I said, "and plenty of guys would take one look at her and go to ten. Either way, a delta of three or more is always a little interesting."

"It turns out the beautiful Missus Teller is a socialite. *Baltimore Magazine* did a puff piece on her and some other people. 'Thirty Under Thirty.' They didn't come out and call her a party girl, but it wasn't hard to read between the lines."

I sipped some more coffee. "That was my evening. What do you think it all means?"

"Good work, first of all." T.J. smiled again. "Taken separately, I'm not sure either is super significant. Together, though, they paint a picture. They're both used to a certain lifestyle and social standing. I wonder if the wife knows about the . . . entertainment at these parties."

"You think Teller himself indulges?"

I hadn't considered the possibility before. "He doesn't seem like the type to deny himself something. I guess he'd need to make up a reason to disappear for a while, but with a bunch of his workers there, it's probably easy."

"What do you think, boss?"

"Maybe I should have gone into construction," I said. T.J. cleared her throat. "The same thing I thought before, really. They're both used to their lifestyle and place within the local scene."

"Which means either of them could kill to protect it."

I nodded. "It does."

———

Father Cooper,
You need to stop. You're endangering people . . . most of all yourself. This is your only warning.

"The handwriting is really neat," I said.

"Neat enough to be written by a woman," T.J. said. She'd wheeled herself to my desk while we looked at the letter Father Cooper went to some lengths to hide. "I'm sticking with my original observation."

"You just want Mary Teller to be the killer."

She shrugged. "I don't know her enough to like or dislike her. I think we've learned enough to say she makes a credible suspect."

"Listen to you. 'A credible suspect.' You should work for a private investigator or something."

"Do you think she's not a suspect?"

"I'm waiting for the swimsuit round of the competition," I said.

T.J. punched me in the shoulder. "It would be nice if we got a sample of her writing to compare."

"I think it's a lot more likely she wrote the note than whoever the cops currently have in jail."

"Some gang member, right?"

I nodded. "I volunteered at the Esperanza Center for a while . . . even after I started working as a PI. Most of the people there didn't know much English. None of them could have written a note like this. The command of the language and the penmanship both would have been beyond them. I can't imagine any of the gangbangers Father Cooper was helping could do any better."

T.J. slapped the top of my desk. "We could pull up her driver's license. Her signature might match the writing here."

"It might," I said. "Even if it does, you can't presume she's the killer. She might have written the note, and her husband went to Saint Ann's to kill the priest."

"It would still mean she's involved." T.J. pushed off with her legs and rolled her chair back to her own spot. "I'm going to check." I'd taught her how to get to records held by the MVA, including the ones the administration didn't set up for people like us to find easily. A minute or two later, she frowned and said, "Huh."

"What?"

"Her name is listed as Mary C. Teller. No middle name. Just an initial. The MVA asks for a full name."

"It's unusual," I agreed.

"I emailed you a screencap of her license." T.J. wheeled again to my desk. "Let's compare the handwriting."

"Something neither of us is really qualified to do," I pointed out.

"Let's try anyway."

I opened the photo. Mary Teller managed to look good even to the MVA's cameras. This was a rare feat indeed. Even I looked a little less handsome on my license. I zoomed in on the signature, and we both scrutinized the letters. "I guess it's a match."

"Looks like it to me," T.J. said.

"If you start talking about the swoops on her letters, I'm calling bullshit."

She grinned. "Nothing like that. They do look pretty similar. Look at the M in Mary and *most*. One's obviously taller, but otherwise, they're basically identical."

She was right. "True. But anyone who took a cursive class will make letters in a similar way." T.J. crossed her arms. "I'm not saying she's a bad suspect. I just don't think comparing a short letter to her signature is enough for us to say she's more."

"Yeah, right," my secretary said with a smirk. "You only want to see *more* of her in the bikini part of the competition."

"It might help rule her out," I said. "You never know. It would eliminate concealed weapons at least." T.J. shook her head but couldn't stop the corners of her mouth from turning up. "We'll look into her along with her husband. They both had motive."

"There's someone else I want to look at, too."

"Who?"

T.J. sighed. "Velvet."

———

"I don't even know her real name." T.J. frowned. "Kind of silly, isn't it? She and I spent a couple years working together, and all I know is her street name. Hell, she still thinks my initials stand for Tami Jean." Her expression soured.

"She's probably easy to look up," I said. "Don't worry about the details. You two did what you needed to do to survive bad situations."

T.J. blew out a deep breath. "I know."

"If this case is stirring up a bunch of shit you'd rather not deal with, you can take some time off."

"No." She shook her head hard enough to wag her ponytail. "Let's put this damn thing to rest. Then, maybe I'll take a vacation with the bonus you'll pay me."

"I hear Back River is especially fragrant this time of year."

She chuckled in spite of her serious look. "Go to hell."

"When I looked into Libby's disappearance," I said, "I also did some research into you, Velvet, and Barbie. Whatever I found should be in the case files." I opened a shared folder I created on my network storage.

"Which I recently reorganized for you," T.J. said as she rolled her chair next to mine. "What would you do without me?"

"Have a lot more money and be slightly less organized?"

She punched me in the shoulder again. "It was rhetorical."

"I want to add 'have fewer bruises' to the list."

"There it is." She pointed at the folder labeled *LIBBY PARSONS*. I remembered the case and still wished I'd been able to get to poor Libby before her life went completely off the rails. At least T.J.—one of the unfortunate girl's friends and coworkers at the time—got off the streets and turned out all right. I reminded myself I couldn't save everyone as I opened a Word document. My notes about meeting with the young prostitutes were toward the bottom.

"Amy Velarde," I said. "Looks like she's about a month older than you."

"I'm going to check her socials." T.J. wheeled herself back to her own desk. A moment later, she waved me to her desk. "You need to see a couple things." The first thing I spotted was her most recent Facebook update. About a half-hour ago, she checked in from a local cinema and mentioned treating herself to a movie and popcorn. T.J. clicked on the Pictures section.

"Wow." Three images of Mary Teller were the first to come up. The fourth was of Velvet herself wearing an identical dress to the one Mary sported in one of the photos. "I don't think I ever noticed it before, but there's a resemblance."

"Yeah," T.J. said. "Mary is a little taller and bustier, but Velvet does look like her."

"This could mean a few things," I pointed out. "I'm not sure any of them are good."

"I know where she lives. We should check out her place." When I didn't answer right away, T.J. shrugged. "She's at the movies. Be gone at least another hour and a half. Her place isn't all that far."

"All right. Let's go."

———

The Courtland looked more like a boutique hotel than an apartment. When I shared this observation with T.J. as we approached, she said, "I thought the same thing. Great minds think alike."

Unlike a hotel, we couldn't simply walk in. The door remained locked. We knew Velvet was out, so hitting her button wouldn't help. "You think whoever's at the desk keeps track of people coming and going?" T.J. asked.

"Doubt it," I said.

She pushed the button for reception. A man answered a few seconds later. "Can I help you?"

"Hi, we're here to see Miss Velarde. She's not answering."

"She's expecting you?"

A camera rotated above us with a faint whirr. T.J.'s eyes flicked up to it. She put her arm around my waist, and I slipped mine around hers. "Yes," she said, adding a smile. "My boyfriend and I go way back with her."

"All right," the man said. A buzzing sound echoed from the intercom speaker. I grabbed the door and pulled it open.

"You know which one is hers, I take it," I whispered as we walked inside. The fellow working the desk sat at the far end of the lobby. It was past the initial hallway to the left. T.J. waved at him and made the turn. I followed.

"I saw it from the outside, but I can guess." She stopped at the door to 104 and grinned. "Would I lead my boyfriend astray?"

"I suppose not." I scanned the hallway for cameras and spotted one at the far end. It did a circuit, taking in the entry-way, foyer, and corridor. When it pivoted away from us, I took out my snap gun and popped the lock in a couple seconds. We were in Velvet's apartment before the camera could make it back to us. "Not very big." I kept my voice low. We didn't know how many neighbors were home.

"Definitely not," T.J. whispered. "I'm sure she pays a lot more than I do, too."

"Having the word 'Luxury' on the façade adds a lot to the rent," I said. It showed in the interior. The space itself was fine though almost certainly not worth the monthly price. It was a basic rectangle with nice enough laminate floors. Velvet didn't own much furniture. The tan leather couch had seen its better days. A small coffee and end table at least matched. A TV I pegged at forty inches hung on the wall. No paintings. No pictures, though I didn't expect any considering Velvet's profession likely stemmed in part from a difficult home life as a girl. The kitchen was small but functional, and the appliances went well with the cabinets. A backsplash reinforced the idea of the Courtland being an upscale place.

We moved through the bathroom. Everything looked new enough, and Velvet kept it clean. An open door on the other side led to the only bedroom. Velvet owned a queen with a long dresser and two matching nightstands. A small desk on the far wall drew our attention. "What the hell?" T.J. muttered as we walked across the carpeted floor. A large poster-sized collage—helpfully labeled *Amy's Vision Board* in fancy letters across the top—stood atop the desk. Much of it was covered in high-end dresses and clothes with a few pictures of Mercedes and Porsche cars.

There were also a dozen photos of Mary Teller.

They weren't taken from social media or some article, either. These were candids. Mary didn't even look at the camera in most of them. She wore a nice dress or a sharp blouse and skirt in all of the shots. T.J. slid the closet door back to reveal Velvet-sized versions of the outfits Mary Teller wore. "This is super weird," T.J. said.

"I guess it's nice to have something to aspire to."

"Melinda encourages it, even though I'm not sure Mary Teller is someone to model yourself after."

"It's clear she's significant to Velvet," I said. "They look similar for starters. Any differences in appearance are easy to gloss over . . . especially when the outfit matches."

"I was referring to the fact she could be married to a murderer . . . or just might be one herself."

"If she is," I said, "your friend might be in over her head."

CHAPTER 19

"I THINK we need to talk about your friend," I said.

T.J. returned to the living room and dropped onto the tan leather couch. I sat beside her. "I'm not sure how much there is to tell." She sighed. "You know we worked together for a while. Once I got out, I lost touch with her . . . and basically everyone else from my old life."

"For the best, I'm sure."

"Yeah," T.J. said. "There was plenty of baggage I wanted to leave behind. Some of the people were worth something, though. Velvet was one of them. Every now and again, I'd wonder what happened to her. Until a few days ago, I hadn't seen her since Melinda got me out."

"And she just pops back into your life?" I said.

"What do you mean?"

"It all seems a little coincidental. You're getting food near your apartment, and she happens to be across the street. Then, after you can't find her, she shows up at your door. I know it doesn't always feel like it, but this is a big city. Lots of streets and neighborhoods. Why was she there?"

"I don't know!" T.J. barked. She frowned and continued in a more normal and civil tone. "I don't know. I was surprised and happy to see her. She seemed happy to see me, too. I guess I never thought much about the oddness of the timing." T.J. paused. I didn't say anything. Velvet was her friend, and she needed space to work all this out for herself. "What's her angle, then?"

"Her angle?"

"Yeah. Let's say it wasn't a coincidence. What's she doing looking for me?" T.J. pointed toward the bedroom. "There's practically a fucking shrine to Mary Teller in there. Even if Brent and Mary are murderers, and Velvet caught on to it, why would she try to take down someone she clearly looks up to? It doesn't make sense." She was right. It didn't add up. "Besides, she would need to know where I lived and worked."

"Those two data points probably aren't hard to get," I said, "but I see what you're saying. If she reinserted herself into your life for a reason, it requires a few logical leaps."

"Even your hatred of coincidences can't bridge that gap," T.J. said.

I nodded. "What the hell is up with the shrine?"

"No idea. I guess she idolizes Mary for some reason."

"Have to be better role models out there," I said.

"Didn't you ever look up to someone when you were younger?" she wanted to know.

"Sure. For a while, I really wanted to be like David Beckham." I chuckled at the memory.

"The soccer player?"

"He's the one."

"Why? And don't say for his wife."

I grinned. "I was too young to truly appreciate her. No, I played soccer when I was a kid."

"Then what happened?"

"I realized I'd never be a great player." T.J. raised an eyebrow. I moved my hand in a slow circle around my face.

"Couldn't risk the moneymaker. Not on some random header off a corner kick."

She shook her head and smiled in spite of herself. "But you played lacrosse."

"With a helmet on, yes." I focused us back on the reason we'd come to the Courtland—which was not my illustrious athletic career. "You don't remember Velvet talking about anyone glamorous or fixating on a celebrity?"

"No. Mostly, we were trying to survive. Hell, I think Velvet and I were the only two clean girls in Weasel Boy's stable at one point. The rest all dabbled in meth or worse." I remembered hearing him offering to pay the girls in drugs. It was just another way to keep them in his thrall. Wherever Weasel Boy was, I hoped someone punched him in the face a lot. "It felt like swimming against the tide at some point."

"No doubt." I stood. "We should probably go. Don't want the guy at the desk to get too nosy." I glanced around the place. There wasn't an abundance of places to hide something. "You think there's anywhere we need to search?"

"I doubt it." T.J. got to her feet, too. "I snapped a picture of the vision board and all. Maybe it'll be relevant. If nothing else, it might be a conversation piece for later."

I made a circuit of the small apartment again but agreed with T.J.'s assessment. We wouldn't find anything else here. Considering I had zero idea what to do with the significant discovery we'd already made, this was probably a good thing.

The guy at the desk glanced up as we transitioned from hallway to lobby, but he didn't do anything else. Not even a little wave as we left. Luxury accommodations at The Courtland were lacking. We stood on the sidewalk outside the building and waited for traffic to ease. A black Lexus sedan sat a couple car lengths behind my Audi. It looked like a newer model of the car I drove for years. Once the threat of being run over passed, T.J. and I crossed St. Paul and got into the S4.

"What's our next move?" she asked as I pulled away from the curb.

"We need to figure out why Velvet is back in your life," I said. "Yeah, I hate coincidences. Maybe this is one, but something tells me it's not." T.J. fidgeted in the passenger's seat. "What?"

"Nothing."

"No, it's something."

"It's not good for Velvet," she said.

"If she's a killer, we shouldn't care what's good for her." I expected a rousing defense from T.J.—shouting about how Velvet could never be a murderer. When she remained silent, I knew something was really off. "You have some reason to suspect her, don't you?"

My secretary remained quiet for a few seconds. Then, in a quiet voice, she said, "Remember the cigarettes we found?"

"At the brother's house?" I asked. She nodded. "Yes."

"Velvet smokes them, too."

"You didn't think this was relevant before now?"

"I don't know," T.J. said. "I'm not sure what it means . . . or if it even means anything. I don't know how to feel about Velvet. Ever since I saw her light one up, I've been conflicted. She never struck me as a killer when we were working together. What would make her one now? Especially of a priest."

"Good questions," I said as we sat at a red light. "I think you need to ask her when you see her again."

"I'm not sure I want to."

"You need to. She might be innocent, and if she is, she's going to need a lifeline. Whatever's going on, I think she's in too deep."

T.J.'s voice dropped to a whisper I struggled to hear. "You think she's in danger?"

"If she's not the murderer? Yes. Definitely."

We lapsed into silence again. I checked the rearview mirror. The Lexus sedan remained behind us even though we'd driven close to a mile away from The Courtland. "You think someone could be watching Velvet?" I said.

"If she's in trouble?" T.J. shrugged. "Yeah, I'm sure someone would be."

"We've already met one bent cop."

"You need to go to Rich about him."

"Eventually," I said. "At the moment, I think we have a more pressing concern."

"What do you mean?" T.J. turned her head enough to look into her side mirror. "Is someone following us?"

"Did you see the black Lexus parked behind me when we came out?"

"No. I'm not much of a car person."

"You don't need to be." I drummed my fingers on the wheel at another light. The sedan was three vehicles back in the next lane. It provided an easy spot to keep an eye on us. So far, the driver didn't try to escalate the situation. He could have made a phone call, however, and more people could be coming to close in on us.

"What are we going to do?"

"First things first," I said. "I'm going to try and lose this tail."

———

We pulled away from the light. I shifted into second gear. Traffic was heavy enough to prevent me making a quick getaway. The guy following us remained three cars to the rear. He was pretty good at following. I only spotted him outside Velvet's place because he drove a Lexus. If he'd sat there in a battered old Chevy, I might never have noticed. "Is he still back there?" T.J. wanted to know.

"Yes. Driving the speed limit in a straight line isn't exactly an evasive maneuver."

"You think you can lose him?"

"I've done it before," I said. "This guy seems more competent than most. If I had the preference, I'd rather learn who he is and who's paying him."

"I can answer the second part for you," T.J. said. "One of the Tellers."

"Which?"

"I don't know." She let out a loud hissing breath. "It was easier before Mary went and made herself a suspect." Before I could contribute to the conversation, she added, "I know you're going to say the individual companies stood to lose more. You're right. Yet someone must've complained. A foreman loses a bunch of work for his guys, what's he going to do?"

"Stab a priest?" I offered.

"Maybe. Or he blabs to Brent Teller, and we know the ultimate result."

I swung a left from St. Paul onto Baltimore Street. Traffic remained moderate. I figured it would. The Block—a haven for nightlife and prostitutes—lay a few intersections ahead. It was early for ladies of the evening to be plying their trade, but I still spotted one as we drove. T.J. gripped her door handle hard. "Sorry," I said. "Didn't think you worked around here a lot."

"Not often," she said. "Just don't like the place. He still behind us?"

I confirmed the Lexus remained about the same distance on our six with a quick check in the mirror. I didn't want to tip the driver off. "He is. Let's see how he feels about driving near police headquarters."

It didn't seem to bother the guy. I made a right to go south on the narrow one-way Frederick Street to see if he would continue to follow us. No other cars turned behind me until the black Lexus appeared in the rearview a couple seconds later. He pulled closer now. Maybe turning onto a road like this clued him in to the fact I knew he was there.

Frederick terminated at Water Street, so I made a right and then another onto Gay Street heading north again. "He must know you're onto him now," T.J. said.

"I'm sure. Let's see what he does."

The next intersection was Baltimore Street again. I made the right. This time, I headed past police headquarters. The sedan remained behind us, the driver having abandoned all pretense of blending in to traffic. At the next light, I picked up President Street heading south. It would take us farther in to the city. Port Discovery zoomed by on T.J.'s side. Enough other vehicles shared the road with us to put the Lexus a couple cars behind mine again. The problem was most of them were SUVs. My sedan—like our pursuer's—stuck out in the crowd. I shuddered.

"What?" T.J. asked.

"Just realized I might need to get an SUV to blend into traffic better."

"You poor baby."

"It's one step above a minivan."

"I'm sure Audi sells a few."

"They do," I said. The light at Eastern Avenue went

yellow. I sped through the intersection, dropped down to second gear, made the turn on screeching tires, and kept going. The Lexus still followed. He kept his speed high, in fact, and the chrome grill of his car kept getting closer in my mirror. No one else was behind us. The sedan accelerated and rammed into the rear of my car. Our seat cushions and headrests did their jobs when the impact rocked us back.

"We need to do something else," she said. "Losing him isn't working."

"This bastard is paying for my body work," I said.

The Lexus remained right behind us. "You got any other bright ideas? He might have called for reinforcements by now."

"I thought about it." I hit the *Phone* button on the console's multimedia controls. "How about we do the same?"

CHAPTER 20

AS WE PASSED La Scala restaurant on the left, I dialed Rollins. We first became acquainted when I hired him as a bodyguard during an especially dangerous case three years ago. Since then, we helped each other on occasion. Thankfully, his assistance almost never came with an invoice attached. He answered on the first ring. "What can I do for you?"

"I seem to have sprouted a tail," I said.

"You need help getting rid of him?"

"Yeah. Bastard already rammed my car. If we catch him, I'm taking his credit card."

"Where are you now?"

"On Eastern Avenue. We just passed La Scala."

"Stay on it. See you in a few." He ended the call. I stopped for the red light at Central Avenue. The Lexus tapped my bumper as the driver stopped behind us. Even with the windows closed, I heard his V6 revving. In a straight line, my car with its supercharged engine would be faster. However, the confines of Baltimore streets—especially with early afternoon traffic added in—nullified this advantage.

Our sedans were of similar size, so I couldn't outmaneuver him. The hope was Rollins—and his oversized pickup—would be too much for the guy to handle.

A few blocks later, I heard the distinctive rumble of his truck's massive motor. He came down Caroline Street and swung onto Eastern Avenue behind the Lexus. Rollins drove a large Ford F-250. It was jet black, rode on tires too large for any normal vehicle, and featured one of those metal rams on the front. Despite being huge and heavy, its V8 engine made it pretty fast. It made the perfect truck for the kind of work he normally did. When the signal at Bond Street went from green to yellow, I fought the urge to mash the accelerator. Instead, I pressed the brake and clutch and brought the Audi to a stop. The Lexus driver did the same.

Rollins remained right behind him and made sure to ram his bumper. I saw the sedan rock in my rearview mirror. It moved forward a few inches but didn't tap my car. The driver glared into his mirror. Rollins' engine revved loudly. When the light went green again, I drove away at a moderate pace. The big pickup kept the Lexus pinned in. I waved to the fellow behind me and got a middle finger in response. We remained on a major street, however, and Broadway—which would lead into the crowded heart of Fells Point—loomed a couple intersections ahead.

I made a hard left onto Bethel Street. It was one way headed north. A parking lot on the right butted up against the rear of the Esperanza Center. The other side of the road was residential. Despite being at a disadvantage now, our tail remained behind us. I wondered if he called anyone to help like I did. At Bank Street, he broke away with a hard right. T.J. held up her phone and snapped a picture. "I think I got his plate," she said.

With the immediate threat over, I called Rollins again. "Thanks for the help."

"Don't sweat it. I know how problematic it can be to spring a tail."

"Want to join us back at the office? T.J. got the car's tag."

"You think it'll be legit?"

"Doubt it, but we might as well check. Most of these guys aren't on the Mensa roster."

"All right. See you there." He ended the call again.

"You think the plates are stolen?" T.J. asked.

"Or the car," I said. "Or maybe both. There's always a chance this guy got blinded by the thought of a nice payday and brought his own ride. It's why we check."

"What if it's another cop?"

"Then, we'd have to go to Rich."

"I hope it's not," she said. "For a few reasons, but mostly because I want to keep this one in-house."

"I knew I hired you for a reason," I said.

———

Rollins joined us at the office, parking his XL pickup next to my car. On our way in, Manny waved me to him. I sent T.J. and Rollins upstairs ahead of me with instructions to make coffee. I joined Manny in his small office. Even with the door closed, the hustle and bustle of a body shop made it through. I'd been dreading this conversation and hoped he wouldn't be giving me the boot. "I guess I never figured how dangerous a business like yours could be," he said in a voice carrying a light Hispanic accent.

"I did go into it with you."

"I know. I'm not accusing you of anything." He sighed.

"This is the second shooting we've seen here, and I can't keep having the cars in the lot under fire."

"Let's just get down to it," I said. "Are you kicking me out?"

"No," he replied after a couple seconds of keeping me in suspense. "I probably should. I thought the camera system would be a nice deterrent." I neglected to mention how T.J. and I accessed it to get an ID on the most recent guy to pepper the lot with bullets. "Now, I'm adding a wall to the parking lot."

"It's why the construction van was here."

"Si. They're going to start tomorrow. It'll be made of stone and ten feet high. When it's finished, we'll lose a parking spot and a little maneuverability in the lot, but I think the tradeoff is worth it."

"How much is all this costing?" I asked.

Manny smiled. "Enough. If you want to stay, we're going to sign a new lease agreement. It'll run for a year, and your rent will go up by four hundred dollars a month." Considering the extra risk my business brought to Manny's shop—and his employees—I considered this fair. "My guys will leave cars behind the wall before we close in case anything happens. I'll need you and your secretary to start parking farther down."

"All right." He produced a new agreement. I read it over and signed it, and then Manny did, too. We shook hands. "Thanks for understanding."

"You do good work for people who need it," Manny said. "I know you've been to the Esperanza Center, too. Keep it up." I must have looked confused because he added, "People talk to me."

I told him I would continue to set a standard of excellence, and I left to rejoin my colleagues upstairs. The smell of brewing coffee up here was far better than the aromas of metal shavings and oil from the first floor. "What was that all about?" T.J. wanted to know. "Is he upset about the shooting?"

"He has every right to be salty about it," I said. "We're not getting the boot. He's adding a wall to protect the cars, we'll have to park farther down, and I'm paying an extra four hundred a month in rent. Let's make sure we send a nice bill to the archdiocese when this is all done."

"You got shot at again?" Rollins said.

"Yeah. This time, the gunman was a bent cop."

He whistled. "You go to Rich?"

"Not yet."

"Why?"

I shrugged. "Not sure how this guy fits into everything yet. When I have a better idea, then maybe I'll bring in Rich. He'd probably punt it to internal affairs anyway."

The coffee finished brewing. T.J. poured three mugs. Like a philistine, Rollins took his with no cream or sweetener. He sat in a guest chair near my desk. Rollins was a little over forty and black. He wore his hair short like a lot of guys who left the military. Thanks to his training, he was the stealthiest man I'd ever known. I'd bet good money he could sneak past a guard dog with a steak in his pocket. Today, Rollins wore dark blue skinny jeans, low-cut boots, and a white track jacket with pink trim. "Was your bent cop driving the Lexus?"

"I didn't get a great look at whoever was behind the wheel," I said.

"Me, either," T.J. added. "I'm going to run the plate." She pushed her chair in front of her desk and got to work.

"Doubt it'll get us anywhere." Rollins kicked his New Republic brogans up onto my desk. "Your assistant was giving me some of the details. You like the union boss for it?"

"He's a suspect," I said. "Not sure if he's the best one."

T.J. sipped her coffee. "C.T. thinks men who worked for the individual contracting companies would be more likely to act out."

"Their financial motive is more direct."

"This guy run a tight ship?" Rollins asked.

I shook my head. "Not from what I can tell. There isn't a great deal of discipline among the folks at the office. Could be much different on job sites. He's big into looking the part and having a big fancy office, parading his wife around, making appearances. I think he's mostly a politician."

"Politicians murder people sometimes," Rollins pointed out.

"So do doctors," I said. "I'm still keeping my next GP appointment."

"The plate is stolen," T.J. said. "It belongs to a twenty-year-old Ford Aerostar . . . whatever the hell that is."

"Minivan," Rollins and I said at the same time.

"What about the car?" I said.

My secretary shrugged. "Don't know what it is."

"Lexus sedan. Looks pretty new. I'd say it was compact to midsize. Call it an IS and see if you get anything." She tapped away at her keyboard and shook her head a moment later. "Nothing in the last week."

"Could be a new theft," Rollins suggested. "Owner might not have seen it yet."

"Possible," I said. "It doesn't help us, though. We don't know who followed us or the person who ordered it done."

Rollins finished his coffee and set the mug down. "Your cases generally go like this?"

"Pretty much, yeah."

———

Rollins left a few minutes later. I ordered pizza for delivery and even got a few extra pies for the workers downstairs as a *mea culpa* to Manny. While we waited, I also checked for Lexus IS sedan thefts and came up with nothing. Did I get the model wrong? I keyed in two others and got a couple hits, but they were for the wrong colors. Either our pursuer drove his own car—with enough brains to use a stolen tag, at least—or Rollins' theory about the theft going undiscovered for now was correct.

I turned the Velvet situation over in my mind. T.J. knew her a lot better than I did, of course. She'd never struck me as a malicious person, so I also couldn't see her as a murderer. Something weird was definitely going on with her Mary Teller obsession. Even if the union boss' wife was a socialite who went to all the best parties around—something I would need to check on—did it make her worthy of emulation? I shrugged. I'd never been a twenty year-old girl in a competitive and risky profession.

When the pizza arrived, I snagged ours and told Manny he and the crew could enjoy the rest. T.J. and I each enjoyed some pepperoni and extra cheese. "What do you think is really going on with Velvet?" I mused as each of us grabbed a second slice.

T.J. shrugged. "I wish I knew. Do you think she's important to the case?"

"She's a distraction for you . . . so in a way, yes. When we add in the fact she smokes the same cigarettes we saw at a murder scene and has an unhealthy obsession with a possible killer's wife, I still get to yes. If nothing else, we might need to save her from herself at some point."

"I think she's just caught up admiring someone glamorous."

"I hope so."

"Maybe she's waiting for the swimsuit portion of the competition like you," T.J. said.

"Who could blame her?" I said. T.J. didn't seem interested in continuing the conversation, and I didn't want to push it. She had a job, an apartment, and some stability in her life for the first time in years. Dwelling on her past wasn't easy no matter how brave a face she tried to put on. Once we finished our late lunch, I kept looking into Lexus sedan thefts and expanded my search to surrounding states. Still nothing which fit the vehicle we saw.

With some access to the BPD's systems restored, I checked their records to see who partnered with O'Hearn over the years. He'd worked with several men and a few women. The driver of the car which rammed mine looked male from what I could see in the mirrors. It could have been any of the faces looking back at me from my screen or none of them. Nothing in the individual officers' files jumped out at me as something alarming, but O'Hearn's also looked clean, and he was dirty.

"I'm going to head out," T.J. said a while later. It was a little early for her, but I knew this case had given her a couple rough days and nights.

"All right. See you tomorrow."

She flashed a quick smile, wished me a good night, and left. A minute later, I watched through the window as her Mustang left the lot. No one took off after her. When I sat in my chair again, an obvious fact hit me, and I felt like an idiot for not seeing it sooner. We'd been considering the Tellers and Velvet as completely separate issues. If T.J.'s old friend were obsessed with Mary Teller, they almost certainly crossed paths at some point. They were both local. This didn't need to be a case of idolizing a celebrity from afar. Velvet's job could have put her in the same swanky ballrooms Mary Teller enjoyed.

With T.J. gone for the evening, this would be my best chance to do a deep dive into Velvet.

CHAPTER 21

VELVET MAINTAINED A WEBSITE. It was clever in not coming out and saying exactly what she did or offered, but reading between the lines would be easy for most men. A few of the photos still bore the watermarks from her OnlyFans page. They all stayed in the PG-13 kingdom while leaving little to the imagination. The resemblance between Velvet and Mary Teller struck me as strong. Once you got past a decade of age and a couple inches of height, they looked a lot alike.

It sparked an idea which I didn't like. My laptop runs a suite of tools used by hackers and security specialists around the globe. I've added a few customizations and new programs of my own, as well. One scraped popular social media sites. It scanned for connections, dates, posts, images, videos, and pretty much anything else about people's lives they shared with the world. In the case of most folks, they broadcast too much information about themselves. I found Brent Teller on four major platforms. He made no effort to hide himself or lock down his accounts. I set a few basic parameters and turned the tool loose.

Not surprisingly, Brent connected to Mary on all four. This included LinkedIn. His profile declared him to be the "Leader of Construction Union 79 in Baltimore." Mary's offered the nebulous "Administrative and Social Media Professional." My experience with LinkedIn has taught me people who put "Professional" at the end of some word salad absolutely did not work with distinction in the field they claimed. In this case, the title was ambiguous enough to sound important—every company needed a social media presence, after all—while also providing no real indication of experience or competence. The employment history on her page showed her as working for the union since her husband became the boss.

Her Instagram page was full of selfies and photos with other people in social settings. As I expected, Mary looked terrific in a bikini, and there were dozens of examples to prove it. She also loved fast cars, even posing in front of a McLaren she called her baby. A few more posts showed her behind the wheel of the car. If she in fact owned it, the gig of being the union leader's wife paid really well.

Mary also provided another good data point for my program. She'd amassed a ton of followers—her beach pictures probably chief among the reasons—and I cast a much wider net on my next run of the program. When all the bits settled, I ended up with a bunch of data. Many accounts connected to both Brent and Mary on multiple platforms. Some appeared to be friends of the couple. Others were workers in the union ranging from grunts new on the job to people in the executive leadership chain. I wondered how Brent felt about laborers following his wife on Instagram. Maybe he considered her bikini photos some kind of morale boost for the workers.

I couldn't prioritize people close to one or both of the

Tellers versus workers they knew from the union. If they were guilty in this whole mess, anyone in their circle could have also been involved. When I added the parameter of a connection to Amy Velarde, all my results disappeared. So much for trying to find the obvious tie-in. I cleared this and stared at the results again. Some of these people had been linked to one or both of the Tellers for years. Father Cooper's murder was a little over two weeks old. I sorted my results by recent activity.

This helped but not as much as I expected. The Tellers had some chatty friends. When I was about to click on the first name, I heard footsteps on the metal stairs. They sounded light but also solid like a woman in heels. Maybe Mary Teller came to confess her guilt and shoot me. If she did, I would get her first. I took a 9MM from the top drawer of my desk and held it as the door opened.

———

Gloria walked through the door carrying a brown paper bag inside a white plastic one. Sure enough, the outer bag bore the name and logo of a local Chinese restaurant. "I was in the neighborhood." She set the bag on my desk, noticed the pistol, and frowned.

"Delivery people get really insistent for tips," I said. We kissed.

"Everything all right?"

"Sure. Never know who's walking up the stairs."

"At a hundred and thirty pounds in heels?"

"Assassins come in all sizes and shapes. Even one as pleasing as yours."

"You know exactly what to say to a girl," my wife told me

as she ripped open the paper bag. The scent of fried rice filled the area.

"Did you order in Cantonese?" I asked.

"No." Gloria rummaged around near the microwave and coffee maker. "I'm not you."

"How fortuitous. I'd be miserable if I were married to myself." She continued searching. "I think plates are on top of the fridge." Gloria grabbed a couple. Our small appliance sat atop a single counter. Its drawer held a box of plastic utensils, and she brought the ones we would need.

"Good thing I'm happy, then," Gloria said. While she set out the plates, I removed the contents of the brown bag. I took out a sleeve of spring rolls, two large paper containers of fried rice, and two covered plastic bowls. "Kung Pao and orange chicken. I figured we could share."

"Sounds great." I let Gloria grab some first and then loaded up my plate with a spring roll, rice, and a generous portion of each entree. Despite having more food than her, I knew I would finish first. Armed only with a fork, I dealt with chunks of chicken as they came. Gloria used a plastic knife to cut them at least twice. "Thanks for bringing this by. I hadn't really given a lot of thought to dinner."

"What are you working on?" Gloria asked between mousy bites.

"The priest murder," I said. "Just trying to make some connections."

"Have you?"

"Maybe too many. I was about to start reviewing them when I thought a killer approached."

She grinned. "Sorry to disappoint you."

"You could at least carry a knife next time," I said.

"I'll consider it." Gloria paused for another nibble. She'd

eaten maybe twenty percent of the food on her plate. I approached a third. "You going to be a while?"

"I don't know. It depends on what I learn."

"Want to go back to your place tonight?"

"Sure."

"I'm warming up to the idea of keeping both for now," she said. "This isn't the best market to look at selling."

"Good," I said. "We'll make it work. I might need a little more closet space at your house."

Gloria grinned. "You just might need to fight me for it."

"Don't think I won't. I take my clothes very seriously."

"I know you do," she said. "I've seen the contents of your closet and drawers."

We ate in silence for a few minutes. I'd almost finished everything on my plate, and Gloria still had at least a quarter of hers left. "You have any strong suspects?" she wanted to know.

"A couple," I said. "T.J. is keen on one. I'm not convinced, but I haven't produced a better one yet. I was hoping my recent searches would point me in the right direction."

"It's hard to think very many people would want to murder a priest."

"It certainly is."

She patted my hand. "You always figure these things out. I know you'll find who killed him. Maybe T.J. has been right all along."

"Maybe," I said. "Don't tell her. She'll ask for another raise."

Gloria set her fork down, leaned across the desk, and kissed me. "Your secret is safe."

———

After Gloria left, my work resumed.

Many of the accounts I found provided a recent update. I opened the Facebook page of a union worker named Jimmy Zoukas. His feed was unremarkable. He made a post last night called "Killer Party," and it included a few videos. I opened the first one. No time or date stamp appeared. Everyone in the shot was dressed to the nines. A fancy party of some sort. Music and voices talking provided a loud sound-track. I didn't recognize the venue.

I did, however, recognize Mary Teller. She wore an expensive black dress cut low enough to put most of her chest on display. Considering she smiled at everyone, she welcomed the attention. A little unsteadiness in her gait indicated she'd probably knocked back a few before the video began. Over the background noise, a man I presumed to be Zoukas said, "Damn, I'd fuck her."

The camera followed Mary Teller as she moved across the ballroom, eventually breaking away from the crowd to stand off to the side. A man followed her. The video zoomed in a little. It looked like O'Hearn. He and Mary engaged in a quick conversation before he pushed her up against the wall and kissed her like a familiar lover. "Unexpected," I muttered to my empty office. I took its silence as agreement. Mary wrapped a leg around his waist, and one of his hands cupped her ass.

After another minute of making out, they broke away and walked off together. The shot followed the pair as they entered an elevator. Before the doors closed, O'Hearn again shoved Mary Teller to the side of the cage and kissed her again. Their destination left little to the imagination. "Wow," Zoukas said in narration, and I agreed. "Lucky guy." The clip ended.

The next followed Mary as she emerged from the elevator. She smoothed the front of her dress and fussed with her hair before entering the ballroom proper. There, she found her husband, kissed him like she didn't just have sex with another man upstairs, and chatted with a middle-aged couple Brent talked to. The union boss didn't seem to care about his wife dressing provocatively. I wondered if his *laissez faire* attitude extended to extramarital dalliances. Whatever the Tellers and the other couple talked about got lost in the noise of the event. The video ended a second later.

One more remained embedded in the post. I played it. This one followed Brent Teller as he moved through the venue independent of his wife. He approached another woman in a similarly low-cut black dress. I paused. "Shit," I said as I realized it was Velvet. I resumed playback. Velvet and Brent Teller chatted for a moment. Despite being under twenty-one, she held a glass of champagne, and her easy laughter suggested it was not her first of the evening. Teller put a hand on the small of her back as he leaned in closer to whisper in her ear. Whatever he told her made Velvet put her drink on the nearest table.

Teller checked the room before leading her off to the side where Mary and O'Hearn went. A similar scene played out. He pressed Velvet against the wall, kissed her, and groped her. Neither seemed to be aware someone captured everything on a cell phone. They trotted to the elevator, made out while they waited for the car, and couldn't keep their hands off each other once they walked into it. The video ended after the doors closed.

"What the hell?" I wondered aloud. The post got shared a couple dozen times. I cross-checked the names, and at least half were members of Local 79. All were connected to both Brent and Mary Teller on at least one social platform. Mary didn't strike me as the kind of woman who would want her husband leaving the party to have sex with an escort even if she engaged in her own infidelity. In the twenty or so hours since this post went live and made the rounds, she must have seen it.

Velvet seemed obsessed with Mary Teller for reasons I didn't understand. Maybe one of them had something to do with her husband. I didn't take nearly enough psychology classes to fathom what Velvet might have been after, but whatever she wanted, she was in over her head. The Tellers were craven politicians, and T.J. and I both liked them to varying degrees as potential suspects in the murder of a priest. Anyone who would murder a man of the cloth wouldn't think twice about also knifing a prostitute.

I grabbed my keys and left the office.

———

I made good time getting to The Courtland. As I curbed the S4, I noticed the same Lexus sedan from before parked across the street. "Shit," I muttered as I got out of the car and sprinted across Saint Paul. Before, T.J. and I needed to get the front desk guy to buzz us in. I didn't want to wait. Velvet might not have the time. This time, fortune smiled upon me as a woman walked out of the building when I approached. I slowed my pace so as not to appear like a maniac. Once she reached the sidewalk, I grabbed the door before its pneumatics let it close and headed inside.

I rushed down the corridor to find Velvet's door ajar. Never a good sign. Two men emerged as I walked closer. Neither were armed, but one had blood on his beefy hands. They both smiled like wolves as they blocked my path. "Get out of the way," I said.

"You can either fight us or save the whore," the closer one said. "I doubt you have time for both."

When the bloody-fisted fellow smirked, I turned to face him and kicked him in the balls. His friend slinked past me. I grabbed the guy by the back of the head and punched him hard enough to break his nose with a satisfying crack. "Fuck off," I said as I shoved him down the hallway. "Plenty more for you later." He still couldn't straighten up, but he moved toward the front entryway with surprising speed.

I let him go and dashed into Velvet's apartment. The front room and kitchen were empty. I jogged through the bathroom and found her on the bedroom floor. Her face was a bloody mess. Bruises already formed on her arms where her attackers manhandled her. Velvet's shirt was torn and hung off her body, exposing her bra. She wore a pair of black gym shorts which were bunched up near the tops of her legs. A pack of Virginia Slims gold menthol 120s lay on the floor. Velvet's eyes widened when she saw me. I knelt beside her. "It's all right," I said in a quiet tone. "You may not remember me, but I'm C.T. T.J. works for me."

"Good . . . timing," she managed to say.

I took out my phone and dialed 9-1-1. When I requested an ambulance, the operator told me it would be fifteen minutes. "For fuck's sake, I'll drive her myself," I said and hung up. While she'd taken quite a beating, Velvet didn't appear to be in any immediate danger of dying. No need to wait for the paramedics with Mercy Medical Center a few blocks down Saint Paul Street. "I'm sorry for what happened to you. I need to pick you up and get you to the hospital." Her head bobbed a fraction. I put one arm under her shoulders, the other under her legs, and lifted. Velvet wasn't very big or heavy, but she felt like a dead weight.

Carrying her slowed me somewhat, but I ran as quickly

as I could out of the building. A break in traffic allowed me to dash across the street to my car. I set Velvet down across the back seats, climbed in, and pulled away in front of a line of impatient horns. The light at Pleasant Street flicked to red. I downshifted and made the turn anyway. A few seconds later, I swung a right into the emergency entrance at Mercy.

CHAPTER 22

T.J. COULDN'T SHAKE the feeling Velvet was in trouble.

She'd kept some of her suspicions from C.T. His heart was in the right place, but he didn't understand what they'd been through together. Girls like Velvet and T.J. got good at spotting bad situations and adapting to them once they arose. It was a simple question of survival. She dashed off a quick text. *Hey, I'm a little worried about you. Hope you're OK. Hit me back.*

It was past time for dinner. T.J. checked her fridge. She heated up a couple of hot dogs in a small skillet, put them on the freshest bread she could find—the buns were definitely past their sell-by-date—and added a handful of potato chips to the plate. It wouldn't be the healthiest meal she'd eaten recently, but she didn't want to lose time fixing something. Besides, she didn't keep a lot of produce in the apartment. It was expensive. She wanted a raise, but with Manny adding four bills a month to the rent, would it be possible? C.T. was a generous boss, but he ran a business, not a charity.

Velvet never replied. T.J. finished her meal and tossed the paper plate in the trash. She sent another quick message. *Hey. What's going on? Want to know you're OK.* Considering

Velvet still took some escort work, she could have been on the job. T.J. didn't like waiting. She thought of what her employer would do. For all his talk about being patient, he favored taking action. The situation certainly called for it.

T.J. opened her laptop. C.T. had shared some programs and scripts with her and taught her how to use them. She could track Velvet's cell phone via a simple app. A few seconds after she entered the number, the map showed her device in the vicinity of The Courtland. T.J. frowned. If home, Velvet should be able to answer a text. A call went straight to voicemail. This was odd. T.J. opened a program to scrape social media sites, exploit connections, and compile research on people.

She still suspected the Tellers of a few shady things, so she entered both of their names plus Amy Velarde. A bunch of mutual connections—mostly for the union boss and his wife—scrolled past. T.J. checked each one. There were quite a few professional connections on LinkedIn, but many union workers at least followed their boss on Facebook. A significant number also followed Mary on Instagram, and a quick look at her feed showed why. "Here's the swimsuit portion of the competition," T.J. muttered. Mary Teller would certainly accrue some high scores. Brent must have known a bunch of thirsty union grunts followed his wife. Maybe it was all part of his vanity. They could only lust after her pictures online, but he got to go home with her every night.

She sighed. "Fucking *men*."

After tweaking her search options, T.J. discovered a bunch of users shared a trio of popular videos. One attached all three to a post which proclaimed *Two hot brunette bitches get macked on at the same wild party! Crazy!* The top comment predictably called both women whores. T.J. didn't want to click on *Play*, but she also knew it was inevitable.

———

Wherever they were, the people in the video were having a good time.

They were all dressed in suits or tuxes for the men and nice dresses—and even a few gowns—for the women. Just about everyone carried drinks in their hands. T.J. couldn't pick out any of the conversations, but she recognized the song. It had been popular in clubs for at least a few years. She'd snuck into enough of them in her day.

The cell phone camera settled on Mary Teller. Anyone who followed her on Instagram would love her black dress. It showed as much of her breasts as most bikini tops would. It also hugged her form. When she turned around, T.J. noted both the absence of a panty line and the number of men who made no effort to hide their admiration of her ass. Mary seemed to know everyone. She could have a future as a politician's wife. Her steps looked a little uncertain as she walked. While she didn't currently have a drink, she'd clearly put a couple away already. A voice said, "Damn, I'd fuck her," and T.J. figured the sentiment went for almost every man in attendance.

Whoever filmed Mary followed her as she left the ballroom. She ran into the cop who fired at C.T. and T.J. outside the office. "O'Hearn," T.J. said in a venomous whisper. It didn't take long for him to push her against the wall and begin a heavy makeout session. They pulled themselves away from each other long enough to get in a nearby elevator. There, the making out resumed before the doors blocked them and someone commented how lucky O'Hearn was.

Now, O'Hearn's involvement made more sense. Maybe he worked off the books for money, but he clearly enjoyed a few other perks, as well. What would Brent Teller think of this? Would his ambition mean he was fine with his wife sleeping around so long as her paramours benefited the couple in some way?

The second video showed the aftermath. Mary walked off the elevator and neatened her appearance before re-entering the ballroom. T.J. had done the same thing before. It wasn't quite a walk of shame, but it came pretty close. Mary found her husband and kissed him. *Hi, darling. I just let a man fuck me upstairs. Don't worry, he can help us. How's the party going?* The Tellers chatted with another couple as this video ended.

One more remained. "What the hell could this one show?" T.J. wondered aloud. It didn't take long for the clip to provide an answer. This time, Brent Teller left the soiree. Outside the ballroom's main door, he met a woman dressed much like his wife. It wasn't, however, and T.J. didn't even need to pause or zoom to know it was Velvet. She could tell by the way the woman moved. Following a brief conversa-tion, Velvet tabled her drink and walked away with the much older Brent Teller. Something crawled in the pit of T.J.'s stomach. She regretted her dinner choice already.

Teller steered Velvet to the nearest wall where he kissed and groped her like a teenager who's waited all night for his parents to leave. T.J. knew the type well, unfortunately. Most men in this category were at least Teller's age. They disap-peared into the elevator like Mary and O'Hearn did, and the way they were all over each other before the doors closed told T.J. this was not their first rendezvous. She wondered if they would end up in the same room Mary and O'Hearn recently used. The union would have only rented so many. "Gross."

Her cell phone ringing nearly made T.J. leap off the couch. She hoped it would be Velvet, but caller ID showed C.T.'s name and photo. He couldn't want anything good at this hour. Still, T.J. tried to summon a little optimism. Maybe he'd made a break in the case. "What's up, boss?"

"Velvet's not the killer," he said.

"What?" T.J. chided herself for not sharing more about her suspicions. "Is this about the cigarettes?"

"No. It's about the fact two guys just beat her half to death." T.J. swallowed hard and couldn't put any words together. Thankfully, C.T. kept talking. "I found her in time. She's probably lucky there's a hospital a few blocks away."

"You dropped her off?"

"Yeah," he said. "I didn't stick around. The cops would have questions, and I don't know the answers. I'm in the parking lot. It'll take them some time to treat her and get her in a room. I'll pop back in and see her later."

"I'll be there, too," T.J. said. She ended the call. Her head spun. While she'd never thought Velvet made a great suspect, she didn't want to see her friend get cleared like this. Based on the videos T.J. just finished watching—which got shared hundreds of times—the person who would want to hurt her the most was Mary Teller. C.T. would have come to the same conclusion. She looked at her watch. Doctors would need to treat Velvet. Cops would want to question her under the circumstances. She wouldn't be in a room for at least a couple hours.

T.J. resolved to be there.

———

T.J. passed the time seeing who else shared the videos. It got circulated by lots of workers in the union. Thanks to the nature of social media, a bunch of people who had nothing to do with Local 79 would've seen it by now. T.J. wondered who filmed the videos and what his or her agenda was. She didn't want to presume the first person who posted them also worked their phone like a camera, but she took note of the name anyway in case it became important. If he turned up dead, the Tellers would be the obvious suspects.

She couldn't wait any longer, so she drove to Mercy. A few texts to Velvet went unanswered. Whoever worked reception in Emergency could not have been less helpful if she'd tried. She provided short non-answers to every question T.J. asked. No, she didn't know where Amy Velarde was. No, you can't go see her. Finally, T.J. inquired if the cafeteria remained open and received a curt yes in reply. She headed there.

Due to the hour, much of the food service stopped. The only options were refrigerated, microwaveable, or drinks. A few people sat at tables. Most of them were employees. T.J. made herself a coffee, paid for it, and scanned her options. A tallish dark-haired doctor in a white coat faced away from T.J. and talked to an older colleague. She wanted to find someone lower on the totem pole. A nurse in the back corner repeated the cycle of looking at her watch, scowling, and checking out something on her phone. She didn't want to go back to work. T.J. headed to the woman's table before she changed her mind.

"Can I ask you something?" T.J. said. "Sorry to barge in on your break. It'll only take a minute."

The nurse, a short, round-faced blonde, rolled her eyes. "What?"

"The woman who's at reception in the emergency room isn't telling me anything."

"Yeah." The employee snorted. "She's a bitch. I don't think I could help you find someone, though."

T.J. dropped onto the uncomfortable wooden chair. It would look less weird to anyone else if she were sitting, too.

"Maybe just tell me where to start looking. My friend caught a beating, and I'm sure she would've been admitted. I just want to know what floor she'd be on."

"Unless she needs the ICU, they'd probably admit her on three," the nurse said. "Visiting hours are long over. I'm not sure how you'll get up there."

"Let me worry about that. Maybe you could open the right stairwell door for me."

This got a small smile. "Maybe I could."

A few minutes later, T.J. followed the nurse out of the cafeteria. They diverted from the way she came. After a right turn and then a left, the short lady swiped her ID and opened a door. It led to stairs going up. T.J. mouthed her thanks and ducked inside. She dashed up to the third level and peered through the small window in the metal door. The coast looked clear, so she opened wide enough to squeeze through and made sure the door closed quietly.

She stood in a short corridor. The elevator was on the same wall. Two much longer hallways led to patient rooms. T.J. glanced around one corner, saw a nurse, and headed for the other corridor. Thankfully, it was empty. She checked the walls near each room. Small dry-erase boards showed patient names. Around the midpoint, she passed the empty nurses station. Toward the far end, one of the boards read VELARDE, AMY. T.J. scanned the hallway, saw no one, and slipped inside as quietly as she could.

Velvet lay in the first bed. The other was empty. She was either asleep or unconscious. Bruises and a little blood covered her face. Her upper left arm stuck out from the blanket. More bruises encircled it. Someone held her down while she took a beating. Or worse. The monitor let out a soft beep in time with Velvet's pulse. At least her vitals looked good. A tear slid down T.J.'s cheek, and she wiped it away. "Not the first time we've been here, is it?" she whispered.

T.J. squeezed Velvet's hand. "We're gonna find who did this. I already have a pretty good idea, but we'll get them. I'll make sure they pay for what they did to you." T.J. wiped her eyes again and left the room. In her distracted state, she almost ran somebody over.

CHAPTER 23

I CARRIED a coffee cup in each hand, so I couldn't really steady T.J. as she nearly bowled me over. "I'm sorry," she said, and her eyes narrowed as she recognized me. "What the hell are you doing here? And why are you dressed like a doctor?"

"Pretty sure I'm here for the same reason as you." I handed her one of the paper cups, and she took it. "As for my threads, someone left his office door open." I wore a standard-issue white lab coat which fit me pretty well. In case I ran into anyone who would know Doctor Kumar—including the man himself—I turned his photo ID badge around. "I saw you in the cafeteria, by the way. Good idea to talk to a nurse who looked like she didn't want to be here."

"You were the doctor talking to someone else." She punched me in the shoulder. "You could have just told me you were here."

"It was more fun this way." We walked along the hallway. "How's Velvet?"

"Sleeping," T.J. said. "Maybe she's unconscious."

"She was awake when I brought her here."

"What happened?"

"I found some videos online. One of them showed Velvet getting into an elevator with Brent Teller. They were all over each other. I thought she'd be in danger, so I went to her place. Two guys were leaving. I ran in to check on her."

"I found the videos, too. What do you think it all means?"

"I haven't come to any conclusions yet," I said. "You saw the one of Mary leaving with O'Hearn?" T.J. nodded. "It's an awfully sordid web. She might be able to get O'Hearn to do her dirty work by sleeping with him. Doesn't really explain Velvet's involvement. Once Mary knew about it, I think it's safe to conclude she wasn't happy."

"I figure she sent the two guys you saw," T.J. said.

"Logical conclusion. We still need to . . . don't let me catch you up here again after visiting hours." T.J. shot me a confused look until her eyes fell on the nurse walking our way. Before the schoolmarm-looking woman could add anything, I held up a hand. "I'll make sure she leaves." The nurse sneered at T.J. and bobbed her head. We reached the end of the hallway without running into anyone else.

"We need to what?" T.J. asked as I opened the door for the stairwell.

"We need to keep investigating," I said. "The Tellers look good as suspects, and I think at least one of them is responsible for putting Velvet here. Doesn't mean they killed the priest, though."

"It's personal for me. They put Velvet in the hospital. How would you feel if someone did this to Joey?"

"Pissed," I admitted. The scene played out when I first met Melinda. Someone beat her and my longtime friend Joey Trovato badly enough to put them in the hospital. I found out who did it and made sure the guy took his meals through a straw for the next several weeks. It didn't exactly mark the high point of my career, however. "The best thing to happen is if we can do both at once. Figure out who killed Father Cooper and nail the Tellers for this." We exited onto the first floor. I headed to the right. Doctor Kumar's office door remained ajar. I peeked inside. It was empty.

"No one's coming," T.J. whispered. I snuck inside long enough to hang his lab coat back where I found it. We reversed course and headed for the exit through the emergency room.

"Promise me you'll keep a level head," I said.

"Yeah."

"I mean it. I don't need you flying off the handle because you're pissed about your friend. Take a few days off if you can't keep it in check."

"I'll be fine," T.J. said with an edge in her voice. I chalked it up to a mix of determination and being angry at me for threatening to sideline her.

"All right."

"Was it the same car outside her place this time, too?"

"Yes," I said.

"You think it's O'Hearn's?" I shrugged. "Didn't you see our shooter get into a gray sedan, too?"

I'd never thought about it before. "Lot of gray or black sedans out there. Besides, O'Hearn wasn't one of the two guys who roughed up Velvet. They looked like garden-variety goons, not cops."

"They're bastards," T.J. muttered.

"Agreed. Let's get back to work, then."

————

T.J. and I returned to the office. We gathered around my desk and watched all the videos together. As someone who toiled alongside Velvet in a variety of settings, I wanted my secretary's perspective on working an event like this. "You get hired under the guise of entertainment," she said. "That keeps it legal in case anything comes under scrutiny." She snorted. "You'd be surprised how many of these gigs get paid out of corporate accounts that a bunch of people can review and even audit later."

"I probably wouldn't, actually," I said. "I went to college with a few guys who would do exactly what you described. All right . . . if we presume Brent Teller is the one who signed the check, how many girls would he get besides Velvet?"

"There's no way of knowing. Let's watch the videos again. We'll check out the people other than her and the Tellers." I cued up the first one. T.J. kept a running verbal count of the men she saw. I reminded her to include the one who shot the footage. The other videos only showed us one guy we didn't note the first time. "So that's fourteen men. The Local 79 roster is pretty big. We only saw a small slice. Some of them would have brought wives and girlfriends."

"So?"

"Sometimes, women take advantage of the entertainment, too," T.J. said. "It helps if they're drunk, and a few guys are cheering them on."

"The ballroom itself looks pretty big on the footage. You think we could estimate about a hundred and fifty people?"

She shrugged. "Yeah, that's reasonable."

"Obviously, not all of them are going to disappear with a girl working the event," I said. "Like you mentioned, some came with their significant others."

"If I had to guess, I'd say four girls worked the party. So Velvet and three others."

"Would she know them?"

"Maybe," T.J. said. "They probably didn't all get booked at the same time. Higher-end escorting is different. More exclusive. Smaller stables of girls, including some out on their own like Velvet seems to be. All four could have been hired separately."

"Let's watch again," I suggested. "Maybe we can spot them." We went through the trio of clips an additional time. Mary Teller dressed like an escort—and certainly behaved liked one—but we couldn't count her. After the last video ended, we only found one woman who might have been paid to attend.

"The others could have been upstairs with some of the men," T.J. said. "Hell, it's even possible Velvet was there alone."

"She definitely seems to be interested in Mary Teller. Do you think she would have snuck in somehow?"

T.J. shook her head. "I doubt it. If she wasn't hired to be there, my guess is she worked over someone in the union. She slept with him a couple times and got him to take her as a date. Probably even for free."

"However she got there," I said, "the union boss certainly seemed happy to see her."

"The fact she was cosplaying as his wife might have helped."

"Sure, but there's a decade in age and a few inches in height between them. Even if he'd already tied half a load on, Teller knew who he was making out with in the elevator . . . and who he was taking upstairs."

T.J. frowned. "I wonder if he booked Velvet personally."

"You mean specifically to take her to a private room at some point?" My secretary nodded. "If he did, I imagine his wife would be pissed."

"Let's not forget her dashing off with O'Hearn," T.J. said. "I've . . . run into my share of powerful and self-important men. The double standards they apply to themselves are really something."

"I know," I said. "My parents have made acquaintances of a few similar assholes over the years."

"Looks like the Tellers are the ones most likely to be upset by what happened. Even though someone in the union filmed these videos, and a bunch of guys shared them, I can't see some random worker being pissed off."

"I agree. The problem is either Brent or Mary could have wanted to go after Velvet." When she raised an eyebrow, I added, "Self-important men also like to cover their tracks. Doubly so when their wives might be pissed. There's basically a hundred percent chance Mary has seen the videos."

"Might not have been his first elevator ride with a hooker, either," T.J. said.

"True." I looked at my watch. "I think this is enough excitement for one night. Tomorrow, let's go back to Local Seventy-nine. They won't want to see us but too bad. We'll try to clone the boss's phone while we're there and see who he's talking to and about what."

"All right." T.J. stood. "Thanks for helping Velvet. I know you could have gone after the two guys who were there."

"Wasn't really a consideration," I said. "Her life was more important."

She smiled. "Not everyone would think so. I'm glad you do." She leaned down and hugged me around the shoulders. "Good night."

"See you tomorrow." T.J. left and locked the door behind her. Her sudden and unexpected display of gratitude or affection showed me how much this case affected her. Velvet's presence alone was a distraction, but her getting tangled up in everything else clearly wore on T.J. I wanted the case to be over for a whole host of reasons, but its negative effects on my secretary ranked at the top of the list.

CHAPTER 24

IN THE MORNING, I left a sleeping Gloria in bed and headed out to the mean streets of Federal Hill. Brooklandville was nice enough for a constitutional, but nothing beat my home turf. Between the park and the harbor, it was hard to find better. After a quiet half-hour, I walked up Riverside Avenue and walked back into my house. Gloria remained upstairs. I set the coffee to brew while I took a shower.

When I emerged, Gloria was no longer in bed. I got dressed and found her inhaling the aroma of a fresh mug of coffee in the kitchen. She kissed me before I could pour myself one. I searched through the fridge and pantry to see what I might make for breakfast. Gloria busied herself looking at something on her phone while I set six strips of bacon in a cast-iron skillet. When they finished, I set them on a plate and cracked four eggs to fry in the remaining grease.

A few minutes later, I carried two plates of multigrain toast, bacon, and fried eggs—over medium—to the kitchen table. Gloria's portion was identical to mine except I only gave her one piece of bread. Watching her take mouse bites of a second was a bridge too far. Gloria topped off both our coffees and joined me. We ate in silence for a couple minutes before she asked about the case. "I think it's taking a toll on T.J.," I said.

"How?"

"She's run into a coworker from her former life. This woman also seems to have some involvement in what we're investigating, but we don't know how much yet." I paused, unsure of how to explain whatever Velvet's role was in the whole mess. "You've heard of a vision board, right?"

"Sure," she said. "It's always sounded like a fancy name for a collage."

I grinned. "Pretty much. Anyway, T.J.'s friend Amy . . . Velvet . . . really wants to be like the union boss's wife. The woman is all over her vision board. It's a little creepy."

"It could be a little dangerous, too."

"Yeah. We came across some videos from one of their parties. No dates, but the decorations in the room make me think it was a couple months ago. Anyway, the wife makes out with the bent cop who shot at us before heading upstairs with him. Later, the union leader does the same with Velvet."

Gloria froze with a fork halfway to her mouth. "Really? That's crazy."

"It is," I said. "I know T.J. wants to do the right thing for her friend, but at this point, I don't have any idea what the right thing even is."

"You think the wife knows what's going on?"

"Amy caught a pretty bad beating last night. Someone knows."

"I think you're right to be concerned for T.J. Did you tell her to take some time off?"

"I asked her if she wanted to. She doesn't."

Gloria sliced her eggs into tiny slivers. She ended up with at least three times as many pieces as I did. This method worked for her, but the idea of eating like a rabbit would infuriate me. "She's trying to be tough. Probably doesn't want to disappoint you."

"I know," I said.

"You're protective of her," Gloria said. "Sounds like you should be right now. If things get much worse, you might need to sideline her."

"I hope it's not necessary. She's had a few pretty good insights." Gloria started to talk around a small mouthful of food, but I continued. "I know," I repeated. "The boss needs to be the adult in the room."

"Even when you don't want to."

I tore off a large bite of toast. "Sometimes, adulting sucks."

Gloria smiled. "Ah, the wisdom that comes with being over thirty."

———

T.J. and I drank coffee and strategized. "You're going to clone his phone?" she asked.

"More or less," I said. "We know he'll be there. Mary's presence is something of a wild card. If nothing else, it lets us make a judgment on his status as a suspect."

"You think he'll reach out to anyone like O'Hearn?"

"Maybe. Hell, Mary's the one who took him upstairs. She might have him on a short leash."

"You going to get him via Bluetooth?"

"Not this time." I sipped some hot java. "Users and carriers are getting better about locking it down or at least minimizing discoverability. No, I'm going with a good old piece of mobile malware. You can do a lot with it, but I'm only interested in knowing who this asshole talks to."

"How do you plan to get it to him?"

"A couple ways," I said. "I'll try a text at first. If it fails, there are some zero-click exploits using tools like WhatsApp."

"I'd like to watch the master at work," T.J. said.

"Pull up a chair, then." While she wheeled herself beside me, I launched an app called Crocodile on my laptop. "This enables you to do all kinds of mobile attacks. The problem with an actual SIM swap is he'll notice. A guy like Teller lives on his phone, so if his service goes out or even gets degraded, he's on the horn with support. If we manage to infect it and just eavesdrop on his calls and messages, though, he shouldn't catch on."

"You have his number?"

I jutted my chin toward the business card on my desk. "Self-important people always include their cell numbers on these things."

"Yours is on your business cards," T.J. pointed out.

"The pattern holds," I said. Within the program, I crafted a text to come from a spoofed number. It included an image which carried an extra payload. If Teller opened it, the malware would run on his phone. If he didn't, I would try another delivery vector.

"How do you know he'll read your message?"

"I don't. I'll have to make it enticing." I showed her the body of the message I would send. *OMG dude, is this your wife? You really married up, bro. LOL. Hit me back.* The selected image came from the puff piece T.J. uncovered about Mary Teller. She remained beautiful—I doubted the woman could take a bad photo—but she wore a pantsuit and made no attempts to draw attention to her more prominent assets.

"So you're hoping he'll think it's some buddy of his whose number he doesn't have?"

"Basically," I said. She frowned. "Do you really think he doesn't know guys who would send a text exactly like the one I wrote?"

"I'm sure he does," T.J. said.

"All right." I sent it via the app. "Let's head on over and try to get him angry. If we're going to snoop on all his communications, they might as well be interesting." This time, T.J. drove us to the headquarters of Local 79. While we were en route, my phone buzzed from a notification.. "He opened the message and the picture. We're good."

"That was fast," T.J. said.

"I told you . . . he knows a bunch of grown-up frat boys."

"So what now? Do you see everything he does on your phone?"

"No." I patted the Android tablet on my lap. "It's on here. I could send it to my phone, but I'd rather wait until we leave his office."

T.J. guided the Mustang into a spot on the crowded lot, and we walked inside. As usual, Rebecca the receptionist maintained a very loose hold on things, and men worked really hard to appear busy.

"I don't think Mister Teller wants to see you," she said. Her face suggested we wasted her time. From where I stood, it didn't seem very valuable.

"I don't think I care what Mister Teller wants," I said. "This is a murder investigation, and more people are in danger." Her expression didn't change. "If you want to summon a couple guys from the back to deter me, go ahead, but you'll have to tear them away from the games on their phones first." She rolled her eyes. "At least they're not playing paper football this time." We headed up the stairs.

Brent Teller's brows knitted when T.J. and I walked in,

and then he looked like he'd eaten a bowl of lemons for break-fast. "What the hell do you two want this time?"

"You're a popular man," I said. We moved to the chairs on the other side of his desk. "Mind if we sit?" Before he could answer, I dropped onto one. T.J. did the same.

"Of course I'm popular." Teller wore a blue button-down and black pants. "I make sure thousands of hard-working men and women get the money and benefits they deserve."

"Wow. You running for mayor? I'm ready to vote."

He flashed a politician's quick grin. "I just might one day."

"Don't get your hopes up," I said. "I don't vote. I would say it's not personal, but it kind of is."

Teller crossed his muscular arms. "I was hoping I'd seen the last of you. What are you doing here?"

"When I said you were popular, I didn't only mean it in the conventional sense." I took out my phone. This was the reason I didn't put his communications onto it yet—he would need to see it and maybe even hold it. Downloading the videos of Teller and his wife would be enough. I started with the clip of Mary. "Maybe I should say your wife is the one with a lot of fans." The footage of her and O'Hearn making out against the wall played. "Can't say I blame the guy. She's a good-looking woman."

Teller clenched his fists, and the sounds of his deep breaths proved louder than the playback. "There they go into the elevator," I said.

"So what?" he demanded. I spread my hands when he didn't say anything else. This spurred him on. "You don't know where they were going."

"I don't know which room," I said. "True. We know what they were going up there to do, though. The only question is whether they tore each other's clothes off before they even opened the door."

"What's your point, Mister Ferguson?" Teller asked through clenched teeth.

"I haven't been married as long as you. You might even say I'm still a newlywed." I cued up the footage of Teller with Velvet and turned the phone to face him again. "My wife and I are pretty competitive . . . but not like this. We don't do revenge games. She looks like Mary, at least."

"Enough." Teller pounded the desk, and I was surprised it didn't crack. "So you found a few videos. They could be fakes."

"They're not," I said.

"They've been shared hundreds of times," T.J. added, "by a bunch of people you're connected to. You might be mad, but this isn't the first time you're seeing these."

I went back to the video of Mary and O'Hearn. "You know who he is?"

"No," Teller said without really looking at my phone screen.

"You sure?"

"Positive." He smirked. "Whoever he is, I'm sure Mary is the best lay he's ever had. You want me to be mad at her? Throw something across the room?" He took a deep breath and shrugged. His voice was a little quieter when he talked again. "If Mary went upstairs with him, I'm sure she had a good reason."

"What about her?" I switched to the clip of Teller and Velvet.

Teller scoffed. "No idea. Whores like her are a dime a dozen. The men like to have some . . . entertainment for their big parties. Who am I to say no?"

"It's funny you jump right to assuming she was hired to be there versus being someone's girlfriend."

"Look at how she's dressed. You saw the way she was all over me. Mary doesn't really care what I do. If some pretty whore wants to take me upstairs, why would I refuse?"

T.J.'s breath hissed beside me. I squeezed her forearm. We didn't need her blowing up right now. "Mary doesn't care what you do?" I asked.

"Nope."

"Including sleeping with escorts?"

He shrugged. "She knows a man in my position sometimes has to do certain things to keep up appearances for the workers."

"The young lady you disappeared with caught a bad beating recently."

The news made Teller pause but only for an instant. "I hear it's a dangerous profession."

"Especially if a jealous wife sends a couple of her brawny paramours after you," I said.

Anger clouded Teller's features, but he didn't take the bait. "I'm sure Mary wouldn't lower herself to deal with such a girl."

"Fuck you!" T.J. shot to her feet, knocking the chair over and jabbing her finger at Teller. He took it with the calm smirk of a man who thinks he's untouchable. Her face turned red as she continued her tirade. "You don't get to beat people or stab them and get away with it. We're coming for you and your wife, you prick."

"Good luck," he said.

I stood, grabbed T.J.'s arm, and steered her toward the door while she seethed.

———

T.J. let out an inarticulate yell in the parking lot. A couple passing pedestrians stopped to look at her before continuing on their way. She stomped around the blacktop, scanned the area, and planted a hard kick to the door of a black BMW 7 series. I approached the sedan from the rear. Its license plate read 79BOSS. "At least you found the right car," I said. We were probably fortunate the alarm didn't go off.

"What a bastard." She stared at the Bimmer—and the noticeable dent in the driver's door—and stalked away.

"He said those things for the reaction. Once he knew you gave a shit about Velvet, he exploited it."

"Well, it worked." T.J. walked toward her Mustang, and I followed. "Does this mean I'm weak? On the bench for the rest of the case."

"No." I grabbed her shoulders and looked her in the eyes. They were wet and about to overflow. "It means you're human, and you care about people. You have to in this line of work. It's better if assholes like Teller don't see you sweat very often . . . but whatever. It's done. He knew we were looking at him already, so it's not like he learned anything new."

T.J. nodded. "Thanks. Sorry I flew off the handle." She wiped at her eyes with the sleeve of her black sweater.

"Forget it. Let's see what our favorite union boss is doing about our visit." We climbed back into the car, and I configured Crocodile to send Teller's communications to my phone. In its app, we could see any texts, emails, or other messages he sent or received, plus listen to his phone calls. All remained quiet as T.J. backed out of the spot and we exited the lot. Several Greektown restaurants tempted me into an early lunch, but T.J. guided us back toward the office.

A couple minutes later, Teller sent a message via Whats-App. Crocodile showed me the number as opposed to any contact entry he had, but I recognized the digits as O'Hearn's from our deep dive into him.

> It's BT. We have a situation. Need you to work some overtime.

I'm always up for overtime. What's going on?

> A couple people are nosing around even after the incident the other night. You sure the other guys who worked overtime are good?

They don't work with me directly, but I've heard they are.

> We need a different strategy. A more permanent one. I have two jobs in mind.

Let's meet and discuss in person.

> Need to talk ASAP.

Fine. You know where to meet me. See you in a couple hours.

> Make it 3. I'm busy.

The communication stopped. T.J. read it at a traffic light. "We going after O'Hearn?" she wanted to know.

"We could," I said, "but no one has committed a crime here yet."

"They're talking about us."

"You and I both know it. Proving it would be a much different challenge. These two would say they were talking about a rat problem behind the headquarters or something. Everything is vague enough to give them plausible deniability."

"We can't just sit back," she said.

"I agree."

"They both seem to know where they'll be meeting."

"But we don't," I said.

"True," T.J. said. "We need to get in front of this . . . and fast."

CHAPTER 25

AT THE OFFICE, T.J. and I decided to divide and conquer.

She would stake out Brent Teller's house, and I would do the same with O'Hearn's. Before we left, I set up Crocodile on her phone so she could also see any communications from Teller when I did. She set off in her Mustang, and I drove the S4 home to pick up my second car. It was a late-'eighties Chevy Caprice I only broke out on special occasions. Years ago, I acquired it from a chop shop owner after doing him a favor, and he gave me a break on the price of souping up the car and making it resistant to small arms fire. It was big, ugly, heavy, and painted a few different shades of blue, but it did its specific job very well.

I drove the blue beast to O'Hearn's house in Highland-town. The neighborhood encompassed several blocks directly to the east of Patterson Park. O'Hearn's rowhouse stood on South Ellwood Street. He would have a fairly easy drive to Greektown and the Local 79 office. Just head south to Eastern Avenue, turn left, and he'd be there in a mile or so. I curbed the Caprice across the street and about four houses to the north.

The spot afforded me an easy view of O'Hearn's home.

Thanks to the time of day, someone driving by would find plenty of parking. A few hours later, this would very much not be the case. Like most rows of houses, an alley ran behind these, and residents often converted some or all of their meager backyards into parking pads. I did it, and it remained a great decision. I didn't know if O'Hearn made the same choice. If he did, there was a real risk he could leave his house without me seeing him.

At the moment, I saw no lights or signs of activity. I got out of the car, jogged across the road, and entered the alley. Most houses opted for the parking pad. O'Hearn did, as well, but his sat empty. I reversed course and took up my perch in the driver's seat again. My phone buzzed as T.J. sent a text.

> All quiet here.

> > Same. O'Hearn's not home.

> You think they already left?

> > Considering the timeline, they wouldn't need to unless they were meeting someplace far away.

> These people might be assholes, but they have a nice house. I'm tempted to pay some kids to TP it later.

> > It's your money.

I grinned. It would be just like T.J. to do it, too. Part of me hoped she did. In their exchange, Teller told O'Hearn he was busy. I suspected part of it was a power play—the union boss struck me as exactly the type who enjoyed making others wait for him—but he could have had legitimate work to do. Either way, he may not have needed to make a trip home. T.J.'s odds of running into Mary Teller struck me as higher. Who the hell knew what she did during the day?

I waited. Nothing happened. Thirty minutes became sixty and then ninety. If Teller and his favorite bent cop were going to meet, they would need to leave soon. If O'Hearn was already out, of course I'd never see him. I checked the back of his place again and found it the same as before. The witching hour came and went with no signs of activity. The pie place on the corner about a hundred yards behind me sounded really good right now. Before I could give in to temptation, however, a message from Teller came in.

Where are you?

No response came. T.J. called me. "You're seeing this, right?"

"Yep," I confirmed. "Still no sign of O'Hearn."

"I haven't seen Teller, either. His car is still here." She chuckled. "Someone's looking at the door."

"He must have taken someone else's ride."

"I've been here the whole time. I haven't even left to pee. I would've seen him leave."

"I'm sure there's a back exit," I said. "Past all those guys who are wasting space and oxygen on the first floor. He could have ducked out there, gotten into a waiting car, and he's gone without you even knowing he left."

"He's a slippery bastard if he did all that," T.J. said.

"He also knows two smart people see him as a suspect in at least one crime. He's going to be cautious. Even if he were normally reckless, O'Hearn could have given him some pointers to stay under the radar."

"What do you want to do now?"

"Let's wait another fifteen minutes," I said after considering my options for a moment. None were good, so I went with the least sucky choice. "If there's still nothing, we'll pack it in and go back to the office. These two are somewhere, and we'll put it together."

"All right." She ended the call. I waited the additional quarter of an hour. Nothing happened. On my way back to the office, I detoured through a drive-through for a late lunch. T.J. wouldn't complain.

———

For the second time in as many days, T.J. and I huddled around my desk to look at lascivious videos. She munched on her last few French fries as I played the first clip of the infamous three. "You think O'Hearn's disappearance has something to do with these?" my assistant asked.

"We don't know if he's really disappeared," I said. "If he has, though, he's on camera groping Teller's wife and heading upstairs with her. Even the oldest nun in the world knows what they were going there to do. Men have killed other men for less. Whatever use he provided by doing things like shooting at us could have ended pretty quickly once Teller saw these videos."

"Now we want to know where this took place."

"Right. Whoever first shot these was smart enough not to tag a location and to remove any identifying information from the clips themselves. No one who shared it mentioned where it was."

"And what happens when we figure it out?"

"Teller and O'Hearn seemed to know where they were supposed to meet," I said. "What if it's the same place? What if he went back there to meet someone else?"

"Like Mary?"

I shrugged. "Or anyone else who might want to kill him."

"You think O'Hearn is dead?" T.J. wanted to know.

"I think he's a man who's very likely outlived his useful-ness to a pair of craven assholes. If they were responsible for murdering a priest in literally his own backyard, they won't think twice about knifing a cop somewhere."

T.J. tossed her empty fry container into a paper bag and then disposed of the whole thing. She leaned closer to the monitor. "I don't see much to identify it yet."

"Me, either," I said. "It's a hotel ballroom. Absent any signage, they pretty much all look the same. Even the staffs tend to dress alike for fancy get-togethers."

"I guess you would know," she said, shooting me a grin. "All the fancy fundraisers your wife drags you to."

"It's a gift . . . and a curse."

The first video ended. We watched it again and failed to note anything of significance the second time, as well. "Let's try the next one." This clip showed Mary Teller and O'Hearn getting into the elevator. Before the doors closed, they continued their make-out session. "Pause it," T.J. said. I did. She pointed at the screen. "The signs near the elevator."

"They don't identify the venue." I knew where she was going with this, but I wanted her to reach the conclusion on her own. With enormous effort, I feigned ignorance.

"No, but each place's will be distinct. A different shade of gold for the placard. The letters are taller or shorter. You know what I'm getting at."

"I think I do." I managed to suppress a grin. Good for her. I took a screenshot of the signs near the doors and saved them in a shared folder. T.J. wheeled herself to her own desk, fired up her laptop, and got to work. I imagined she would take what I sent her and run reverse image searches on it. While we might not get a specific location as the result, we would probably learn which chain hosted the gala the night everyone seemed to head upstairs for extracurricular entertainment.

"It's the Hyatt," T.J. said a moment later.

"Makes sense. Nice place. Easy to find. Close to the interstate if people are coming from farther away."

"You think O'Hearn is there now?"

"No idea," I said. "So far, we know he's not at home, and he's not at the Local 79 headquarters. Considering he might be anywhere else in the city right now, I think we should eliminate reasonable options."

"Let's go to the Hyatt, then."

I grabbed my keys.

———

The clerk at the luxury hotel wasn't eager to cooperate.

"I can't disclose our guests," he said. His name badge identified him as Darren. He looked a few years younger than me, was tall and very thin, and his brows never lifted from their position of a scrutinizing frown.

"Of course not. What would Mister Hyatt think of you?"

"You're not the police."

I showed him my credentials again. It seemed to have no effect. "True," I acknowledged. Considering the time of day, a lot of people waited with suitcases, children, and other burdens in the lobby. I could use this to my advantage. "However, I have reason to believe someone here is in trouble." I raised my voice so everyone in the area could hear. "Are you really going to tell me you don't care about a dead body in one of your rooms?"

Chatter arose behind me. Darren winced. T.J. smiled. "Perhaps you have a picture of the person you're wondering about," the clerk said in a much quieter tone than I used. "I'd be happy to take a look at it."

"Sure." I pulled out my phone and showed him a photo of O'Hearn out of uniform. "Have you seen him recently? Especially today?"

"I have." Darren grabbed a small plastic key, entered some data, and swiped it through a reader. "The gentleman is in room three-ten."

"Thanks," I said. T.J. and I headed away from reception. A woman standing with her husband and two young kids stopped us. The man was checking something on his phone. The children—a boy and a girl who both looked to be under eight—tried to see what their dad was up to.

"Is there really a dead body here?" she asked.

I shrugged. "When it's your time, it's your time." We walked to the elevator. Behind us, the woman urged her husband to find another hotel faster and how could they possibly let their children stay here now?

"Darren is going to hate you," T.J. said.

"He should realize his job doesn't require him to be a barrier to people asking questions."

"You think that family downstairs is going to stay somewhere else?"

"My guess is it depends how easily they can cancel their reservation here. If it's quick and free, probably. She won't want to take the chance her children are on the same floor as a corpse even though people die in hotels every day."

We stepped out of the car onto the third story. The map on the wall showed the elevators in the approximate center of the floorplan. A long table stood against the opposite wall. It held a single flower in a tall, slender vase. "Luxury is all in the little touches," I said, and T.J. snorted. Signs indicated the room we wanted would be to the left. We headed that way.

Once we reached the door for 310, T.J. checked the corridor in both directions while I knocked lightly. No reply came.

"He could be in the shower," she suggested.

"I doubt it." I drew my pistol and stood to the side of the entry. T.J. moved behind me without me needing to tell her. With my free hand, I used the key card. The lock whirred, and the tiny red LED light flashed green. I pushed down on the handle and threw the door open. No bullets came flying out at us. This was a good sign. Before the door could swing shut again, I moved into the way of it. The room looked empty. I smelled a hint of copper. We were too late again.

O'Hearn's corpse lay on the bed. A single stab wound tore his white shirt just above his stomach, and it looked like most of the blood from his body was now around him on the queen. The pink comforter got turned very dark in spots. "Shit," T.J. muttered. She checked the rest of the area. "Bathroom's clear." I saw a rectangular bulge in O'Hearn's right front pocket and fished out his mobile. It was an old and original iPhone SE. With no further threats, I put my gun away. I swiped up on the screen. This model was way too old for FaceID, but it still wanted a four-digit passcode.

"We'll need to try to unlock this back at the office," I said. "Check the desk. See if he left anything." I opened the two drawers of the nightstand and found nothing but an unused copy of the Gideon *Bible*.

"Nothing," T.J. said. "The little writing pad is still intact. I don't think he did anything here."

"Except bleed out."

Several sets of footsteps approached. At least four people stomped toward the room. "Shit," I echoed. "It's probably the cops. They're going to have some questions." The noise stopped at the door. I took O'Hearn's phone and dropped it down the front of my pants, untucking my shirt to cover anything which might look unusual.

Four officers burst into the rooms, guns drawn. T.J. and I both raised our hands. "Freeze!" the closest one shouted. The quartet—three men and one woman—surveyed the scene. "You know who this is?"

"I do."

"You kill him?"

"No."

He jerked his red-bearded chin at another officer. This one was black and brawny. He looked like a slightly smaller version of Captain Leon Sharpe. "Arms up," he barked as he patted me down. "He's got a gun."

"And a permit for it," I said.

The officer disarmed me. He found a knife in my pocket and also took my phone, wallet, and keys. He wanted no parts of frisking me where O'Hearn's phone currently resided. I hoped no one tried to reach him. My crotch ringing wouldn't be a good look. "This the knife you stabbed him with?"

"You see any blood on it?"

"You could've wiped it off."

"We just got here," I said. "Literally a few minutes before you did. Talk to Darren at the front desk." A reedy Asian officer turned away and spoke into the radio on his upper chest. He swung back a minute later and nodded.

"You're still going to need to come with us," the first cop said.

CHAPTER 26

T.J. STOOD and watched helplessly as the beefy cop showing a shiny black dome joined his redheaded Irish partner. She remained with the wiry Asian, his slicked-down dark hair a contrast to the stocky blonde's pale Scandinavian features. "Wait in the bathroom, Nguyen," the female officer said. As she moved closer, T.J. could read the name *WILSON* on the board above her breast pocket. "I need to search you," she added once the other door closed.

"Fine." T.J. kept her arms raised. Wilson performed an extremely thorough pat-down. If the mood in the room had been a little lighter, T.J. might have made a crack about buying dinner before feeling her up. Considering a fellow cop lay dead on the bed, she didn't think the comment would go over well. Wilson took the few things T.J. carried in her pockets and also explored every nook and cranny of her purse. She dropped everything into a large plastic bag.

A loud knock came on the door. "It's fine," Wilson called. "You can let them in, Nguyen." He emerged from the restroom to admit two guys in white medical examiner suits.

"Did you know the dead officer?" T.J. asked in an attempt to build even a whisker of rapport with the businesslike

Wilson. Her throat felt dry. She'd been frisked by too many cops over the years.

"Not well." After a pause, Wilson added, "You're not under arrest, but you need to come with us to the station. I don't have to cuff you, but I will if I think you're going to force my hand. You going to play nice?"

"Yeah."

"All right. Let's go." She moved past the bed and gave T.J. a moderate shove in the back. It wasn't necessary. Nguyen walked out first. T.J. reminded herself she wouldn't be with these two long. They would ride to the precinct. She'd done nothing wrong—a first in all her encounters with the police. They didn't hold any leverage over her. No trying to make a deal in exchange for other girls or her pimp.

They rode down the elevator in silence. A few stragglers in the lobby watched as the two cops walked T.J. outside. She climbed into the rear of their cruiser on her own accord. No pushes to the back this time. T.J. buckled herself in. As usual with these vehicles, the occupants of the front were shielded from the presumptive criminals they drove around via wire and plexiglass. It had been a couple years since T.J. got forced into the back of a patrol car. Those cops were jerks. They didn't wait for a female officer to come, and they enjoyed the pat-down a little too much.

"How do you know the deceased?" Nguyen asked as they drove away.

T.J. said nothing.

After a moment, Wilson chimed in. "You're not gonna talk to us?"

"I doubt it would help," T.J. said.

"You're not under arrest," Nguyen said.

"And you're not my buddies . . . no matter how many times you try and butter me up. You're taking me to your precinct. You want me to talk? Ask some good questions there."

"We got a few minutes," Wilson said. "Might as well use them. You don't want us to record you as being uncooperative, do you?"

"I'm not under arrest." T.J. shrugged. "Write me down however you want."

"This is a chance for you to tell us what you and your boyfriend were doing in that room." T.J. didn't take the bait. In truth, Wilson wasn't very good at this. Some of the vice cops who'd corralled her in the past—even the ones who didn't get way too hands-on—were way better at prying and cajoling information out of people.

T.J. realized there was more to it now. Previously, whenever she'd been in the back of a police car, there had been a good reason for it. She'd been caught doing the wrong thing in the wrong part of town. Today, she and her boss were investigating a murder case. Two more bodies had dropped since they started. Nguyen and Wilson didn't seem too broken up about another cop being dead. Maybe O'Hearn was a dick, or perhaps his fellow officers knew he was bent.

The trip took longer than T.J. wanted. It wasn't very far from the Hyatt to police headquarters. Nguyen drove slowly, however. Whenever a light went yellow, he would hit the brakes immediately. This made him a rarity among his fellow policemen in T.J.'s experience. It also meant he was milking the drive . . . trying to buy time so he and Wilson could have a fishing expedition.

T.J. wasn't biting.

"Don't want to talk?" Nguyen asked. He drove past Baltimore Street. T.J. made enough trips to HQ with C.T. over the last several months to know he should have taken the turn.

"Can I get an Uber?" she said. "I like my chances of getting there faster."

In the mirror, Nguyen smirked. Wilson remained stone-faced. T.J. wondered if the woman were even capable of humor. It took an extra minute or two, but they got to their destination. The two cops walked in with T.J., and they all took the elevator to Homicide. Wilson steered T.J. toward the closest interview room. Rich's office was clear across the space. "Sit here," she ordered. "A couple detectives will come by to ask you some questions."

T.J. again didn't answer. Wilson slammed the door. This was no different than the other interrogation rooms T.J. spent time in before. Her pulse quickened, and she took deep breaths to calm herself. The police didn't have anything on her this time. They'd be clueless about O'Hearn, and it would be up to her and C.T. to fill in the gaps. T.J. knew they would keep her waiting. Under arrest or not, it was a common tactic. Probably the most popular one in the playbook.

She leaned back and kicked her feet up on the desk. If they were going to make her wait, she would do it in style.

———

As T.J. expected, no one came in for a while. She didn't let it bother her. At least this little room was nicer than previous ones she'd been in. She used the downtime to think about the case. It was better than memories of being in other police stations. O'Hearn died much the same way Steven Cooper did. One fatal stab wound. T.J.'s quick look at O'Hearn's body showed a small gash. Whoever killed Sean Cooper also used a slender blade, though they did it many times in his case.

These things all pointed to the same person. T.J. suspected Velvet for a while. She didn't want to, but her friend fit the evidence. More recently, she'd come to suspect Mary Teller. The small blade suited a woman rather than a brawny guy like her husband. He'd take a sledgehammer and bludgeon someone to death, then flex over the body afterward. The problem was that C.T. and T.J. didn't have any good evidence pointing to Mary. It was all circumstantial . . . like it had been with Velvet.

Whenever they both got out of here, Mary Teller needed to be their focus. By now, wife and husband could be long gone. They certainly had the means to flee and the money and ambition to be successful somewhere else. The interrogation room door swinging open interrupted T.J.'s thoughts. Two white male cops walked in. Both wore white button-down shirts with boring ties but no jackets. One of them looked familiar. "Tamera," the one with sandy blond hair said.

T.J. shook her head. "Adams, right?"

"You remember." He plastered on a fake smile and sat in one of the two chairs across from her. The other cop wore a more dour expression. "I'm touched."

"You were in vice," she said, "and you actually weren't an asshole. Kind of remarkable."

"How about you? Seems like you've really made something of yourself."

"It beat the alternative."

Adams opened a file folder. A photo of O'Hearn dead on the hotel bed was the first thing inside. "Life's been going pretty well for you, Tamera. I'm impressed." T.J. remained silent. As she expected, Adams kept talking. "It's something of a surprise, then, to find you in a hotel room with a dead cop. Did you know he was on the force?"

"I knew his name, too. O'Hearn."

"You go there to fuck him?" the other cop asked.

T.J. ignored him. Adams stuck to the relevant details. "Why were you and your boss in a hotel room with him?"

"We'd just gotten there," T.J. said. "Your colleague got stabbed earlier."

"The ME's initial guess is two hours before." The older cop glanced sidelong at Adams. "We don't think you killed him, Tamera. It was never your style."

"You got quite a history with us, though," the other detective said. He was probably in his forties. Between the receding hairline, chubby face, and shirt he needed to size up, he didn't represent the best the BPD had to offer. Rich could do better in his homicide unit. "Bunch of arrests for hooking . . . some before you were even eighteen. You ever have to get rough with a john?"

"We had someone who did that for us."

"But he couldn't go with you all the time. Be pretty awkward if some guy is keeping watch while you're . . . well, you know."

"What's your point, Detective?"

"You ever use a knife?"

"I'm tempted to right now," T.J. said. She shifted in the uncomfortable metal chair and took her hands off the table. The middle-aged cop scowled. Adams tried to hide a smirk. "No. I've never stabbed anyone."

"Where's O'Hearn's phone?" Adams asked.

"No idea."

"Wasn't found with his body. Our people have thoroughly searched the room. It's not there."

"Maybe whoever killed him took it," T.J. said.

"You have it?" the second cop wanted to know.

"The lady officer on the scene searched me quite well. The only cell I had was my own."

The guy grinned like a wolf staring down a sheep. "She look everywhere?"

"Fuck you. What are you, twelve?"

Adams held up one hand toward T.J. and the other toward his presumptive partner. "Enough. You didn't see a phone at the scene?"

"No," T.J. said. Her hands gripped the sides of the chair hard. She didn't want to be here anymore. Adams wasn't bad, but the other guy was really pushing her buttons.

"Your boss didn't pick it up?"

"I'm sure someone has searched him by now." She leveled her eyes at Adams's partner. "Maybe you'd like to stick your hand up *his* ass instead." The man's face reddened.

Adams intervened again. "You know something you're not telling us, Tamera?"

"O'Hearn was dirty," T.J. said.

The older detective slapped the tabletop. "Bullshit."

"How many cops walking the straight and narrow get stabbed and left to bleed out in hotel rooms?"

"Probably not many," Adams said with a sigh. "I can't tell you much about O'Hearn. Was kinda hoping you could fill in some gaps for me."

T.J. shrugged. "Don't you guys have a whole division for dealing with crooked coworkers?"

Adams stood. His partner followed his lead after fixing T.J. with an ineffective stare-down. "It's good to see you've turned your life around, Tamera. Stay out of trouble." They left, and the door swung shut behind them. T.J. was left to wait alone again. Adams was a good cop. He'd been one of the few nice ones she encountered in vice. Most detectives there didn't like the job or the people they met. Even back then, T.J. got the impression they wanted to be somewhere more glamorous. Adams did the work. He arrested people—including T.J.—when he needed to. He acted like he cared, though. He told her she needed to get out of the life, and now that she did, his happiness for her seemed sincere.

The BPD didn't know anything, but T.J. got the impression they suspected O'Hearn was dirty. Adams's partner was angry at the accusation but never tried to deny it. Maybe internal affairs already had a case going. If so, did other cops sniffing around lead Mary to kill O'Hearn? It had to be Mary. When T.J. got out of here, she would prove it. By herself if necessary.

A few minutes later, the door swing open, and Rich Ferguson walked in. He'd kept his suit jacket on. As usual, he wore a serious expression. "What the hell have you gotten into?"

"I like Adams," T.J. said. "However, his partner's an asshole. If he works for you, you can do better."

"I don't think you're in a position to be my human resources department." He crooked his finger at her. "Come with me."

"Am I free to go?"

"No," Rich said.

CHAPTER 27

I'D BEEN in interrogation rooms before.

The first time came in Hong Kong, and the overseas version—complete with overzealous officers in love with using their fists and nightsticks—wasn't an experience I cared to repeat. Since I've worked this job, I've been hauled in for questioning a few other times. Both city and county cops paled before those in China. Here, they loved to make people wait. I've gotten good at waiting over the years. Few people can count ceiling tiles faster or more accurately than I can. I don't put it on my business cards or brag about it, but I'm something of an expert.

O'Hearn's phone remained where I stashed it. I made sure my shirt covered the area again. Sitting close to the table would help. I'd never gotten a chance to turn it off at the scene. I could only hope O'Hearn kept the phone in silent mode. Efforts to stonewall the cops about where it was would evaporate if he got a call or text. I wondered if T.J. sat in a room nearby. Riding in the back of a police car and getting shoved into an interrogation room probably conjured up bad memories for her.

The door opened, and Sergeant Paul King walked in

carrying a manila folder. No one else came with him. I must have looked surprised, because he said, "When you make sergeant, they let you wipe your own ass *and* talk to people by yourself."

"I hope you've done the first part already."

The door swung shut with a loud *thunk* as King sat opposite me at the small table. Despite this whole area being renovated within the last couple years, the interrogation rooms were largely unchanged. They got better lighting, but they remained small and cramped by design. The cynic in me realized more bulbs overhead simply allowed people a better look at their grim surroundings. "Why were you and your secretary in a hotel room with a dead cop?"

"We'd just gotten there. You're making it sound like we spent hours with him."

King waved a hand. "Whatever. No one thinks you killed him. Timeline aside, why were you there?"

I pondered how much to tell King. He was a good cop, and I would count him among the small number in the building I could trust. At the moment, he was doing his job. The fact we were friendly wouldn't matter when the corpse belonged to a fellow member of the BPD. Even if King didn't suspect me or T.J., he wouldn't want the runaround, and he didn't deserve it. "O'Hearn was dirty."

"You know this for sure?"

"You don't seem surprised," I pointed out.

King shrugged. "Answer my question."

"We can infer it from where and how he was found. The Hyatt's a nice place, but how many clean cops get stabbed a single time and left to die on a bed somewhere?"

"I'm not asking for your inferences," King said. "I can make my own. You told me he was dirty like it's a fact."

"Remember when T.J. and I got shot at a few days ago?"

"It might surprise you to know I don't follow your every move . . . but yeah. I heard."

"O'Hearn was the shooter."

King's eyes widened. "No shit?"

"No shit," I echoed. "I recently helped the guy who owns the building upgrade his security system. We pulled a few stills from the cameras. Pretty sure it was him."

"Thank you *so* much for telling us in a timely manner."

"What would you have done if I had? Punted it to IAD?"

"Probably," King said. "It'd be their case. At least we'd know."

"O'Hearn never struck me as exceptional." King crossed his arms. "I didn't know him well, but I never got the impression. He's probably been crooked for a while. My guess is your beloved colleagues with internal affairs already knew about him."

"I'm not at liberty to disclose such sensitive information," King said, though he used the file folder to hide a quick thumbs-up from the camera. "We found a knife on you. Small lock-blade model. Could be the right size."

"Like I mentioned to the officers at the scene, let me know when you find any blood on it. Your kitchen knife theory was better." My mind's eye chose this moment to replay a memory of Mary Teller walking into her husband's office. She wore a great black dress with red trim and looked stunning in it. After a brief exchange with her husband, she picked up a slender letter opener and used it on an envelope. Like kitchen knives, a lot of people could own a similar instrument, but it would fit. Keeping it in her husband's office would even deflect suspicion from her.

"What are you thinking?" King wanted to know.

"I think you're fishing in the wrong river with old bait," I said.

"Help me out, then."

T.J. would be locked onto Mary Teller as a suspect. She made a good one, but I wanted to finish this and wrap up the case for Father David. He'd hired me because the police hadn't come up with anything. "Brent Teller."

"Who?"

"Union boss. Local Seventy-nine. I like him in the murder of the priest."

"How the hell does this connect to O'Hearn?"

"He did some work for them. Security mostly. I guess they leaned on him when they needed something more." I debated telling King about O'Hearn and Mary's affair. She wouldn't be the first beautiful woman to use sex as a means to control a pliable man. I wanted to save Mary for T.J. and me to take down, however.

"Why would this union guy kill a priest?" King asked.

"Problems with the contract," I said. "Father Cooper ended up giving a bunch of work to people in the church who needed it."

King frowned. His folder remained closed. I wondered if he carried it in here for show. "All right. There may be something we can use here. Sit tight." He left the room, and I went back to waiting. I already knew how many ceiling tiles hung overhead. I'd even confirmed the count three times. The floor was solid concrete. I spotted a few pockmarks in the surface. It would take longer than counting tiles, at least.

Before I could get very far, the door opened again. Captain Leon Sharpe's massive frame filled the jamb. I wondered if any suspects were foolish enough to try and get past him. "For a smart person," he said, "you sure are an idiot sometimes."

"Nice to see you, too, Leon. If this whole police thing doesn't work out, maybe you can write greeting cards."

"You should have told us about O'Hearn."

"Why? So neither of us could have been in control of the investigation?"

His answer came in the form of waving a hand toward the door. "Come with me."

Lacking a better option, I got up and followed the captain.

———

I shadowed Sharpe to Rich's office where my cousin and T.J. already waited. The captain joined Rich on the business side of the desk. "I like you both," he began, "but this is pretty dumb. You come across a cop you think is dirty, you let us know." I started to repeat my comment of moments ago, but Sharpe held up a large hand. "Right. We wouldn't be in control of the investigation. I understand your point, but sometimes, we all need to use proper channels."

"This probably isn't O'Hearn's first time wandering off the straight and narrow," I said. "IAD must have a file on him already."

"Not the point," Rich said. "Clean or crooked, we're always going to want to investigate a dead cop."

I shrugged. "No one's stopping you."

"We have someone in custody." Rich frowned at the proximity of the much larger Leon Sharpe. He sat and crossed his arms. "The gangbanger."

"I told you when you arrested him he didn't do it," I said.

"Either of you got a better suspect for us?"

"Brent Teller," T.J. said. "He's the union boss for Local Seventy-nine."

"Why the hell would he want to kill a priest?" Rich wanted to know.

"Problems with the contract," I said. "It seems the archdiocese is something of a fickle client. Father Cooper ended up giving a lot of work to people in his parish . . . many of whom were immigrants. It's money out of the union's pockets."

"And the companies who actually do the work," Sharpe said. "You look into those?"

"We did," T.J. said. "No one firm was out a major amount."

"I might still like the gang kid," Rich said. "Clearer motive."

"How?" I asked. "Everything points to Father Cooper being a friend to immigrants and refugees whether or not they were in gangs."

"You're presuming the banger would be a rational actor."

"Well, I guess I'm presuming most people don't bite the hand that feeds them. I think Teller is a much better suspect." Not as good as his wife, of course, but I was still saving Mary for T.J. and me. If it turned out she didn't do it, the BPD would end up with the right man in custody.

"This Teller might be a bit of a stretch," Sharpe said. "We'll bring him in to be thorough. Sweat him a little. A man with his connections would lawyer up right away, but I'm sure we'll get some details out of him." He leaned down, put his fists on Rich's desk, and stared at T.J. and me. "Maybe you gave us someone good, but a cop is still dead. I don't want you two nosing around anymore. Who hired you?"

"Another priest in the archdiocese," I said.

"Tell him you gave the police a suspect. Case closed. Collect your check and move on. We'll take this one from here."

"But we—" T.J. started to say.

"I said," Sharpe broke in, "we got this one." When she

frowned, he added, "Considering all you've done and especially haven't done, young lady, we could probably charge you and your boss with obstruction of justice."

"We'll stay out of it," I said.

"Good." Sharpe stood up straight again. "Get your things and go."

We collected our belongings from the desk sergeant and headed for the exit. "We're really going to let him put us on the bench?" T.J. asked as we crossed the lobby.

"I'm not sure we had a choice in the matter. Besides, what we said back there and what we do can be two different things."

"You told Sharpe we were done."

I pushed the front door open and swept my hand for her to walk through. "I had my fingers crossed."

"They might have let us walk out," T.J. said, "but I'm going to guess your cousin and his boss are still going to be suspicious of us."

"He doesn't work for Sharpe," I said. "You're right, though. I pretty much presume the BPD is giving me the hairy eyeball most of the time."

"What are we going to do, then?"

I pointed to the far side of the building. "Let's talk over there. We still have a phone to inspect."

———

"Don't you have a Lysol wipe?" T.J. frowned as I fished O'Hearn's phone out of my pants. "Maybe some bleach?"

We stood in an alley near police headquarters. I swept the area with my free hand. "If you can find some, you're welcome to use it."

"Gross."

"I'm not asking you to hold it. I'm also not a leper."

Her expression didn't change. "Can't they track his phone?"

"Yeah."

"You're not worried?"

"The location data isn't super precise. As far as they can tell, the stupid thing has been in their own building for a while now." The device prompted me to enter an unlock password. I tried a few of the most common—1111, 1234, 4321—and got nowhere. Most iPhones will auto-wipe if someone guesses wrong a certain number of times. Ten is typical, but if O'Hearn set his to five, I needed to make better guesses.

"You know his birthday?" T.J. asked.

"Offhand, no. Use your phone and get it from our office." She opened an encrypted tunnel and connected to her laptop like I showed her. From there, it took T.J. a few minutes and a little trial and error to find what she needed.

"Got it. June thirteenth."

I keyed in 0613, and the phone still refused to let me in. "I'm not sure how many tries we have left. It may only be one."

"You think this is his only phone?"

I shrugged. "No idea. It's pretty old. Small, too. I'm sure it doesn't get the operating system updates anymore."

"Maybe it's sort of a burner."

"Could be," I said. "Carriers have been incentivizing new models for a couple years now. If this is meant for limited use, I think we can presume who gave it to him." T.J. nodded in agreement. I entered 6279—which spelled *MARY* on the keypad—and the phone unlocked.

"Good guess," T.J. said.

We checked the contacts first. There were only two—

Maria's Pizza and B's Bistro. I found the distinction between Mary and Maria interesting. Same name but a different language. I recalled something from the first time we saw her. Maria versus Mary would explain it. Text threads corresponded to each entry, but the one obviously belonging to Mary Teller was much longer. It was also filled with far more interesting content, including many pictures of Mary wearing nothing at all. The photos were also saved in the camera roll.

"What a pig," T.J. said with a snort.

"I don't know many guys who wouldn't save these," I said.

"Rollins wouldn't."

"Fine. I'll add a heterosexual qualifier to my comment." I scrolled through the collection of pictures.

"You're going to start oinking soon, too," T.J. said.

I stopped when someone else appeared. "Look. This is Velvet." Her resemblance to Mary was profound even in varying states of undress. "Brent probably sent those."

"So what do we do now?"

"I'll text you a few of the pictures."

She wrinkled her nose. "I don't want them."

"Upload them to your computer," I said. "We might be able to use them later. I'll screencap some of the texts, too." I spent a couple minutes sending images to T.J. She spent a couple more forwarding them to a shared folder on her laptop.

"All right," she said when everything finished. "Now what?"

"I'd love to toss this in the trash, but we need to clone it. There's a convenience store a couple blocks east of here. Can you pick up a burner?"

"You mean on The Block?" T.J. asked with a little tremble in her voice.

"Yes," I said. T.J. clenched her hands into fists. "If you want to get out of the office and be more involved, you're going to have to do things which scare you sometimes." She remained rooted in place. "You can get the phone or stand here and hope the cops don't figure out where O'Hearn's cell really is."

"Is this tough love?"

I shrugged. "Call it whatever you want. It's reality." T.J. still looked like she had no interest in moving. "When I got shot, I spent a while doing the physical recovery. The mental part took a lot longer. Even after I got back home, I still reached out to the shrink I worked with at the rehab place. Her name was Parrish. She was entirely unimpressed with my usual bullshit." T.J. smiled for the first time in a while. "I've never been a big fan of folks in her profession, but she was good. One of the things she made sure I learned was realizing it's a process and not just one single hurdle to overcome."

"You're not very good at pep talks, you know," she said.

"I guess I won't go into coaching after I retire."

"Fine." T.J. took a deep breath and finally unclenched her fists. "I'll get the damn burner." She headed out of the alley and made a right. Good for her. I probably wasn't very good at pep talks, but T.J. needed to move past some things if she wanted to be more active in what we do every day. This case already dredged up some aspects of her past. Might as well rip the band-aid all the way off.

A couple cops walked by on Baltimore Street. I acted like I was on the phone, and they paid me no mind. Nothing else of consequence happened until T.J. returned a few minutes later. She handed me a package containing a nondescript Motorola Android phone. "Everything intact back there?" I said.

"I only burned two places down."

"We must strive for moderation in all things." It took longer than necessary, but I finally extracted the phone from its complex plastic prison and turned it on. It had about thirty percent charge. Good enough for now. With hands on O'Hearn's mobile, this would be easy. "Physical access trumps everything," I explained to T.J. "It's irrelevant what settings O'Hearn enabled on his cell. I unlocked it, and I'm holding it. None of what he did matters."

"You going to clone it?"

"Yes. Keep an eye out for nosy cops." She did, and the process completed after a few minutes.

"What now?" T.J. asked again.

"We leave the original here. I want to try and draw Mary in first. We don't know for sure if she's killed anyone. Hell, her lawyer would deny this contact is even her. Let's see what happens." With all content from the iPhone now on the Android I held, I opened the messages between O'Hearn and the alleged Maria's Pizza. They talked about a great many things. Italian food, however, was not on the list. Most of it consisted of flirting and sexting with a few cryptic messages about taking care of problems thrown in for good measure. The most recent text asked O'Hearn to meet in the usual spot to discuss a business opportunity. Considering the time-stamp, this probably led to his demise.

I tapped out a message while T.J. watched. *You didn't finish me. We'll need to talk soon or I go to the cops.* I sent it and added a separate message. *By the way, you owe me a new shirt.*

"Why talk about his shirt?" T.J. wanted to know.

"Playing a hunch." I tossed O'Hearn's phone into a nearby dumpster. "Let's get out of here."

CHAPTER 28

WE CAUGHT an Uber back to the Hyatt and then returned to the office. The burner remained silent. I connected it to a charger once we were inside. It chirped and buzzed a few minutes later. Mary responded in two separate messages.

> Maybe I underestimated you. Let's discuss our future together.

> Happy to get you a new shirt, baby. What size do you use?

"See?" I said as I dropped into my chair. It felt about fifteen thousand percent better than the hard plastic monstrosity at the BPD.

T.J.'s eyes scanned the messages a few times, but she shrugged. "See what?"

"We suspected this Maria's Pizza contact was really Mary Teller. Here's your proof."

"Where?"

"Think back to the first time we visited Local 79," I said. "Teller was giving us his usual political spiel. Then, his wife walked in."

"That's when you really started paying attention."

I grinned. "To her especially. He mentioned something about a guy needing a polo for an event the same night. You remember her response?"

After a few seconds, T.J. said, "What size does he wear?"

I shook my head. "What size does he *use*?"

"So she's not the most precise speaker."

"It's the way in which she's imprecise. You take Spanish in school?"

"Sure." Her eyes lit up as the realization hit her. "*Usar*. It means to wear."

"Right," I said. "And because it looks a lot like 'use,' many native Spanish speakers will refer to things like the size they use versus the size they wear."

She grabbed her chair and wheeled it to my desk. "This means Mary wasn't born here."

"My guess is O'Hearn knew her real first name was Maria. It's why he created her contact entry like he did."

"Does this help us?" my sleuth-in-training wanted to know.

"Probably. We can figure out who she really is later. For now, we need to keep stringing her along. She thinks she's talking to O'Hearn. Once the story gets out about him being in the morgue, we lose her."

"You should answer her, then."

I jotted off a reply which included my best guess as to O'Hearn's actual shirt size.

> I'll take an XL. Might even need a 2X to cover the bandages.

> Sorry, lover. I thought you were a loose end.

> Why should I meet you again? You tried to kill me once. Almost got there.

I was wrong. You know Brent. Always filling
my head with lies. He knows about us.

> I told you he did.

He's unaware I know about the whore he's
been fucking. She got a beating. I probably
should've stabbed her, too.

> This isn't convincing me I should ever see
> you again.

Let me make it up to you. You know how
good I am.

> I doubt I could survive much right now.

We'll take it easy and slow, then. Whatever
you need, lover. Give me a chance to show
you how sorry I am.

> Fine. Come by my house tonight at ten.

See you then. XX

"She's not going to go alone," T.J. said.

"Neither am I. You're coming with me."

"Can I kick that bitch's ass?"

I chuckled. "Fine with me."

"You know she might not buy this." T.J. frowned. "Mary strikes me as calculating. What if she stabbed O'Hearn and waited while he bled out on the bed?"

"She'll know this is a ruse, then." I shrugged. "It's a risk. I doubt she would've come alone either way. If she knifed him and ran, and he somehow made it out alive, she'd bring muscle to make sure he didn't survive the second time."

"Maybe it'll be the same guys she sent after Velvet."

"I hope they're the ones. I didn't have time to deal with them then."

T.J. cracked her knuckles. "We'll be ready. I want a piece of Mary . . . or whatever the hell her name is."

————

Her name, in fact, was Maria Cabrera.

She'd taken some steps to make this hard to find. Uncovering the details took us a while, but we had time until the big meeting at ten. Maria arrived in the US from Argentina when she was twelve. "Pretty remarkable," T.J. said. "I don't recall hearing her speak with an accent."

"She doesn't. If she didn't talk about people using shirts, I don't think I would have been suspicious."

T.J. joined me in perusing pictures of Maria. "She doesn't really look like a Latina."

"A lot of Argentinians are Caucasian," I said. "Like Lionel Messi."

"Who?"

"Soccer player," I said. "Pretty famous one, too."

T.J. put her hand over her heart in mock surprise. "Have you moved on from David Beckham?"

"He was *so* twenty years ago."

I texted Gloria and told her it would be a late night, but we would wrap up the case. She wished me good luck and promised to save me some dinner. T.J. and I ordered Chinese for delivery and strategized while we studied pictures of O'Hearn's house and property. He lived not far from Rich, actually. I wondered if my cousin knew he shared a ZIP code with a crooked cop. His home was much smaller. It was a basic Cape Cod model with a medium driveway, porches in the front and rear, and a decent-sized fenced backyard.

"You think the police have already been there?" T.J. asked.

"Probably. It's one of the reasons I wanted to wait until ten. Gives them time to finish."

"You don't think the house being a crime scene will deter Mary . . . or Maria?"

"We'll get there early. You gonna eat the last spring roll?"

"Yes." T.J. dragged the tiny plate closer to herself. "You already had one."

"So did you," I said. "They come three to an order."

"We'll cut it in half, then." She used a plastic knife to chop it down the middle. I grabbed my portion. "You can't have my duck sauce, though."

I wrinkled my nose. "It's all yours. Poor ducks."

She snickered, and we continued our recon of the grounds. "They could come from the back," T.J. said as she pointed at my screen. "That grassy alley gives them access."

"You're right. They'd be smart to use it. We need to presume they're looking at a map, too."

"I can be back there."

"No," I said. "I don't want you to take the risk. We'll set up a camera to cover it. You can watch on your phone. Let me know when the goons are about to crash the party."

"I don't mind mixing it up."

"My name is on the door. I'll take the chances. Once I handle the muscle, if you want to run in and kick Maria's ass, I'm all for it."

"Count on it," T.J. said. We did a little more research, and I made sure to pack what we needed. Some strong Velcro strips would hold the camera in place. We would park close enough for T.J. to connect her phone and surveil the rear of the place. At the appointed time, we left for Hamilton. Most houses on the street were either dark or only left one light on. O'Hearn's place stood toward the far end. We parked in front of the neighbor's house. I walked the perimeter, didn't see anyone, and headed to the back.

There were two entrances from the rear. A sliding glass door led in from the patio, and a conventional door provided access from the back porch. I checked both and found them locked. Anyone breaking in would be more likely to try the porch, but I affixed the camera between the two. This way, no matter what Maria's enforcers did, we would see them. I made sure the device was set to transmit and confirmed connectivity with T.J. We kept the line open. Once we were good, I conducted a nosy neighbor check, pulled crime scene tape from the front door, and popped the lock with a snap gun.

Then, I waited. O'Hearn didn't have any ceiling tiles to count. I didn't want to turn a light on, anyway. So far, we'd managed to avoid tipping off the neighbors. I didn't know how much longer this would hold true, but I wanted to keep it going as long as I could. I checked my watch periodically. Just after I confirmed it was 9:55, T.J. told me two guys approached the back door. The darkness inside didn't allow me a good look at the house. I moved toward the rear. A long table told me I stood in the dining room. I flipped the light on. I've always found it much easier to beat up goons when I can see them.

A pair of hushed voices came from the back. The dining room opened into the kitchen. I stood next to the doorway off to the side. If the enforcers came in, they wouldn't see me at first. "Any sign of Maria?" I whispered to T.J.

"I certainly don't see a McLaren out here," she said. "A car did pull up across the street a couple minutes ago. I didn't catch anyone getting out, but she could have let them off farther down."

"Okay. I think they're about to crash my party. If you see her approaching, let her come. We don't want to spook her."

"Fine," T.J. said with a sigh.

A loud cracking came from over my shoulder. One of the musclemen must have kicked the door in. One set of footfalls sounded across the kitchen followed closely by another. They didn't even bother to close up after themselves. Maybe Maria planned to follow them at a set interval. These two idiots would rough up the already-wounded O'Hearn, and his lover would come in and finish him off.

I kept my right hand near my pistol just in case and raised my left arm. When someone's head appeared in the doorway leading to the kitchen, I leaned out and struck, clobbering whoever it was flush in the mouth with my elbow. He didn't fall, but he turned away and bit off a string of curses muffled by the hands covering the lower portion of his face. I moved over to fill the space as the other goon came forward.

He was one of the men from Velvet's apartment . . . the one who didn't get a broken nose. "Told you I'd have more for you," I said.

"Where's the cop?"

"Not here. You get to deal with me instead."

He shrugged and came at me with a right cross. I blocked it along with the two punches which followed it. He was no slow lummox, at least. My foe turned his hips each time. Someone taught him how to throw a punch, and he possessed the size and strength to get some good power into them. After I deflected a left hook, he wound up for a big right uppercut. I moved to the side, and his fist slammed into the drywall.

His hand went through it up to the wrist. When he tried to pull it free, it didn't come. I capitalized by kicking him in the ribs, grabbing the back of his head, and slamming it into the moulding until he went limp. The other guy remained in the kitchen. The room was pretty clear except for a couple of pans on the stove. I approached warily. Sure enough, he lashed out with a knife as I drew closer.

I stepped back from the cut, and it missed by maybe a couple inches. As I retreated another pace, I grabbed the closest skillet. This guy wore tape on his nose. I smiled. "How's your face?"

"Fuck you."

"At least I couldn't make you any uglier."

He swung the knife again. I ducked this time. He'd grabbed a typical kitchen blade. It only added a few inches to his reach. When he reached back to swing it again, I stepped forward and transferred the pan to my left hand. My upraised right forearm deflected his strike, and before he could try to twist the blade and still get me, I hit him in the side of the head with the skillet. It wasn't a hard shot, but it was enough to stagger him.

I took it in my right hand again, wound up, and let him have it square in the face. The clang was very satisfying, and he dropped like he'd been shot. With both of them down, I asked T.J., "Any sign of Maria?"

"Not yet."

"Let's get things moving, then." I grabbed the unconscious goon's phone.

———

His mobile was a lot newer than O'Hearn's. It wanted his face to unlock. I held the screen near him and got access once the device sorted everything out. Sure enough, this guy had been texting with Maria—or simply Mary as she appeared in his contacts. I scanned their recent messages to get a sense of how my mystery assailant talked. Then, I sent her a message.

No dice on the cop, boss. Got the nosy investigator we saw at the whore's place instead.

After a moment, she replied. *I'll take the consolation prize. Headed to the back door.*

"She'll be on the move," I said into the open connection.

"I see her," T.J. said. "You want me to follow her?"

"Let her get behind the house. I'd rather she not spot you." I left the two unconscious goons in the kitchen and took up my post in the dining room again. Maria would probably be carrying her trusty knife. She came here to finish O'Hearn, however, and as far as she knew, the blade didn't do the job the first time. Something stronger might be in order. I drew my pistol and waited.

Her heels clattered on the concrete outside. "I'm coming your way," T.J.'s voice warned through my earpiece. When Maria's shoes hit the tiled kitchen floor, I stepped out of hiding, keeping my gun behind my back for now.

"You," she said.

"Hello, Maria." She narrowed her eyes. A slender blade extended from her right hand. Maria wore tight jeans and a white blouse over a black tank top which accentuated her cleavage. If she brought another weapon, I couldn't see it. "Surprised I know?"

"Let's say I've taken care to leave the past behind."

"Not well enough. We're aware of what you've done. O'Hearn must have been disappointed when you stabbed him. He probably expected another roll in the hay."

"Is he dead?" she asked with the sincerity of a reporter mailing in her last day on the job.

I debated telling her the answer for a second. "Yes," I said after a little deliberation. She might as well know the depths of her predicament. It could goad her into a mistake. "The police are going to be very interested in arresting you. He might have been dirty, but O'Hearn was still a cop."

"Maybe we can work something out." Her voice took on a lower and sultry tone, and I would have to admit it was alluring. "I've seen the way you look at me."

"Kind of hard to avoid it. You don't exactly dress modestly."

She pushed her breasts up. They didn't need the help. "Like you Americans are fond of saying . . . when you got it, flaunt it."

"I'm sure you'll be very popular in a women's prison," I said.

Maria brandished the knife. I inched to the side and held up my 9MM. "We also have a saying about not bringing a knife to a gunfight."

"You wouldn't shoot me," she purred, still going for seduction. T.J. crept into my line of sight, but I kept my eyes trained on Maria. She made it easy, after all. "I'm going to walk away. A real man won't shoot me in the back." She retreated a couple of steps. T.J.—who wore sensible tennis shoes instead of three-inch heels—moved silently into the room. Maria turned and gasped in surprise. Before she could do anything, T.J. kicked at her hand. The knife fell to the kitchen floor with a loud clatter.

"You hurt my friend," she said with a fierceness I'd never witnessed before.

"The whore?" Maria spat. "Pick better friends. I should have told these two to kill her and not just beat her up."

To her credit, T.J. didn't wait. She took a single stride closer and booted Maria hard in the midsection. The older woman folded in half. T.J. punched her a few times before grabbing her ponytail and dragging her farther into the kitchen proper. Maria shrieked, but T.J. ignored her. She used her grip on the black ponytail to slam Maria's head into the fridge. T.J. let her go, and she sagged to the floor. The lights were still on, but barely.

"Go to hell," T.J. said. I tossed her a zip tie. She locked it in tight enough to draw blood.

"Let's make a late-night delivery to police headquarters," I said.

T.J. hauled the woozy Maria to her feet. "I'd prefer to think of it as taking out the trash." I held the woman upright while T.J. used a paper towel and Ziploc bag to collect the fallen knife. As we walked through O'Hearn's house, my assistant asked, "Can I stuff her in the trunk?"

"No."

"Please?"

"I know it's tempting, but we're going to do this one right."

"Fine," she grumbled. "How did I do back there?"

"No offense," I said, "but you still punch a little like a girl."

"I'm working on it."

"I can tell."

"The next time I punch you in the shoulder, I'll be sure to do it like a man."

"I'd rather you didn't," I said.

CHAPTER 29

SINCE WE WERE ALREADY in Hamilton, we drove by Rich's house. I was careful not to mention why, and T.J. stayed silent, too. My cousin wasn't home. He worked more hours after his promotion to lieutenant. I hoped it wasn't taking a toll on him. We left the area, and I called him. "I was about to head home," he said.

"Stay there," I told him. "If Sharpe's still around, try and get him to stay, too. T.J. and I are making a special delivery."

"They've kidnapped me!" Maria hollered from the backseat.

"What's going on?" Rich wanted to know.

"We're bringing you the person who really killed O'Hearn . . . and both the Cooper brothers, I suspect." Maria quieted down, and her eyes glared at me in the rearview mirror. "You might want to let the gang kid go."

"Sure. Any other professional advice you have for me at almost eleven o'clock?"

"Yes. Add some new suit colors to your repertoire. Your look is getting a little stale." He hung up. "Some people can't take constructive criticism," I said.

"You think I killed the priest?" Maria asked.

"And his brother," T.J. said. "Can't have family nosing around."

"What are you going to do if I kick your windows out and yell for help?"

"If you damage my car," I said, "*I'm* going to punch you."

"Looks like someone already did." She grinned. "Pity."

"Don't worry. I'll take it out of your bank account. You won't be needing it."

She snorted. "You couldn't."

"I probably could. In the event it failed, I'd take a lacrosse stick to your precious McLaren."

Maria's expression turned sour. "Leave my car alone."

"Why not a golf club?" T.J. asked.

"What am I?" I said, "a retired orthodontist? I'm about thirty years too young for golf."

"Why do you think I killed the priest and his idiot brother?" Maria demanded.

I matched her stare in the mirror. "The stiletto blade, for one." T.J. held up a Ziploc bag with the weapon inside. "I'm willing to bet O'Hearn died from the same knife."

"You left cigarette butts at the brother's house, too," T.J. said. "It's enough for a DNA test."

Maria spat out some choice curses in Spanish. I learned them all in high school. Our teacher for sophomore year taught them to us so long as we promised not to dime him out to the administration. His rationale was we would learn them on our own anyway because it's what teenaged boys did. Maria didn't have much else to say when her streak of profanity ended. The ride down I-95 into the city was blessedly silent.

I parked near police headquarters. T.J. hauled Maria out of the back and kept a tight grip on her arm as we walked to the building. A couple cops shot us funny looks. "She killed

O'Hearn," I said, and they glowered at her. Inside, I explained what was going on to the officers on the first floor, and they let us through. One ogled Maria the entire time. She didn't offer any indication she noticed.

We stepped off the elevator and walked into the homicide bullpen. Rich met us near the doors. "This is the second cop killer I've delivered," I pointed out.

"Good," he said. "After the third, you get a free hamburger." He jerked his head toward a brawny uniformed officer who stopped staring at Maria's chest long enough to steer her toward an interrogation room. "You want to sit in?"

"You bet."

"Me, too," T.J. added. "That bitch hurt my friend."

"Fine," Rich said. "Wait in the break room. Make yourself useful and brew a pot of coffee while you're there."

"With pleasure," I said.

The swill in the break room was a couple hours old and had the consistency of well-used motor oil when I poured in down the drain. I ran the disposal an extra few seconds to rid the room of the memory of such dreadfully neglected java. I made a fresh pot and waited. The aroma drew a couple cops in. They all checked the progress and walked away. I figured they would return in a few minutes.

T.J. and I snagged the first two cups. Styrofoam, in this case, and with the blight to civilization known as powdered creamer, but I believed in the saying about beggars and choosers. In the end, the coffee was adequate. I cared most about it being hot and caffeinated, and it ticked both those boxes. The officers I saw checking the pot's progress a couple minutes prior now helped themselves. One was even courteous enough to thank me. I raised my cup to him.

Rich poked his head in. "We're ready. King and I are going to question her. You two are welcome to join us, but you'll be standing." He sniffed the air and smiled. "You really made a fresh pot?"

"I had to," I said. "The other one probably counted as a hazmat violation."

"Thanks. We'll start after I fill my mug." He returned to his office long enough to retrieve a black ceramic cup, added coffee almost to the top, and took a sip. I couldn't imagine drinking it black. "Not bad. Let's go."

We followed Rich into an "interview room" as the police liked to call them. Maria sat in a metal chair on the far side of the table. Her right arm was handcuffed to a bar. Rich dropped onto a nicer chair beside King. He went over the minutiae for the recording—date, time, suspect, she's been Mirandized, and all those fun bits necessary for court. "All right, Maria," my cousin said. "You're accused of a few extremely serious crimes. Why don't you tell us what happened?"

She scoffed and leaned back as much as the inflexible chair and cuff chain would allow. "Why should I talk to you without a lawyer?"

"It's your right," King said, "as we explained to you."

"Then, I'll wait."

"You should know your husband has also been here," Rich said. "Considering the money involved in the contracts, we didn't think you acted alone. In fact, we were onto him before you. He's already told us a great deal." I doubted this was true. One of the great power imbalances in the system was the ability of the police to lie to suspects with no repercussion. I didn't know how I felt about it in the broad sense, but in this situation, I was fine with just about anything which put the screws to Maria Cabrera a little tighter.

"I'm not sure what advice a lawyer would give you," King added, "but being the second person in the interview room is always tough." He shrugged. "It's your call."

Maria lapsed into silence for a few seconds. Her posture changed, and she leaned forward. This gave both men at the table a great view down the front of her tank top—a deliberate choice on her part even if she wouldn't admit it. Neither said anything. "I guess I'll talk to you for now," she whispered. "I might change my mind later."

"It's fine if you do," Rich told her.

More silence prevailed. Maria sat more upright. Maybe she realized allowing glimpses of her cleavage wasn't having the desired effect. After a long, deep breath, she started talking. "The priest needed to go." She didn't expound on the comment. It was like she expected us all to nod along and agree.

"Why?" King asked. "The jobs he was giving away?"

His question earned a snort in response. "A very simple way of looking at it."

"Why don't you explain it further, then? Use small words if you want so we can all keep up."

I grinned. I couldn't see Rich's face, but I imagined him scowling. He wasn't above lying to the suspect to coax her into talking, but he didn't bring much sarcasm to the interrogation room. Some people have weird priorities. "On some level, yeah," she said. "We didn't like him giving work away. The union earned those contracts. The companies who were supposed to do those jobs expected to earn their money."

"Contract squabbles happen," Rich said. "I can't imagine you'd kill a priest over it."

"That's not all." Maria shook her head. "Brent likes to

drink. He says he does it socially, but it's more. One night, he'd had a few too many, and he went to the church. We'd just lost some funding from the archdiocese." She waved her free hand. "They're a terrible client. Anyway, he goes to Saint Ann's and talks to the priest. Ends up going to Confession."

Rich jotted a note in his small spiral book. "I guess he told Father Cooper some things he shouldn't have."

"Yeah. I only found out when he sobered up the next morning. The idiot told him everything."

"What do you mean by everything?" Rich asked.

"Brent believes in what he does. He wants to help the workers. He also knows he's in a unique position. After his first couple years were good for everyone, he got re-elected. He . . . made sure to get a bigger cut of everything."

"You were grifting," I said.

"Yes, but not in an obvious way. Brent raised his own salary. He also got a discretionary fund for administrative support and special projects. Six hundred thousand a year."

"Let me guess," King said. "You get it all."

"No. I get about sixty percent." I wondered where the rest went as Maria fell silent for a few seconds. "There are four guys at headquarters. They work in the back behind the secretary. They pretend to, at least. We call them consultants in various aspects of running the union. In reality, they're on the books to be muscle."

"Doing what?"

"Whatever we want. Leaning on someone. A little extra security. Beating up a hooker who's sleeping with your husband."

"You bitch!" T.J. shouted. Maria smiled.

I grabbed T.J.'s forearm, squeezed it, and leaned closer. "Rich will throw you out if you keep yelling."

Sure enough, my cousin turned to give us a pointed look. "We good?" T.J. nodded. At least now, the guys in the Local 79 office sitting behind Rebecca who weren't doing anything made sense. They drew paychecks to twiddle their thumbs until needed. He turned back around and gestured toward Maria. "Continue."

"They're former union members who got kicked out for . . . various violations. Brent pays them each sixty thousand a year to ask how high when we tell them to jump."

"Nice work if you can get it," Rich said. "And an even nicer paycheck for you. What do you do to earn three hundred and sixty thousand?"

"I help out in the office," Maria said. "I also make sure contracts have a little wiggle room in them. We can usually nab a percent or two. As long as the job gets finished on time and within budget, no one really cares."

"The companies doing the work don't catch on?"

"If it seems like they're getting wise, we split it with them. Small businesses always want cash."

"Did you actually kill Sean Cooper?" Rich said.

"And his brother," I added. "And O'Hearn."

Maria smiled again and leaned forward. She made sure the arm resting on the table pushed her breasts up a little more. "I think I'd like to talk to my attorney now."

———

Once Maria lawyered up, King went to make the call, and Rich suggested T.J. and I leave. When we were back in the homicide bullpen, I said, "Rich mentioned they brought Brent in, too."

"You think he was telling the truth?"

"About the basics, yes."

"Should we look for him?" she suggested.

"I knew I hired you for a reason." Rich was experienced enough at interrogation to keep people who knew each other far apart. We started our search clear on the other side of the floorplan. It held three interview rooms, as well, and Brent Teller sat by himself in the middle one. T.J. scanned both directions, gave a quick head bob, and we walked in.

"The hell are you doing here?" Teller demanded. "You a cop?"

"There's no need to hurl rude accusations," I said. I dropped onto the chair opposite him, and T.J. sat beside me. "Maria pretty much came out and said she killed the priest."

He nodded. "Yeah." Teller let out a mirthless snort. "Told me I shouldn't have confessed to everything. I said he wouldn't tell anyone."

"He's not allowed to. Sanctity of the confessional."

"Right." The disgraced union boss pointed at me to emphasize this. "You get it. He'd take whatever I mighta told him to his grave. Even if the cops leaned on him, he wouldn't spill. I tried to explain this to Mary . . . Maria, but she wouldn't hear it."

"She have a bad experience with the clergy back in Argentina?" I said.

"Seems like you know a lot about her."

"We weren't writing a puff piece," T.J. said. "We actually did our research."

Teller sighed. His hair was a mess, he sported a five-o'clock shadow, and his clothes looked like he'd worn them to sleep off an all-day bender. "I still don't know Maria's full story," he said after a moment. "She's told me a lot, but she still holds some things back. I know she grew up in Argentina. Her family was pretty well-off for a while, and then, they lost everything."

"You know why?" I asked.

He shook his head. "She's never told me. I admit I'm not familiar enough with the place to have a good guess. Maria was ambitious. The early part of her life probably taught her almost anything was possible. She came here as a teenager to flee poverty. She hated the thought of losing money . . . of even being middle class. Once we set ourselves up well, she wanted more and more."

"You don't seem to lack for ambition yourself."

"True. I don't think I would've pushed as hard on my own. When I got re-upped by the union, Maria worked out a couple ways for us to get more money without anyone really noticing. We were doing fine already." He snorted again, and his face darkened. "At least she got her precious fucking McLaren out of it."

"If you're looking to unload it on the cheap . . . " I said.

Teller showed a brief grin. "Anyway, she told me the priest needed to go. We couldn't count on him to stay quiet. I figured she would use a couple of the guys we pay to be muscle. Rough him up some, make sure he knew to keep his mouth shut."

"Then, his brother started asking questions," T.J. said.

"Yeah. Her idea, too. I didn't know she'd killed either of them until after the fact."

"How come she didn't also stab Velvet?" I said.

"I told her I'd go public with everything if she did. Look, we've both had a little fun on the side. I know she was sleeping with a cop. She knows I indulged in the girls we hired for the parties. It all worked, but I wasn't about to let her kill someone else. Especially not a girl who had nothing to do with anything else."

The door swung in, and Captain Leon Sharpe stared at us. "You pass the police exam all of a sudden?"

"Pretty sure I could," I said. "Is it multiple choice?"

He jerked his thumb over his shoulder. "Out. We don't need you talking to our suspects."

I pointed to the camera in the corner and its steady red light. "Watch the playback, Leon. Maybe make yourself a bag of popcorn first."

"Out," he said again while trying not to smile.

T.J. and I left.

CHAPTER 30

T.J. DROVE BACK to her apartment and collapsed into bed.

It had been a late night dealing with the Tellers, and she hadn't slept well since Velvet got attacked—by two of Mary's goons, she now knew. If the police didn't learn the identities of the remaining two and round them up, she and C.T. would. For now, however, T.J. really needed to rest. Once the adrenaline of hauling Maria in and questioning her wore off, she felt like she'd been running on fumes for most of a day.

She slept straight through until her alarm went off in the morning. After a quick shower and a bowl of cereal, T.J. drove to Mercy Medical Center. Velvet was awake and alert and talking to her roommate—an older black woman—when T.J. arrived. A tray of breakfast sat on the table beside the bed. Velvet didn't eat the eggs, but their consistency bore little resemblance to something which came from a chicken. "Hey," T.J. said, sitting on the padded plastic guest chair. "How are you?"

"Alive. Probably thanks to your boss." She paused. Amy still looked like she was on the wrong end of a few punches, but some of the swelling had subsided, and her bruises looked less purple. "You know who those guys were?"

"Not by name. Not yet, at least. They work for the Tellers. Hired muscle to sort out union problems."

"How was I a problem for the union?" Velvet wanted to know. "They paid me for . . . what I do. More than once."

"I think it was Mary," T.J. said. Velvet frowned. "I was in your place. I know you looked up to her, but she's not a good person. Her name is Maria, and she's a killer." Velvet sighed. T.J. added in a much quieter voice, "She said she sent the guys after you because you were sleeping with Brent."

Velvet snorted. T.J. realized she knew her friend's real name and still thought of her by the moniker she used. "That bitch was screwing a bunch of guys behind her husband's back."

"He said they were both aware of what was happening." T.J. shrugged. "I guess Maria stopped being okay with it. She also killed one of her . . . uh . . . chosen men. A dirty cop."

"I'm taking my vision board down."

"About all that." T.J. smiled. "Amy, I think you need to talk to Melinda."

"You know." Amy smiled. "I don't think I know your actual name."

"I've come to appreciate T.J. I think I've made it my own."

"You're right," Amy said. "I need to do something else. Where does Melinda send the women she works with?"

"It depends on where your interests lie," T.J. said. "I just wanted out, and she told me office work was the easiest thing to train me for. So I did it. It's turned out well for me, but I know you mentioned you might want to go in a different direction."

"I would. I'm ready. This was it. Can you make the call for me?"

"You bet."

A hospital staffer came in and collected food trays from both patients. She put them on a large cart and wheeled it out of the room without a word. "I want to get some rest," Amy said.

T.J. stood and squeezed her friend's hand. "I'll come by again tomorrow."

"Thanks . . ." Amy's voice rose at the end.

"Tamera. But you can still call me T.J."

———

T.J. called Melinda once she was back in her car. "Amy's ready to make a move."

"Great," Melinda said. "I'll be able to work with her personally. Does she know what she wants to do?

"Not really." Melinda was such a planner. There were a hundred other questions she could've asked—and she would in time—but she wanted to know the big picture first. "If you asked me to make a guess, I would say something with social media management."

"Lots of businesses could use it."

"I think she'd be really good at it," T.J. said. "You didn't get to meet her for long, but Amy's got the right personality for it. She's also a good photographer."

"How long have you known her name?" Melinda asked.

"Not long," T.J. admitted. "She's just been Velvet for about five years now. She only recently learned I'm not actually Tami Jean." T.J. shuddered at the name given to her by her former pimp's enforcer. She hoped both of them were behind bars where they belonged.

"Names matter. It's why pimps take them away. They want to control every aspect of their girls' lives, and it starts with identities." She paused and chuckled. "I guess I don't need to tell you. Sorry. I've gotten used to explaining the basics to people who simply don't know."

"It's fine."

"When do you think Amy will be ready?"

"She's in the hospital right now. C.T. and I wrapped up a case, and Vel . . . Amy was peripherally involved. She took a pretty bad beating, but I think she'll be all right. Give her a few days."

"I haven't heard very much from C.T. recently," Melinda said. T.J. knew the woman had a crush on her boss at one point. He'd rescued her from the same life she now plucked girls out of. "I take it things are still going okay?"

"Yeah, great." T.J. debated how much information to disclose. She was the Nightlight Foundation's first success story. C.T. seemed to be all right with her getting out from behind the desk here and there and doing some work in the field. Melinda would probably be horrified at the idea. She remained protective of T.J. In the end, she said, "I think he really values the work I do, and he's teaching me more and more."

"It's a dangerous job. Make sure you're careful. I like C.T., but he's something of a risk taker. I still can't believe he wanted to use you to lure out the people who killed poor Libby."

"It was my choice to go along with it," T.J. reminded her. "I got to kick some old perv in the balls."

Melinda cleared her throat. "I'm glad things are coming up roses for you. Please let me know when Amy is ready, and I'll start working with her."

"I will. Thanks." T.J. ended the call. Melinda was still a worrier, but her heart was in the right place. She'd find the right situation for Amy. T.J. smiled as she drove toward the office. When the case began, she never expected to see someone from her past. They wound up helping Amy on top of finding the killer of Father Sean Cooper. Not bad for a few days' work.

Maybe T.J. would even get a raise or bonus out of it.

CHAPTER 31

WITH T.J. COMING IN LATE, I brewed the pot of coffee and was into my second cup when she walked in. "I went to see Amy," she said, even though I suspected it was the reason.

"How is she?"

"Better. Ready to make a change, so I talked to Melinda about her."

"Good," I said. "I'm sure she'll succeed. She just needs some better people to look up to."

"Maybe she'll find some inspiration from Melinda. She's tons better than Maria."

"You may have just given her the most backhanded compliment of all time," I pointed out, and T.J.'s cheeks reddened. "Make sure you let her know she's a superior role model to a grifter and murderer the next time her self-esteem dips."

"I will. We visiting everyone now that the case is wrapped up?"

"You have the bill ready for Father David?"

"I'll print it out," T.J. said. She logged in to her laptop, and a minute later, a document emerged from the preowned laser printer I bought a few years ago. "Might as well watch him sweat when we hand this to him."

"Let's go to Saint Ann's first," I said. We took my car and parked outside the rectory. Father Larry was happy to see us. This marked a new experience for me. He smiled, shook both our hands, and led us to his desk.

"I take it you have some news to share?" he asked.

I nodded. "We wanted to tell you first because you worked with Father Cooper. His killer is in custody."

"Very good news. As much as you may not want to acknowledge it, Mister Ferguson, I know God blessed your efforts in this case."

"Tell him to move a little faster next time," I said. "We could've saved a couple people some serious problems."

Father Larry smiled like a patient parent indulging a child who asks too many questions. "I'll see what I can do."

"The woman who killed him was responsible for other crimes, too," T.J. said. "On some level, it tied back to the construction contracts, but it also ran quite a bit deeper."

"Our parishioners will be glad to know the murderer has been caught."

"You might even tell the old ladies who chided me for cursing how I cracked the case."

"I'm sure they'll be pleased," the priest said. "I don't know if it will change their opinion of you being a heathen, however."

I shrugged. "I'm not sure it's the right term for me."

Father Larry spread his hands. "God will be ready when you are."

"I'm sure he will," I said. We shook hands again and headed to the Esperanza Center. Father David happily ushered us into his office. Today, he wore the traditional black shirt and white collar with a pair of blue jeans. "Not venturing out today?"

He rubbed the denim as he sat behind his desk. "Even I get a casual day here and there. You've come to tell me about the woman in custody?"

"Sounds like you already know," T.J. said.

"I read the news . . . depressing as it is most days."

"Maria Cabrera killed Father Cooper," I said, "along with his brother and a crooked cop who had been working with her. The police can probably find some additional things to charge her with. Between her and her husband, the state's attorney is going to have a busy week."

"I'm glad you were able to determine Father Sean's killer. Everyone at the archdiocese is relieved."

"They may not be when they see the bill." T.J. grinned as she handed it to him.

Father David's eyes widened as he looked it over. "I'm happy for the work you did, but this seems a little high."

"Justice isn't free," I said. "Besides, the archbishop can sell a painting in the Basilica if you need to raise some money."

"Hopefully, we won't need to go quite so far." He folded the paper and set it down. "I'll make sure you get paid. Thank you for everything." We shook hands, and as he grasped mine, the priest added, "We can still use you as a volunteer here, you know."

"Maybe I can recommend someone else."

When we left, T.J. asked, "Who do you have in mind?"

"Your friend Amy is going to need some things to do," I said. "Based on her background, I presume she speaks Spanish."

"She does."

"There you go." We climbed back into the car. "This is a

lot of problem-solving for one day. I might need to take the afternoon off."

"You could at least buy me lunch first," T.J. said.

I smiled. "Fair enough."

———

Later in the day, Gloria decided we should celebrate the successful resolution of the case with dinner. As I was hungry and she offered to pay, I found this to be a splendid plan. I followed her back to her place, and then we took her rocket-like coupe to The Mint Leaf in Hunt Valley. I'd never been there, and Gloria said she'd been meaning to try it for a while. The pleasing brick and pale stone exterior yielded to dark wood floors and tables and Indian-themed artwork hanging from the interior brick walls.

We got a table, and Gloria took in the place. "Looks nice."

"Smells nice, too," I said, inhaling the aromas of saffron, coriander, and other fragrant spices. The restaurant wasn't very crowded. If the meals tasted as good as they smelled, they should pull in more people. "A couple years ago, you wouldn't have wanted to come to a place in a strip mall."

"What can I tell you?" She grinned. "I'm a changed woman." Our waitress filled our water glasses and collected an appetizer order of vegetable samosas.

"I wore you down," I said.

"You should frame it as being persistent." Gloria clinked her water glass against mine.

"The Tellers would certainly accuse me of it."

"They'll be in prison," Gloria said, "where they belong. Oh . . . whatever happened to T.J.'s friend?"

"She's going to work with Melinda. I think this whole situation finally taught her it's time to make a move."

"Good for her." The waitress dropped off our appetizer. Gloria ordered chicken vindaloo. I thought it was a good enough idea to select the same thing. The samosas were large and flaky, though I ignored both sauces.

"I've been thinking about our houses," Gloria said as she finished hers. Now, we were coming to the real reason for tonight's dinner.

"And?"

"It's a lousy time to sell. I think we should keep both. We can afford it for now."

"As long as the archdiocese has a case for me every so often," I said, "we can afford them indefinitely."

She grinned. "You sure you can work with priests so often and not catch on fire?"

"I'll make sure T.J. carries an extra large water bottle."

"You're a city boy, anyway." Gloria pushed her appetizer plate closer to the edge of the table. "I know your house and the location suit you."

"Brooklandville is fine."

"I think it's considerably more than fine," she said, "but I know you don't. It's all right."

"Hitting the mean streets for a run doesn't feel quite the same," I said. "Your streets can only ever be mildly unpleasant."

"I don't know. You've never been there when someone gets cited for not keeping the hedges neat."

I chuckled. "I'm sure it's quite the scene." A busser collected our small plates, and the waitress followed with the full-sized versions a moment later. I took a few seconds to inhale the wonderful vindaloo spices before diving in.

After a few mousy bites, Gloria asked, "This case ended up paying well?"

"Yeah." I stirred some rice into the sauce. "You probably

remember T.J. devised separate rate plans for people versus corporations." My wife bobbed her head. "We charged them at the latter rate."

"They can afford it," Gloria said.

"Exactly."

"You get a few more of these cases, maybe we can even get a vacation house."

"Three?" I said. "We'd either need to sell one or field offers from Bravo to make a reality series about us."

Gloria covered her laugh with her napkin. "The Fabulous Fundraising Fergusons," she suggested as a series title. It probably made too much sense to get corporate approval.

"Going out to dinner like this would be hard. People would be calling us bougie everywhere we went."

"Under the circumstances, I think we'd deserve it."

"You're right," I said in agreement. "We definitely would."

END of Novel #14

Hello!

Thanks for reading *Concrete Angels*! C.T.'s next case features nothing angelic, as two people who apparently didn't know each other are found murdered together. It only gets worse for our hero from there. You can preorder *Conduct Unbecoming* today!

THE END

AFTERWORD

Thanks for checking out this novel! I hope you enjoyed reading the book as much as I enjoyed writing it.

I write mysteries and thrillers with action, snark, and flawed heroes. If this sounds like something you like, you can check out my catalog below.

The C.T. Ferguson Crime Novels:

1. The Reluctant Detective
2. The Unknown Devil
3. The Workers of Iniquity
4. Already Guilty
5. Daughters and Sons
6. A March from Innocence
7. Inside Cut
8. The Next Girl
9. In the Blood
10. Right as Rain
11. Dead Cat Bounce
12. Don't Say Her Name

The John Tyler Action Thrillers

I release 3-4 new novels per year. For the most current list of books, please visit:

- www.tomfowlerwrites.com
- https://books2read.com/tomfowler
- Direct sales - https://tomfowlerbooks.com

(**Note**: C.T. Ferguson appears in *White Lines*. John Tyler appears in *Don't Say Her Name*.)

While these are the suggested reading sequences, each novel is a standalone mystery or thriller, and the books can be enjoyed in whatever order you happen upon them.

Connect with me:

For the many ways of finding and reaching me online, please visit https://tomfowlerwrites.com/contact. I'm always happy to talk to readers.

This is a work of fiction. Characters and places are either fictitious or used in a fictitious manner.

"Self-publishing" is something of a misnomer. This book would not have been possible without the contributions of many people.

- The great cover design team at 100 Covers.
- My editor extraordinaire, Chase Nottingham.
- My wonderful advance reader team, the Fell Street Irregulars.